THE RANCHER TAKES A COOK

TEXAS RANCHER TRILOGY ~ BOOK 1

MISTY M. BELLER

Misty M. Beller
BOOKS

Unless otherwise indicated, all Scripture quotations are taken from the Holy Bible, Kings James Version.

ISBN-13: 978-0-9997012-1-8

To Nana and Pop.
For the love, wisdom and kindness you share with everyone you meet.
I'm honored to be your granddaughter, and I treasure everything you've taught me.
I love you more than words can say.

The Lord is my light and my salvation;
Whom shall I fear?
The Lord is the strength of my life;
Of whom shall I be afraid?

Psalms 27:1 (KJV)

CHAPTER 1

COLUMBIA, SOUTH CAROLINA
FEBRUARY 17, 1865

The acrid air was thick and hazy as nineteen-year-old Anna Stewart struggled to sit up in bed. Confused and disoriented, she looked around. What woke her? Her mind refused to focus.

"Anna..." The voice was distant, as if coming from another world. *Why is it so hot in my room?* Edward must have put too much wood on the fire before bed. She tried to focus on something—anything—but her mind was thick mud and her chest ached.

Need air. The craving consumed her. Bolting from her bed, she ran toward the doorway. *Thud. Clang.* Her hands hit rough wood and warm metal. Scrambling to her right, she tripped and fumbled for something familiar. Panic rose in her chest. The darkness slowed her down like a sea of murky water, then Anna's shin struck solid metal and she lost her balance. The floor rose up to meet her, and she landed hard, a moan escaping between gasps.

"Anna."

Edward's voice broke through the smoke like the sun parting the clouds. Or maybe it wasn't her brother, but God calling her home to heaven. The fog in her mind suffocated every thought. And then strong arms lifted her like a limp sack. Thick, smoky air whispered across her skin as she was jostled down the stairs.

~

Air. Anna gulped in a blessed breath then forced open her stinging eyes. Her chest was on fire and a coughing fit seized her. Sucking in another breath, she looked around in the dim light. She lay on a rough blanket in the grass, with people scurrying around. Confusion muddled her mind as she struggled to sit up.

"Edward?" She croaked past the shooting pain in her lungs.

"Here, sis. I'm here."

Relief flooded her and she twisted around. Concern etched her fifteen-year-old brother's youthful face as he knelt beside her.

"What happened?" Anna rasped.

"It burned, Anna. All of it." Edward's voice cracked. "All of Columbia's been burned to the ground by them heathen Yanks." His words tumbled faster as his brown eyes grew wide.

"Our candle shop?" Her heart thudded faster as she waited for his answer.

"Gone. Everything we own. And Emmett's Dry Goods, too."

"Thank God Mrs. Emmett is away visiting her sister," Anna mumbled. Her mind ached as she forced it to focus on the words her brother uttered.

"Thank God? *Thank God?* How can you thank God when people are homeless or dead all around us? *We* are homeless." The vehemence in Edward's voice wrenched Anna's heart as she stared at the ache in his wide brown eyes.

She pulled him into an embrace and his body went limp. Her little brother... How she wanted to make his hurt go away. But, what now? Surely not *all* of their things were burned. With Papa away in the war, would God leave them totally stranded?

Taking a deep breath, Anna sat back and tried to turn on her soft southern drawl that always seemed to soothe. "C'mon, honey. Let's go home and see what's left."

As she rose, a breeze tickled Anna's ankles. She glanced down at her cotton nightgown, coated in soot and grime and a bit worse for the wear. To maintain a scrap of modesty, she crossed her arms in front of her.

Anna glanced around to get her bearings. People milled around the small grassy area. Most of those present were huddled in little groups—some crying and some appearing to be in shock. Remnants of smoke still clung to the air, shrouding the atmosphere in a dismal cloak.

"This way." Her brother led the way down the muddy street. As they walked, they passed black skeletons of buildings—charred remains sticking out in jagged angles with smoke still rising from their midst. The buildings looked eerily familiar, like dear friends who were disfigured almost beyond recognition.

Edward paused in front of a structure that was almost unrecognizable in its horrid condition. The candle shop and their home. Nothing was left. No bright red sign over the door announcing Stewart's Candle Shop. No second story windows with the pretty blue curtains where their home had been. Just two stairs leading up to the porch and black smoldering ashes. Her heart sank and tightness pulled in her chest. What now?

CHAPTER 2

SEGUIN, TEXAS
AUGUST 14, 1865

The stagecoach shuddered and swayed as it had done for five days now. Wincing at an extra-hard jolt, Anna stared out the window at the group of cows grazing on scattered patches of brown grass. These cows were rather funny looking—scrawny, with long legs, colorful hides, and an immense set of horns that appeared to be almost as long as the cow itself. They were so different from the round, healthy milk cows on the plantations at home.

Home... Anna pushed their former happy life out of her mind. Had it only been a few short years ago when Papa left to fight in General Hampton's cavalry? Now, not only had she lost Mama when she was eleven, but the War had stolen Papa, their home, and everything she cared about in the world. Except Edward.

He slouched against the side of the stage and glared into an unseen distance. His glazed eyes looked like he had passed boredom long ago. Poor fellow. Edward was used to scampering about Columbia, not sitting locked in a stage for days on end.

Attempting a smile for her brother, she forced a tone more cheerful than she felt. "You hungry? I think there are biscuits left from lunch."

His head shot up like a dog who had just got a whiff of the aroma of meat. Anna pulled a small, paper-wrapped bundle from her reticule, and Edward nearly pounced on it. He scarfed down the dried bread, and his enthusiasm brought a genuine smile to her lips. He still resembled an overgrown boy, despite how he'd been forced to grow up these last few years. The baggy cotton shirt, too-short woolen pants, and cloth suspenders, only enhanced his lanky limbs and boyish awkwardness. The clothes had been a donation from a neighbor after all their things had burned in the fire. Something was better than nothing.

Anna shifted to look out the window again. The driver called, "Whoa," and the coach slowed. A tickle of anticipation fluttered in her chest. Had they made it to Seguin at last? It would be such a relief to see Uncle Walter and Aunt Laura again. And this would be her chance to start fresh. Create a new life for herself and Edward.

They entered a pretty little town with white-washed buildings and normal-looking people going about their normal lives. Anna caught a glimpse of a pair of blue uniforms and shivered, shrinking back from the stage window. *Yankee soldiers.* Would she ever be able to look at that awful color without a tremor running down her back?

Anna drew a deep, muggy breath to reinforce her courage then turned from the window to gather her things. She cringed at the needles shooting through her legs, but her seat muscles were still numb. Recent experience had taught her the pain would come later, after the brain-jarring bumps stopped and her muscles had a chance to wake up. A sigh sneaked out before she could catch it.

The stagecoach pulled to a stop next to a tall, two-story building made of the same solid, whitewashed material that covered many of the structures they'd passed. *Magnolia Hotel* was painted in faded red letters over the canopy shading the front door. As Edward helped Anna step down from the stage, the front door opened and their uncle stepped outside, a pleasant-faced man in his fifties. He was followed by their aunt, a willowy woman of about the same age, dressed in a white shirtwaist and lavender skirt. When his eyes met Anna's, the man's face broke into a grin and his voice boomed, "Well, if it isn't the Stewart family." Uncle Walter's smile was infectious, and her mouth pulled into a responding grin.

As Edward stepped forward to shake his uncle's hand, Anna was engulfed in Aunt Laura's warm embrace and the sweet scent of roses. The tenderness caught her off guard and left a burning sensation behind her eyes. How long had it been since she'd felt such a motherly embrace?

Stepping back to hold her at arm's length, her aunt's dark brown eyes twinkled as they gazed into Anna's. "Welcome home, my dear. It is so good to see you." She tucked Anna under her left arm and turned to the lanky boy standing next to Uncle Walter. "And, Edward, if I didn't know better, I would have thought you were your father. You've grown so tall. We'll add some meat on your bones, and you'll be the talk o' the town." Aunt Laura's eyes crinkled around the edges, as they appeared to do often by the deep smile lines etched in her face. "Now let's get the two of you home. Supper's on the stove, and I bet you haven't had a decent thing to eat in days."

Uncle Walter grabbed their single carpet bag with a wink. "The store is just down the street a ways. You won't get to see much of the town now, but you'll have plenty o' time to get a look at things later."

Aunt Laura slipped her arm around Anna's waist as they strolled down the rough board sidewalk. The clang of iron echoed from the livery on their right as a blue-uniformed man stood with his shoulder cocked against the doorway. He glared a haughty scowl as they passed then turned away. Across the street, a young woman exited a shop carrying a toddler in one arm and a basket in the other. A wagon passed them with a golden-colored dog perched on the seat next to a hunched old man, straw hat pulled low to shade his face from the scorching sun.

Uncle Walter stopped in front of a light green building with the words *Stewart Mercantile* painted over the door. "Here we are, folks. Welcome to our humble home." He opened the door for them to step inside.

As they walked through the store, Uncle Walter nodded at a tall, broad-shouldered cowboy standing by the front counter. "Howdy, Jacob. You gettin' all set for the fall drive?" The man caught Anna's attention. It wasn't just his unusual attire that made her stare, but his clear blue eyes framed by wavy brown locks. They were breathtaking. If this is what Texans looked like, it might not be that difficult to live here.

~

Over the next week, Anna and Edward settled into something of a routine in their new lives. Anna took on most of the cooking duties for Aunt Laura and helped with the housework, too, while Edward picked up odd jobs around town. The townspeople seemed friendly enough, and Uncle Walter was a respected member of the community, but all the soldiers milling about made Anna nervous. The War was over and the North said it was trying to re-unite the country. But were the Union soldiers really ready to put the hard feelings behind them? Power had a way of going to a man's head, and some of these men had lived through some gruesome battles.

They may not be ready to forgive a town full of Southern sympathizers.

Anna stepped outside the mercantile and squinted in the bright sunlight. Her wide-brimmed bonnet helped, but this Texas sun was a scorcher. She gripped the package for Reverend Walker's wife in her left hand and recounted the directions Uncle Walter had given her. Right on Crockett Street. Left on Milam. The Walker home was on the corner of Elm and Milam. She enjoyed helping with occasional deliveries for the store, since it gave her a chance to breathe the fresh air and see a bit more of this pretty town.

Making her way down the street, a stirring by the livery caught her attention. Anna squinted to make out what was happening. Three figures in blue pushed something back and forth between them. A gasp slipped from Anna's throat. Not some*thing*, some*one*. She hurried toward the crowd beginning to form around the men. As she neared the group, Anna's chest clamped like a vise. The form these soldiers were tossing back and forth like a rag doll looked alarmingly familiar. Edward.

Rushing forward like a bull, Anna charged through the crowd and planted herself in the middle of the three jeering men. "What are you doing?" she demanded, hands planted on her hips. She drew back her shoulders and forced a hardened look onto her face. "Leave him alone."

The man holding Edward let him drop to the ground in a heap and stepped closer. Out of the corner of her eye, she glimpsed Edward scrambling back. At least he was still conscious. She turned her focus back to the man…and almost cowered. He had a big mop of thick, almost-black hair that swooped down over his eyes, and a full-grown beard. If she could have likened him to an animal, he would have been a bear.

"Well, lookee here, boys. We got us a female to play with, too," the man growled. He reached toward Anna and grabbed her arm with his big paw. She struggled, but his grip was a solid clamp.

In an instant, Edward grabbed the man's free arm to pull him away. "Take your hands off my sister!"

A flash of annoyance crossed the man's face as another of the soldiers snatched Edward and dragged him back. "Sister?" the bear-man sneered, keeping his attention focused on Anna. "You mean your father was a yellow-livered Johnny Reb, too?" Gripping both of her arms, the man jerked Anna to his massive chest. "That's too bad, pretty little rebel. 'Cause we were gonna have some fun with you." The man's tobacco-laced breath clouded her face, and her lungs refused to fill, despite the galloping in her chest.

"Private, unhand that woman." The sharp command forced Anna's captor to look up, thrusting her away from him. Anna wheeled around to face the new threat. Another man clad in a blue uniform sat astride a chestnut horse. His jaw clenched tight, and fire radiated from his glare.

"Corporal. I, uh, was just, uh, reprimanding a civilian, sir. She and her brother were being insolent toward our men, and I was letting her know that behavior would not be tolerated." Some of the bully left the man's tone, but he kept one giant hand clenched around Anna's upper arm.

"I *said* release her," the corporal snapped. The soldier obeyed at last, shoving Anna so she had to scramble to stay on her feet. "I think you've made your point. You men can be on your way, and I'll make sure this woman and her brother don't cause you any more trouble."

The look the Corporal gave her when he said 'this woman' made Anna's blood run cold. His penetrating gaze started at her face then roamed down her body and back up again, hovering everywhere it shouldn't. Anna wanted to wrap herself in a big lumpy blanket, despite the scorching Texas sun.

The bear-man turned with a "hmmph" under his breath and stomped off.

"The rest of you folks, go on about your business," the Corporal said to the crowd that had gathered. "There's nothing more to see here."

Anna spun to find Edward and gasped at his face. Blood trickled from a cut on his lip and another on his right cheekbone. Dirt and hay clung to his mussed hair, giving him a pitiful look.

Grabbing his arm, Anna whispered, "C'mon, let's get out of here. " She glanced back at the Corporal to make sure his attention was distracted then pulled Edward into a group of men that ambled in the direction of the Mercantile. She prayed they could blend with the crowd until they were far enough away from the Yankee Corporal not to attract his attention again. Anonymity was a welcome relief at the moment.

CHAPTER 3

A few days later, Anna stood in Aunt Laura's kitchen, elbow-deep in hot, sudsy water. The pungent odor of lye tickled her nose. The repetitive action of scrubbing kept her body focused, while her mind had opportunity to examine topics she'd pushed aside.

She wrung out Edward's brown work shirt and handed it to Aunt Laura to hang on the line they'd rigged across the kitchen. The patter of raindrops on the roof had forced them to keep the laundry duties inside for the day, but Anna didn't mind as long as she wasn't out under the scorching sun that seemed to be a Texas standard. She wished it was as easy to escape her worries.

The memory of Edward being tossed back and forth between the soldiers, face covered in dirt and blood, was imprinted in her mind. And why had they done it? For no better reason than because he was the son of a Confederate soldier. A man who had taken action to stand for his beliefs, the same way these soldiers had. Of course, her father was much nobler than these good-for-nothing ruffians. He never would have pushed around innocent women or children. Her insides seethed all over again. Were all Union soldiers so mean-hearted? Papa had always said there were good and bad men in every lot. She and Edward would need to be careful to mind their own business until things settled down.

The two women worked side by side, the silence between them companionable. At last, Aunt Laura spoke. "You're not happy here are you, my dear." It was a statement, not a question. Aunt Laura had always been intuitive, and her caring nature made her an easy confidante.

Anna cringed and let out a breath. "Oh, Aunt Laura, I'm just so worried—about Edward, the soldiers, our future. You and Uncle Walter have been so good to us. I hope you don't think I'm ungrateful. But I keep thinking I should be doing something more to protect Edward and make a home for us here. We can't trespass on your hospitality forever, and I'll eventually *have* to find a way for us to have our own home. I just haven't figured out how to do that yet. I keep feeling like I'm missing something —that God has a bigger plan for us, but I can't find it."

"Anna dear, you can't take on the world by yourself. Give it a little time and you'll see that God will work all things together for good, as long as you stay in His will."

The lines around Aunt Laura's eyes deepened. "Edward seems to be enjoying himself, except for his run-in with the soldiers. That boy loves doing odd jobs around town. Did you hear the stories he told at supper last night? He seems to be enamored with the cowboys that come into the blacksmith shop, spinning their wild tales about the cattle and living on the range. It wouldn't surprise me if he joined on to a ranch one of these days."

A new tightness settled over Anna's chest. "You don't think so, do you? I know Edward's a capable horseman. Pa made sure we were both competent in the saddle. But there's no way he could be a cowboy. That's way too dangerous."

Aunt Laura chuckled. She opened her mouth to respond but was interrupted when the door banged open and Edward's lanky form shuffled into the room, one hand over his eye and the other holding his head.

"Edward. What's wrong?" Anna dropped the wet pants she'd been scrubbing and was by his side in an instant, leading him toward a chair. "Here, sit down."

"Oh..." He moaned, plopping down and leaning back to look at her through his one uncovered brown eye.

"What in the world happened to you? Where are you hurt?" Anna perched in the chair across from him and rested a hand on his bony knee.

"It was those blasted soldiers again. I was cleaning stalls at the livery, minding my own business, and two of 'em appeared out of nowhere. I tried to be polite, but they kept insultin' Pa and I couldn't take it no more. I got in a couple good licks, but then one of 'em caught me from behind and the next thing I knew I was on the ground with boots flying all around and into me. I must've got knocked out 'cause when I woke up, Mr. Tucker was swinging a pitchfork and yellin' at 'em to get out of his barn. He helped me wash up, then sent me home."

Anna gasped and sat back in her chair, fire burning her insides. How could anyone be so cruel as to hit an innocent boy like Edward, especially soldiers who'd been put there to protect the town? It was unthinkable.

"Stay right there, dear boy," Aunt Laura crooned, peeling his fingers back to examine the already darkening skin around Edward's eye. "I'll bring you a damp cloth and a poultice for your eye."

Edward nodded and leaned back in his chair with a sigh. "I didn't mean to get in a fight with them, sis. Honest. I just couldn't stand them talkin' about Pa like he was some black-hearted murderer."

The earnest expression in Edward's good eye was more than Anna could take. "I know it, love. You relax now and let Aunt

Laura tend to you. I'll be back in a little bit." She rose and grabbed her bonnet from the peg by the door.

"Where are you going?"

"Army headquarters." Before he could protest, she slipped out the door and held her breath as the latch clicked into place. She had to get away before Aunt Laura returned to the room and stopped her. The wisest thing would be to let Uncle Walter handle the situation, but she was not about to sit back and allow someone else to fight her battles, especially when Edward's safety was at stake.

With a determined step, she strode through the mercantile and out the front door. She was met by a steady rain that drenched her hat and shoulders within seconds. No matter. A little rain wouldn't melt her. Hurrying through the streets while dodging mud puddles proved challenging enough, but she had to glance up periodically to make sure she was headed in the right direction. Uncle Walter had said the soldiers were encamped on Live Oak street, a few roads over.

At last, the double row of tents came into view, and Anna pushed forward. As she neared a larger tent with a sign that read *Headquarters*, Anna began to have second thoughts. What was she thinking, waltzing right in the middle of a Yankee camp, unescorted, and looking like a muddy, wet dog? Probably smelling like one, too. Would they throw her out? Or worse, hold her prisoner?

Taking a deep breath, she sent a prayer heavenward. Lord, You promised You would never leave me or forsake me. Right now, I really need Your help. Please protect me and help me to protect Edward. With a weight lifted from her shoulders, she marched toward the Headquarters sign and knocked on one of the wooden posts holding up the canvas.

"Come in," called a deep voice from inside.

Come in? She had expected to be questioned by a guard and searched, not invited in like an expected guest. Peering inside, two uniformed men sat around a small table, a stack of papers between them. Their eyes connected with her and widened. They rose and removed their hats.

"Please come in, madam." The deep voice boomed from the man on the right as he gestured to the dry ground in front of him. His face looked a little older than middle-aged, but the silver in his hair made him look a decade older than that. The stripes on his blue wool jacket proclaimed him to be a Major.

She approached, eyeing both men as she gave a quick curtsey. One glance at her water-logged and drooping attire sent a pang of regret through Anna's chest. Why hadn't she stopped to grab an umbrella?

"It's not often we receive the honor of a visit from a lovely lady, especially on a dreary day like today. To what do we owe such an honor?"

Heat rose to Anna's cheeks, and she dipped her head, but then Edward's blackened eye flashed through her mind and she raised her chin. "Please pardon my intrusion, Major…" She paused, waiting for him to provide a name.

"Barnes. Major Barnes," he supplied.

"…Major Barnes," she continued. "My name is Miss Anna Stewart and I have an important matter that must be addressed immediately."

"Indeed, Miss Stewart. I am pleased to make your acquaintance," the older man said with a slight bow. "May I introduce you to Captain Randall?" He pointed to the slender man next to him.

The Captain also bowed, his heavy mustache and somber manner giving him the appearance of an undertaker. "A pleasure, Miss Stewart."

Major Barnes turned back to Anna and waved toward a chair near the entrance of the tent. "Won't you please be seated?"

Anna sat and, after inhaling a deep breath, began her tale.

She spoke through the lump in her throat as she recounted the story of the three soldiers who had harassed them on the street then told of the same soldiers who had sought out Edward to taunt and beat him. "Even after he lay unconscious on the ground, they continued to kick and abuse him. Not stopping until the livery owner accosted them with a pitchfork." Anna's voice pleaded as she finished the tale.

The Major's face looked suddenly worn, his eyes tired and sad. "I am so sorry, Miss Stewart, for the ill-treatment you and your brother have experienced at the hands of my men. It is not our intent to be cruel to the people of Seguin but to help restore peace and a sense of unity. It saddens me to say, though, that some of my soldiers still bear a grudge for those who fought against them during the War. I will make every effort to squelch such vile behavior and punish the offenders. I do appreciate you bringing it to my attention."

Anna's shoulders relaxed as relief washed over her. Her mission had been accomplished and this man would help to make things better for them. With a grateful smile she said, "I thank you, Major Barnes, for hearing me out and for your attention to this matter."

Rising, Anna turned to leave the tent but stopped as the Major called to her. "Please, Miss Stewart, won't you stay until the rain stops? If you'll wait, I will have one of my men escort you home."

Now that her errand was complete, Anna had a strong desire to get away from this place and back home where the people were familiar. Not to mention a craving for dry clothing. With as charming a smile as she could muster, she said, "No, indeed, Major. My home is not far from here and a little more rain won't hurt me. Thank you again for your help, and I'll bid you both good day."

With that, she plunged through the tent flap and out into the weather. The rain fell in sheets now, and a bolt of lightning flashed in the distance, followed by a clap of thunder. Gritting her teeth, Anna charged ahead, trying to avoid the streams of water flowing across the muddy street. She kept her head bent low so the rain didn't fall in her eyes.

Suddenly, something struck her waist and the air whooshed out her lungs. Strong arms closed around her, dragging her, and then the daylight disappeared. Darkness smothered like a blinding smoke. Choking.

CHAPTER 4

Anna screamed and a hand clamped over her mouth. Grimy skin reeked like a horse's hoof, churning her stomach. She flexed her jaw but couldn't get her teeth around the rough flesh that pressed over her face.

"Shut up and quit yer fighting," a voice hissed in her ear. The warm breath on her neck made Anna's skin crawl. She stomped with all her might, and satisfaction rushed in when her boot landed squarely on his foot. The man muttered a few expletives that burned Anna's ears.

"Quit, you Jezebel," he growled. "If you know what's good for ya, you'll keep your nose in your own business and quit talkin' to the Major. You tell that brother of yours to shut up, too, or I'll have my men do more than just toss him around." The man let out a sinister laugh that spread goose bumps over Anna's arms. His voice sounded familiar—probably the Colonel who had looked at her so lustfully on the street. She had to get away from this thug and his dark tent.

Lord, please help! Anna's mind screamed. A verse flickered through her mind. *Fear not, for I am with thee. Be not dismayed, for I am thy God. I will strengthen thee, yea, I will help thee. I will uphold thee with the right hand of My righteousness.* Anna's chest loosened, and peace washed through her.

The man shuffled deeper into the tent and pulled her with him. "Now listen here, missy," the voice rasped. "I'm going to take my hand off your mouth for just a minute, and you're going to keep yourself quiet as a kitten, do ye hear? One little sound and you'll regret it for the rest of yer short life." He snickered in the darkness as she nodded. She had to pacify him as much as possible until she found the right time to make a move.

His hand slid off her mouth and he brushed her arm as he reached for something in the darkness. Anna sucked in a breath of clean air, but the arm still cinched around her waist restricted her lungs from filling completely. As the man moved, something metallic-sounding clattered to the ground. The arm around her waist loosened just a fraction as the man bent to retrieve the object, but it was the moment Anna had been waiting for.

Like a nitroglycerine explosion, she slammed both elbows into the man's ribcage and kicked at his knee as hard as she could. She wasn't sure if it was the shock or the pain that caused his hold to loosen, but Anna writhed out of his grip and bolted for the door. He recovered too quickly, though, and grabbed her hair in his fist, jerking her back to him. Anna let out the loudest scream she could muster, freedom slipping away from her.

The man again clamped a hand over her mouth and nose, cutting off her air supply. But it was too late. Heavy boot thuds and men's voices drifted from outside the tent, then the flap opened and lantern light illuminated the area.

Over the next week, Anna kept Edward close to the Mercantile, and she was too shaken up to venture farther than the backyard herself. Major Barnes had informed Uncle Walter that the Corporal had received punishment and been transferred to Virginia for his misconduct, but Anna still worried that another of the soldiers might have taken up his vendetta.

She couldn't stay holed up in her aunt and uncle's house forever, though. More than anything, Anna wanted a home of their own and a livelihood. A *purpose.* How could she earn enough income to maintain a roof over their heads and still have enough for food? Without a large amount of capital to start a new business—which she didn't have—it was impossible for a woman to support herself alone, much less support a fifteen-year-old brother, too. Edward's odd jobs earned pocket change but certainly not enough to live on. Anna had become an excellent cook and housekeeper over the years since Mama passed away, but most housekeeping jobs were live-in positions, and she had to find a way for Edward and her to stay together. *Lord, please send me something. I need to figure out what to do now.*

~

Edward came in for supper that night fairly glowing. He fidgeted during the prayer, and as soon as Uncle Walter's deep baritone voice said, "Amen," Edward looked up at Anna with the shine of a schoolboy who'd just won the spelling bee.

"Guess what?" Without waiting for a response, Edward rushed on. "A couple of cowboys were at the smithy today when I was holdin' horses to be shod. One of 'em noticed how good I was with the animals and asked if I wanted a job as a cowpuncher. His name's Monty and he said he's the foreman on the Double Rocking B Ranch and they need a good cowboy. He said he'll teach me everything I need to know. Isn't that great, Anna?"

Edward's eyes looked at her with brows raised and a grin wrapping his face. She didn't have the heart to tell him no right then. But that was certainly what she planned to say. Absolutely not. The life of a cowboy was far too dangerous. She'd heard the stories of cowboys being horned to death by the crazy longhorn cows or bitten by rattlesnakes or sucked into quicksand or attacked by mountain lions. No doubt about it, Edward would *not* be a cowboy.

He eyed her with brows lifted, waiting for an answer. She looked at him with her most placating smile and began, "That's quite an honor, Eddie, that he thought so highly of your skills as a horseman. I hope you were polite when you told him no."

"No? Why would I tell him no?" A wrinkle formed between Edward's eyes. "He said it pays twenty-five dollars a week. Twenty-five whole dollars. And that includes room and board. I'm to start on Monday."

"Start on Monday?" Anna's pulse leaped as a tingle shot up her spine. This situation was becoming too dire to beat around the bush anymore. "Absolutely not. The work of a cowboy is far too dangerous. You simply cannot."

"But Anna." Edward's tone was steady, but he had a stubborn jut to his chin. "We need the money and it's a respectable job. I'll be careful, and everything will be just fine. You'll see."

In desperation, Anna turned to her uncle. "Uncle Walter, please tell Edward how ridiculous this idea is."

Uncle Walter stroked his chin, creases forming between his dark brows. "I know the Double Rocking B and its owner well. Marty O'Brien is a good man and runs an honest spread. He would watch over the boy and see he receives proper training. Yes, I think it might be a good plan."

Anna sat back in her chair, astonished. She'd always respected her uncle's wisdom and judgment. How could he possibly think this was a good idea? Apparently, she would have to take the matter into her own hands.

CHAPTER 5

Anna settled into the saddle on the bay livery mare and let out a long breath. The leather beneath her and the musky smell of the horse eased the tension from her muscles. She tucked her feet in the stirrups, adjusted her grey skirt, and gathered the mare's reins in her right hand. Straightening her shoulders, she squeezed the horse with her lower legs and relaxed as they walked out of the livery yard.

While she rode through town, Anna couldn't help but stare at the pretty white buildings they passed, some with decorative scrollwork. Uncle Walter had said the white material was called concrete, made out of lime that was harvested nearby. It gave the buildings an unusual solid look and wouldn't burn or rot. That must be why so many buildings in the town were made of the stuff. People called Seguin the 'Concrete City'. There was even a concrete wall around the town.

As soon as she passed through the city gate, Anna urged the mare into a trot, then a rocking canter. She reveled in the breeze playing across her face and the gentle rhythm of the horse beneath her. The bay mare was an older horse, but Anna settled into the ride like coming home.

Even though they'd lived in the city growing up, every Saturday Papa would rent three horses from the livery and he, Edward, and Anna, would go for a ride through the plantation country around Columbia. Anna smiled as she pictured Pepper, the black and white paint mare the livery owner had always saved for her. Pepper had been a small horse but quick and a high-stepper. Over the years, she'd helped Anna develop a solid seat and sit a canter with confidence.

After loping for about fifteen minutes, Anna reined the mare back to a walk. A grin stretched across her face. Even remembering where she was headed couldn't steal the pleasure from this moment.

After Edward's news of his new job, Anna had spent many hours in prayer as she went about her daily work, beseeching God for guidance in the situation. He'd not sent any miraculous signs or changed Edward's mind, so it seemed the only thing she could do was to ride out to the ranch herself and reason with Mr. O'Brien. Surely when he understood how young and inexperienced Edward was, he would override his foreman's decision and fire Edward before he even began to work. Since Edward was to start on Monday—just two days away—time was of the essence.

Too soon, Anna reached the cedar post which held a sign that read *Double Rocking B Ranch,* just like the directions Mr. Tucker had given her. She halted the mare at the post and gazed down the dusty wagon ruts that led to a ranch house and outbuildings. From this distance, it was hard to make out details. No sign of people, but several animals milled about in the corrals near the barn. Anna inhaled a deep breath and let it out, then squared her shoulders and squeezed the mare into a jog. *Might as well get this over with.*

As Anna neared the two-story log house, she marveled at how impressive it looked with its wrap-around porch and glass windows across the front. The structure wasn't as large as the plantation homes back in South Carolina, but it had a rich, masculine look that was comfortable.

Anna scanned the yard. Where was everyone? She dismounted, looped the reins around a hitching rail, and stared at the wooden door to the house. The nerves in her stomach knotted tight. She would have to knock on that door. No problem, though. She would do it for Edward.

Straightening her spine, Anna marched up the stairs, across the porch, and rapped her knuckles on the wood before she could second-guess herself. Within seconds, the door opened and a petite woman with red and grey hair eyed her.

"Well, sakes alive. Come in, come in, lassie."

Before Anna could introduce herself, the older woman wrapped a strong hand around Anna's upper arm and pulled her inside the house. A delicious aroma tickled Anna's nose as the woman led her into a large parlor with a magnificent stone fireplace covering most of one wall. The furniture was rugged but striking, with firm, clean lines and masculine fabrics.

"Why we haven't had such a lovely visitor in ages. Ya must come in and sit a spell. I'm Lola O'Brien, but please call me Aunt Lola. And who be you?" The woman spoke in a heavy Irish brogue, but the accent didn't disguise the kindness in her tone.

"I'm Anna Stewart—"

"Stewart, ya say?" Mrs. O'Brien interrupted with a twinkle in her blue eyes. "Are your folks from the old country? I knew I liked you for a reason."

The woman's grin sent a warmth through Anna. "My grandfather was born in Ireland, but his parents came to South Carolina when he was a boy. Our family has lived there ever since, until recently."

"Aye. Well it's a pleasure, it is, to share your company. Ya must sit down and make ya'self at home while I get us some tea."

The older woman turned and started out of the room, but

Anna spoke quickly. "No, please." Mrs. O'Brien looked back with a question on her face. Summoning her courage, Anna began, "I...I came to speak with Mr. O'Brien about an important matter. Is he home?"

"Nay, Marty's out checking on the men in the south pasture, but I expect he'll be back soon. He didn't take a lunch, so I'm believin' his stomach will bring him back straight away." The twinkle in her eyes was contagious, and Anna squelched a chuckle. "Now sit ye down and I'll be back in a jif."

As the woman disappeared around the corner, Anna eased herself down onto a sturdy-looking sofa and clasped her hands in her lap. The small, spunky Irish woman's assertive kindness had caught Anna off guard, but she couldn't be deterred from the reason she had come. The minute Mr. O'Brien returned, she would discuss her business and leave.

Anna's nerves began to settle, and she smoothed a hand over her skirt. Mrs. O'Brien's voice drifted into the room even before she appeared in the doorway with a cup in each hand. "I put a drop of sugar in your tea. I be thinkin' a lass as sweet as ye wouldn't have it any other way, but if you prefer it without I can bring in a fresh cup."

"No, this is perfect." Anna accepted the cup from the woman's wrinkled hand. Mrs. O'Brien shuffled over to seat herself in a petite armchair that seemed overshadowed by the large pieces around it.

A whinny from the yard caused the older woman to look up from the teacup she'd been stirring, and her ever-present grin widened. "There be my cousin now."

"Your cousin?" Anna struggled to keep the disappointment out of her voice. Where was Mr. O'Brien so she could get this errand over with? "Your cousin lives with you and Mr. O'Brien? It must be nice to have family with you." She attempted a smile, frustration weakening her effort.

The older woman's grin turned somewhat mischievous. "Aye, lassie, family is a wonderful thing. But my cousin *is* Mr. O'Brien. I haven't got a husband—never did have one—so Marty took me in some years back after his precious Katherine passed. Said he needed a bit of a woman's touch with his boy. It was reason enough for me, so I've stayed on, helping where I can."

Anna wanted to melt into the steamy tea she'd been swirling in her cup. "I…I'm so sorry. I just assumed…"

"Nothin' to be sorry about." *Miss* O'Brien scolded. "I wasn't thinkin' about ya bein' new to these parts. Should've told you my story right off."

Just then, the front door squeaked and boots thudded in the hallway. A tall man with broad shoulders and a full head of salt-and-pepper hair appeared in the doorway. His dark blue eyes matched the color of his petite cousin's, and they even held the same twinkle as they took in Anna seated on the sofa.

"Marty, ya must come in and meet our lovely guest." Miss O'Brien took her cousin's arm and pulled him into the room. Anna rose to her feet for an introduction. "Miss Anna Stewart, may I present Marty O'Brien."

The older gentleman approached and bowed low over Anna's hand then rose with the sparkle still securely in his eye and his lips twitching. "What a great pleasure you bestow on us, Miss Stewart. A lovelier creature I've not seen in a month of Sundays. And to what do we owe this honor?" His voice didn't hold the same Irish brogue as his cousin but sounded more like what she'd imagined from a Texas ranch owner—full and vibrant, as if the indoors couldn't contain it.

The heat crept back into Anna's cheeks from the flattery and she lowered her eyes. Her downcast eyes caught sight of the man's dusty cowboy boots, jolting her mind back to her purpose for coming. Setting her jaw and locking her eyes with the dark blue in Mr. O'Brien's, she began, "Mr. O'Brien, I've come to discuss a matter of importance with you."

"Indeed? " His mouth straightened and a brow quirked. "By all means, please come into my office." He held out an elbow for her, as if he were a fine Englishman escorting a lady to dinner. The image contrasted sharply with his bandana, dirty work shirt, vest, and pants—and the dusty boots she had spied before.

Taking his proffered arm, Anna raised her chin and swept forward as he led her down the hallway. He gestured for her to precede him through a doorway, and she entered a smaller room with hundreds of books lining two walls. Through the windows on the third wall, light streamed onto a mahogany wood desk.

He motioned toward a smaller guest chair as he settled in the high-back chair behind the desk. The chair seemed to fit the large man, and he nestled with his hands clasped behind his head. "Now, my dear. How can I help you?"

Anna fought the urge to wring her hands. Now was not the time to show weakness. "Mr. O'Brien, you may have learned from your foreman—a Mr. Monty, I believe his name was—that he has recently hired a new cowboy to work on your ranch. What you may not know, however, is that the new employee is not more than a boy—much too young to work around the dangerous longhorn cattle."

Mr. O'Brien's brows rose. "A boy, you say? And how are you acquainted with this boy?"

Anna's already firm jaw tightened a little more. "He's my brother, and he's a lad of but fifteen years, not even old enough to need a razor." Anna took a deep breath. Logic was probably the best way to approach this conversation. "You see, Edward has always lived in the city and hasn't spent any significant time around cattle. He can handle a horse but doesn't have any experience dealing with wild animals of any sort. I'm afraid he would be a liability to you, and it would simply put him in too much danger. Now I'm sure you can see why I object to his being employed on a cattle ranch."

"I see." Mr. O'Brien had leaned forward during Anna's explanation and his elbows now rested on the desk in a thoughtful pose. "So your brother is not intelligent enough to receive training?"

Anna bristled. "Of course he's intelligent. I'm simply concerned for his safety. Our parents are both deceased and Edward is my responsibility, therefore I must insist you release him immediately."

He leveled her with a kind look, but it held a hint of sadness, too. "Miss Stewart, I won't begin to tell you there's no danger or discomfort in a cowboy's job, just as there is some sort of danger or discomfort in most professions. What I do know, however, is my men are all honest, God-fearing cowboys who put forth a full day's work in exchange for regular pay, hot meals, and my highest regard. I have full confidence in Monty's judgment. If he felt your brother has the qualities needed to develop into a talented cowpuncher worthy of his fellow cowboy's respect, then I believe your brother will be just fine. Monty will make sure he's properly trained, and the rest will be up to your brother."

Anna sat back in her chair and exhaled a breath she didn't realize she'd been holding. Was he right? Could this ranch be a good place for Edward? Releasing her brother's care into the hands of a group of rough cowboys made bile rise in her stomach. Edward was all she had left, her only connection to Mama and Papa and home.

"I have a proposition for you, Miss Stewart." Mr. O'Brien's deep voice broke into her thoughts. "I don't know what your current pursuits include, but I am in need of a cook for my ranch. You met Lola, my cousin, who's been handling all the meals and housecleaning for a number of years now. She's worked hard in her lifetime and is beginning to slow down a bit.

This house is her pride and joy, but I've convinced her to give up the kitchen if we can find a suitable replacement." The twinkle came back into his eyes. "I believe from her introduction that she approves of you, so I'm sure she would be willing to teach you her skills as a cook if you would be willing to learn. That way you could keep an eye on your brother and even make sure we feed him properly." His lips quirked as he spoke the final words.

Anna's mind reeled as she absorbed the offer. A cook on a cattle ranch? She'd been cooking and keeping house for Papa and Edward over the past eight years since Mama died, so she'd developed quite a repertoire and loved being in the kitchen. But that was her own kitchen back at home, not a stranger's kitchen cooking for strange cowboys. And Edward… Taking this job would mean she would see her brother every day and ensure his safety as much as possible. They would stay together.

Anna scrutinized the man across the desk. Uncle Walter had spoken highly of him, and everything appeared to confirm he was a gentleman. And Miss O'Brien was here, so she would have female company as well. Perhaps this could work?

Clearing her throat, Anna tried to sound as business-like as possible. "And how much does the position pay?"

Mr. O'Brien's face broke into a true smile. "Thirty dollars a month to start, then more when you're able to handle the meals by yourself."

"And my quarters?"

"You'll sleep in one of the guest rooms upstairs. I believe you'll find the accommodations satisfactory."

She nodded. "I agree to a trial basis. I will cook all meals for you and your men for thirty days in exchange for room, board, and thirty dollars a month. And I can assure you, I am most capable in the kitchen. You must also agree to allow my brother and me to attend church services on Sundays. At the end of thirty days, we will reassess to determine if you and I are both satisfied with the arrangement. Agreed?" Anna rose and extended her hand to shake on the deal.

"Agreed." He grinned like he'd just caught a two foot fish and rose from his chair to grasp her outstretched hand. "I have a feeling we're going to get along fine, Miss Stewart. Just fine."

CHAPTER 6

Two days later, Anna rocked with the steady rhythm of the wagon as she sat next to Uncle Walter and peered ahead for another glimpse of the ranch house. From the back of the wagon, Edward leaned over the side to catch his own first look at the Double Rocking B—their home for who knew how long.

Butterflies flipped in Anna's stomach. Another temporary place to live. Would they ever truly have a home of their own? Since their home in Columbia had burned and Papa died in battle shortly afterward, she and Edward had stayed with several different families for a few weeks. Then they'd finally boarded the west-bound train on the journey that brought them to Seguin. They'd arrived in town with only the clothes on their backs, although Aunt Laura had soon provided one more set of clothes for each of them. Anna was so thankful for the generosity they had received from friends and family, but she longed to have the means to make their own way. Her heart craved a space to call their own. Maybe this would be a fresh start, the change they needed.

Lord, I'm still not sure if we're doing the right thing here. If this is not Your will, I pray You'll make it clear to me. And please keep Edward safe. A bit of the tension released from her shoulders. No matter what happened, God would be with them.

As they pulled into the yard, Edward jumped out of the wagon before the horses came to a complete stop. He reached a hand up to Anna and helped her down from her seat, but his body twisted around while his gaze scanned the surroundings. His face held the expression of a puppy just released into a new field.

With her feet on solid ground, Anna's attention focused on two figures coming through the open door from the house onto the wide front porch. Uncle Walter's deep voice resonated beside her. "Marty, Aunt Lola. It's good to see you both again."

"Walter, it's always a pleasure." Mr. O'Brien made his way down the stairs and pumped her uncle's hand. Facing Anna, he bowed low like a gallant knight. "Miss Stewart, it's wonderful to see you again as well." Turning to Edward, he extended his hand. "And you must be Edward. I hear good things about you, son. Looking forward to you joining our group." Edward pumped his hand so eagerly that Anna wondered how the older man could keep a straight face.

"Marty, don't keep them standing in the sun." Aunt Lola called from the porch. "You folks come in. I have coffee and cookies awaitin'."

Aunt Lola's bent frame led them down the hall and into a large dining room where three coffee cups were set out on a gleaming pecan wood table. "You men make yourselves at home while I pour you coffee, then I'll take Anna upstairs to get settled in her room." She winked at Anna.

Anna followed the older woman up the stairs. She admired the detailed scrollwork carved into the handsome banister. Someone had obviously put a great deal of time and care into building and furnishing the house, yet it was warm and inviting —as if it were welcoming her home.

"Your room is down at the end of the hall next to mine, so if you ever need anythin', just come and knock hard on me door. Me old ears aren't what they use to be." The twinkle flashed in Aunt Lola's eyes as she turned to smile at Anna before opening the door at the end of the hall. "Here ye go."

As the door swung open, a gasp slid out from Anna's parted lips. This wasn't what she'd expected. The large, sturdy pine bed was impressive in the middle of the room, covered by an exquisite quilt with a star design pieced together in deep burgundies, hunter greens, and royal blues.

"Oh, how lovely," she breathed, stepping forward to caress the soft fabric. A flash of color in the corner of her vision brought Anna's attention to the windows, where curtains of the same rich burgundy material hung from the twin windows on either side of the bed. An arm chair rested under the glass on the left, and a pine bureau and mirror to match the bed sat in the opposite corner. The room held an aura of comfortable luxury.

Aunt Lola's Irish brogue broke into her gawking, "You take your time, dearie, and settle in, then come downstairs when you're ready. We still have a few hours yet, but you can help me get things ready for supper tonight. While we work, you can tell me all about yourself."

Anna moved fast as she unpacked her single spare dress and underclothes, then tidied her hair and washed her face in the basin Aunt Lola had been thoughtful enough to fill with water.

She would like this feisty little Irish woman. She glanced in the mirror to make sure everything was in place, fingering the gold cross that hung around her neck. It had been Mama's, and Papa had given it to Anna for her thirteenth birthday. The necklace and her olive complexion were all Anna had left from her mother. She straightened the cross to lay flat on her brown dress then turned to hurry down the stairs, anxious to say goodbye to Uncle Walter before he headed back to town.

Later that afternoon, Anna stood over the stove stirring a large pot of what Aunt Lola called Irish stew. It was similar to the beef stew she used to make for Papa in the wintertime and smelled heavenly. Her gaze drifted to the pots hanging from hooks in the corner and the large work counter against the wall. This kitchen was larger than what she was used to working in and much better equipped. The variety of pans and utensils would make it easier to cook for a crowd, not to mention the large stove that was already causing beads of sweat to roll down her face.

Aunt Lola charged into the room with wave of her hand. "C'mon Anna-girl. The men are washing up, so let's get this food on the table."

Anna forced down the knot in her stomach. She was about to meet the cowboys for whom she would be cooking. What sort of men would they be? She grabbed the handles on the pot with her apron and carried it to the dining room table, shuffling so as not to spill. The cowboys filed in, nodded, and sauntered around the table to stand behind their chairs, each man holding his hat in his hands. Anna sneaked glances at the four trail-worn men standing around the table. They ranged in height and age, but all had rich black hair and mustaches, with darkly tanned skin. Mr. O'Brien and Edward hadn't come in yet, and she wasn't sure what to do with herself now that the food was set out, so Anna stood by the doorway to the kitchen.

Aunt Lola poured the last cup of coffee and looked up. Awkward silence filled the room. A smirk quirked her lips. "Lads, I'd like ya to meet Miss Stewart. She'll be cookin' for ya from here on, and if this stew is any sign, she has a real talent in the kitchen."

A chorus of "Si" and "Welcome, Senorita" echoed from the men just as Mr. O'Brien and Edward appeared in the threshold.

After Mr. O'Brien introduced her brother, he motioned for them to be seated. "I'll tell you new folks who these cowpunchers are after we let 'em start eating. It's hard to hold 'em back from the grub for niceties." The grin he shared confirmed his teasing.

When they were all seated, the group bowed their heads in unison as Mr. O'Brien spoke a prayer of thanksgiving in his deep baritone voice. Anna peeked at the Mexican cowboys. She imagined cowboys as rough men who had no manners and little respect for God or the law. These men looked the part, but their earnest expressions during the prayer didn't fit her expectations.

At Mr. O'Brien's "Amen, " hands flew everywhere—grabbing biscuits, passing plates, and spooning soup. As soon as the food hit the men's plates, however, it disappeared into their open mouths. For a few minutes, Anna could only stare. They ate almost like savages.

A hand touched Anna's arm. Aunt Lola winked. Heat crawled up Anna's neck and she dropped her gaze to her bowl. It was empty. She'd better get some food before the men ate it all. There would likely be no leftovers.

As the vigorous pace of eating finally slowed, Mr. O'Brien leaned back in his chair and spoke up. "Well now, let me introduce my boys to you both. This here's Monty Dominguez, our foreman. He's been with me since he was old enough to toss a rope, and I couldn't ask for a better friend or foreman. Next to him is Bo, Monty's little brother. Monty finally talked him into comin' over from Mexico a couple years back, and we keep him around to make sure Monty stays out o' trouble." A snort issued from Monty as Bo elbowed him in the side. A grin split the younger man's handsome face.

Mr. O'Brien continued, "And down at the end are Miguel and Donato, Monty's cousins. You'll find most of the cow hands on the Double Rocking B are related to Monty somehow or another. We've decided they're a pretty good family with a healthy dose of cow sense. Besides, it's easier for Monty to keep 'em in line if they're related to him." A round of guffaws and elbow pokes erupted as the men heckled each other. Anna glanced in Edward's direction. A wide grin spread across his youthful face.

After supper was complete and all the dishes washed and put away, Anna followed Aunt Lola into the den for the evening Bible reading. Mr. O'Brien had invited Edward and her to join them for the devotions, after which he'd challenged Edward to a checker match. Her brother had loved the game since he was a young boy and was always looking for a new partner with whom to hone his skills.

The den was a comfortable, homey room with a large fireplace and rustic wood planks covering the walls and flooring. Over the fireplace hung a large painting of a man, woman, and small boy, set in an elaborately carved mahogany wood frame. The man was a much younger version of Mr. O'Brien, with the same dark blue eyes he and his cousin both shared. The blonde woman by his side was lovely, with a joy that seemed to radiate from her as she hugged the young boy. The eyes of both the woman and the lad were also blue but were a lighter sky blue whose crystal clarity might have been a little creative liberty from the artist. Was it possible for real people to have eyes that striking? Altogether, the little family reflected a love that tightened Anna's chest and sent a familiar burning sensation to her eyes.

"Marty had that portrait painted not long after they finished building the main house." Aunt Lola's voice broke into her thoughts. She'd been caught staring.

She opened her mouth to respond but was interrupted by Mr. O'Brien's booming voice as Edward followed him into the room. They all settled into chairs around the hearth, even though the weather was too warm for a fire. Mr. O'Brien filled every inch of a large wing-back chair as he sat with the Bible in his lap and spectacles resting on the bridge of his nose. Aunt Lola, beside him in a worn rocking chair, picked up a bundle of yellow yarn from the basket at her side and began crocheting tiny stitches. Anna and Edward lounged on a strait-back sofa across from them.

As Mr. O'Brien read Jesus' Sermon on the Mount from the book of Matthew, Anna's eyes drifted around the room and rested on an empty wing-back chair beside her between the sofa and the fireplace. Whose chair was that? Probably an extra for guests.

While Mr. O'Brien continued his reading, the sun disappeared into darkness, cloaking the room in a cozy atmosphere like a warm blanket on a cold night. Anna released a long breath, allowing her fears to slip away. It was more peaceful out here on the ranch than any place she had been. Like she was closer to her heavenly Father—as if she could reach out and touch Him. *Thank you, Lord.*

As the morning sky lightened into pinks and oranges the next day, Anna furiously whipped hotcake batter. She'd urged Aunt Lola to sleep late today, figuring the woman hadn't had a chance to do so in many years if she cooked for the men each morning. The cowboys would show up any second ready to scarf down a stack of hotcakes, and she only had one plate piled high for the men. It was definitely more challenging to time the food right when you were feeding eight hungry mouths instead of just Papa and Edward. She'd get better at this, though. That was for sure.

While the last skillet of hotcakes finished sizzling on the stovetop, Anna carried a plate piled with bacon and a large pot of coffee into the dining hall. Mr. O'Brien greeted her from the doorway, his brown hair slicked down and his moustache still damp. "G'morning, Miss Stewart. It smells better than a candy store in here." The resident twinkle in his eye reminded her of Papa. "The rest of the cowboys should be back from the cattle drive any day now, if they didn't get held up anywhere, so I guess I'd better eat my fill now while I can still get some."

Anna's head jerked up from the coffee she poured. "The rest of the cowboys, sir?"

"Yep, my son, Jacob, and ten other cowboys are on the cattle drive, taking our stock to market in Kansas. That's the closest market town with a railroad stop, so we get much better money for 'em there. It took about a month to drive the cows and make it back last year, and they've already been gone longer than that on this trip. I'm sure Jacob has things well in hand, though." The fatherly pride on the man's face sent a pang to Anna's heart. Her father used to look at her with that same expression.

Later that morning, Anna finished wiping down the work counter in the kitchen and glanced around before hanging her towel on a peg. The stove top glistened and the pans were all hung on their hooks. She'd swept and scoured the floors in both the kitchen and dining room until they shone. Possessiveness warmed Anna's insides. This was *her* kitchen now. Her own domain to concoct tasty dishes and desserts that would make the cowboys' mouths water. She'd always loved the response when people enjoyed her cooking, but it would be so much better now that she was able to craft the delicious meals in her own kitchen.

Anna let out a contented sigh and went in search of Aunt Lola. The men had taken packed lunches with them for the day, and supper preparations wouldn't begin until early afternoon. Maybe there was something else she could help with?

Anna found her in Mr. O'Brien's office dusting the shelves and was rewarded with a warm smile. "And how are things, my dear? Thank ye so much for my morning break today. I'm afraid me old bones wouldn't allow for much sleepin' in, but I spent a glorious morning with my Heavenly Father and that was the best gift of all."

Anna returned her smile. "I'm glad you enjoyed yourself. The kitchen is clean for now, so I've come to see how I can help you in the house. Should I make the beds or sweep anywhere?"

"Nay, there's nothing needs doing that can't wait a while. Why don't you take some time for yourself and look around a bit. A pretty young thing like you needs to get outside and stretch your legs. Now get on with ya." Aunt Lola made a shooing motion with her hand.

Anna bit the corner of her lip. "Are you sure I can't help you with anything?" She'd been hired to work, not enjoy the sights.

"If I let you do it all, there won't be work left for me, and me old bones will get lazy." With that, the woman turned back to the bookshelves and Anna had the distinct impression she'd been dismissed.

Despite her guilt over not helping with housework, Anna was excited to explore the place. Edward had been assigned barn chores that morning. Anna had not even been out to gather eggs or milk the cow, and she was eager to see what manner of animals lived on a cattle ranch.

Anna stepped off the porch, tilted her head back, and soaked in the warm late-summer sun. It wasn't quite as scorching as it had been during August when they'd first arrived in Seguin and was a welcome relief after having been in the house for so long.

She strolled toward the corrals near the barn. Half a dozen horses milled around in the larger pen, but one mare's unusual color caught her eye. The horse's body was a mixture of white and black hairs that didn't form a pattern until they reached her rump, which was white with black spots, each about the size of Anna's fist. The mare's face also had a patch of white that splashed over both blue eyes. The horse was striking and unlike any of the solid or paint horses she'd seen before.

Approaching the corral fence, Anna held a hand through the rail and called, "C'mere, girl." She didn't really expect the horse to come, but the animal ambled over with a bored expression. "Hey there pretty girl. How ya doin'?" Anna crooned as she stroked the horse's neck then reached up to scratch the universal favorite spot behind her ears. The mare sniffled a soft nicker and leaned forward to blow in Anna's face. A giddy warmth flowed through her. It was so good to be around animals again.

~

That evening, Anna sat at the dinner table, pleasure warming her as the men dove into the food she'd prepared. Shepherd's Pie was an easy meal to cook but usually a hit with the recipients. For dessert, she would surprise them with fresh blackberry pies made from the berries she'd found in the pasture behind the house.

"Senorita Stewart, you sure do know your way around la cocina," Donato declared, admiration in his voice.

"Yes, ma'am," Mr. O'Brien agreed. "I haven't tasted mashed potatoes this creamy since I traveled back east before the War. You southern gals sure do know how to satisfy a man's belly."

Anna's face heated, but she managed to mumble, "Thank you," before dipping her head to focus on the food on her own plate.

As the conversation turned to horses and cattle, Anna released a breath. The men discussed rotating the horse string kept near the barn for daily use, and the seed of an idea planted itself in her mind.

When the next lull broke the conversation, she spoke. "Mr. O'Brien, would you, by chance, have an extra horse available that I could ride on occasion? Only when I have an extra few minutes between chores."

She shouldn't have asked. What would the man think of her loitering around during broad daylight when she should be working? After all, he was paying her to cook and clean, not go on joyrides across the countryside.

Before she could retract her words, though, he spoke. "By all means. Take Bandita, the Appaloosa mare in the corral. She's a good ride and will take care of you."

Anna's heart leaped at the possibility. "Is she the mare with the black spots on her hindquarters and the white mask across her eyes?"

"The very one. Horses with the spotted color pattern are called Appaloosas after the Palouse Indians that bred them. You won't find a hardier breed around, nor one that can run faster."

Anna couldn't hold back the grin that begged for release. She planned to test that last fact.

CHAPTER 7

The next few weeks flew by as Anna developed her routine. Each day began in the barn, milking the Jersey cow, Stella, and gathering eggs from the chickens, then back to the kitchen to begin breakfast preparations. After the meal, the men filed out to hit the saddle, leaving Anna and Aunt Lola to a silent house. The only exception to the routine was Sundays, when the entire crew donned a fresh set of clothes and headed toward the little white church on the outskirts of town.

Anna's favorite time was the late mornings after the men left for the day and the kitchen was quiet. Aunt Lola usually cleaned upstairs, and Anna could talk to God while she worked. For some reason, speaking aloud drew her closer to her Heavenly Father.

Today, she was elbow deep in water, scrubbing the morning's dishes. "Father, I guess You did know what You were doing when You brought us to this ranch. These God-fearing cowboys seem to be a good influence on Edward, and I think he's enjoying learning to rope and handle the cattle."

Anna swallowed past a lump in her throat. An image flashed through her mind of her lanky brother diving into breakfast that morning with the same gusto the other cowboys displayed. They had all complimented her sourdough biscuits, ham, and red-eye gravy, sending a warmth to her chest that was still there now. This place was beginning to feel like home.

A horse whinnied in the yard, pulling Anna from her reverie. Hmm… It was unusual for Mr. O'Brien to be back so early in the morning. Most days, when he rode out with the men, he stayed out until mid-afternoon, at least. He must have forgotten something. Anna dried her hands on the apron Aunt Lola had given her and scurried to the front door.

As she neared the door, loud male voices carried from the yard. Lots of voices. Curious, she eased the door open and peeked outside. Cowboys and horses filled the open area like bees in a hive. Most of the men wore the dark features of Monty and the other hands, except two men striding toward the porch. Examining them more closely, one of the men was Mr. O'Brien. The other man was younger and a bit taller and definitely more trail-worn, a half-grown beard on his face. Something about him looked familiar. Where had she seen him before?

As the men mounted the porch stairs, the younger cowboy removed his hat and knocked it against his chaps. A small cloud of dust billowed. Anna's breath caught. He was the tall young cowboy in Uncle Walter's store the first day they'd arrived in Seguin.

At that moment, heat rose up her neck. She still stood with the door cracked, and she wasn't the only person aware of her spying. Piercing blue eyes stared at her from under raised brows, just before Anna ducked back inside the house and closed the door. The latch clicked as she leaned against the wall, hand pressed against her racing heart, breath coming in short pants. What had she been thinking to peek through the doorway like a curious child? She was a grown woman who should greet guests with the hospitality and social grace of a southern lady. Of course, she was also the cook, so maybe she would be expected to stay in the kitchen and put together a tray of coffee and cookies. Yes, that's exactly what she should do.

But before Anna could bolt from the wall and down the hall toward the kitchen, the front door opened and in stepped the blue-eyed cowboy with Mr. O'Brien on his heels.

Summoning her courage and pasting on her hostess smile, Anna turned to face the men—and became lost in eyes bluer than a Texas sky on a fall day. Her gaze sank into them, like coming home.

"Miss Stewart, I'm glad we found you." Mr. O'Brien's delighted voice hit her like a shove, pushing her out of her daze. She looked at him, trying to get her bearings. "I have someone special for you to meet." Clapping Blue-Eyes on the shoulder, Mr. O'Brien continued, "I'd like to introduce my son, Jacob O'Brien."

"I...I'm pleased to meet you, Mr. O'Brien." She couldn't read his expression, but she was making a ninny of herself. She had to get out of here soon to regain her wits. Her earlier intention returned, and Anna curtsied. "Please excuse me, and I'll put a pot of coffee on to brew." She fled down the hall before either man could respond.

Jacob's gaze followed Miss Stewart's exit. After two long months on the trail with nothing to look at but filthy cowboys and even filthier cows, he must be hallucinating. He'd expected Aunt Lola's wrinkled smile to meet him. Instead, he'd found a brown-eyed beauty.

Turning from the empty hallway to face his father, Jacob leveled his focus on the man. "Who was that?"

A chuckle escaped Pa's grin. "That, my boy, is our new cook, and she's even better with the food than she is to look at. Makes a blackberry pie that'll send you down on one knee to propose marriage right there in the dining room."

Jacob quirked an eyebrow at him. "I doubt that."

"I see you'll have to be convinced." Pa's eyes twinkled. "Her brother's the new kid you saw in the yard. His name's Edward. Monty hired him on, and she came along to watch after him. I thought I was doing her a favor when I asked her to cook for us, but I had no idea what a treat we were all in for."

Squeezing Jacob's shoulder, the older man continued, "Come on, son. What d'ya say we relax in the den until Miss Stewart brings that coffee."

Anna arranged cinnamon cookies and gingersnaps on a tray while both the coffee and her emotions brewed. Just when it finally seemed God had given them a real home where Edward would be safe and things could feel *normal,* this tall, blue-eyed cowboy appeared to shake things up again. Well, she would just have to ignore him and carry on with her normal routine. She could do this.

Anna poured the coffee into two large mugs, arranged them on a serving tray with the cookies, and balanced the tray in both hands. She inhaled a fortifying breath, squared her shoulders, raised her chin, and marched forward toward the sound of men's voices coming from the den. She was a Stewart, by golly, and she could handle any obstacle that came at her—even in the form of a pair of disturbingly blue eyes that had made her lose her faculties both times she looked into them.

As she entered the den, Anna fixed her gaze on the tray she carried. Out of the corner of her eye, she noticed both men rise as she approached. She eased the tray on the table in front of them. Her senses were painfully aware of the towering presence of the man on her left. She was close enough to catch a dusty, masculine scent—a rich mixture of man and horse. Anna whirled and dashed toward the safety of her kitchen, but Mr. O'Brien's deep voice stopped her in her tracks.

"Miss Stewart, won't you join us for a while? My son has been regaling me with stories from the cattle drive."

Anna wracked her brain for a reason to leave the room, careful to keep her eyes diverted from the younger man standing on the left. Finally, she grasped at what she hoped was an acceptable excuse. "Thank you, sir, but I need to work on lunch preparations in the kitchen. I'm sure the men are hungry from the trail. If you'll excuse me?"

"Ah, yes, of course," the older man responded, nodding. Anna seized her escape opportunity.

In the kitchen, she flew into action. The men most likely *would* be starved from the trail and would appreciate something other than the beans and jerky they had probably packed in their saddle bags. She didn't have time to prepare a hot meal from scratch for so many men, so it would have to be a bit of unusual variety.

She sliced ham onto a plate and thick wedges of bread, thankful now she had spent yesterday afternoon slaving in the hot kitchen to make fresh loaves. She would need plenty for these new mouths. Pulling out cold fried chicken and apple pies from the last night's meal, she scanned the pantry for what else she could feed the men on short notice. Grabbing the basket of vegetables from the corner, she sliced tomatoes and cucumbers, then laid them out on a plate and opened several jars of green beans.

Now for something to drink. These cowboys seemed to be obsessed with coffee, the extra strong variety. After two months of nothing but black coffee on the trail, though, she didn't have the heart to serve it for their first meal at home. Milk seemed a bit too juvenile for strapping cowboys. Scanning the pantry shelves, her eyes lit on the yellow lemons overflowing from a wicker basket. Lemonade was the perfect thing on a hot summer day.

Anna finished setting out the plates and poured lemonade in each of the men's cups. She didn't have an exact head count for the new cowboys, and she wasn't sure if Monty and his men had come in from the pasture, so she set a place at every chair around the monstrous table. Looking around to make sure she hadn't missed anything, Anna nodded silent approval then squared her shoulders and marched to the front door to ring the bell that would signal the hungry men to stampede into the dining room.

And stampede they did. Anna stood by the door as cowboys raced from every direction to form a line in front of the water pump, emerging from the other side with shiny brown faces and damp black hair. Dust still covered their vests and chaps, but they strode to the porch. The sight of the men approaching jolted Anna from her fascination with the scene, and she scurried back into the house to prepare for their arrival.

Each of the cowboys shuffled to stand behind a chair, Monty and Edward among them, and waited for the entire group to assemble. Jacob O'Brien was among them and strolled to the chair on her left, at the end of the table. Anna's shoulders tensed. He seemed to be ignoring her, though. When Mr. O'Brien entered the room, chairs scraped the floor as they all sat. Every head bowed, and Mr. O'Brien thanked the Lord for the safe return of all who had gone on the drive. Anna marveled again at the manners these tough cowboys displayed.

At the "Amen, " the men dove into the food with more than their usual fervor. She glanced at Aunt Lola on her right. The older woman eyed the wild display as well, a grin tugging her mouth. Anna hoped there would be enough food to go around. Should she slice more bread? But the men were beginning to slow as clattering forks and chewing took over.

Sitting back to wipe his face with a cloth napkin, Mr.

O'Brien remarked, "So, Jacob tells me you boys had a few close calls on the trip."

"Si," answered an older man across the table. "The old Shawnee trail was pretty grown up in places, so the dogies would spread out in the brush. Then a big storm hit before we made it to the Red River. It rained for *tres dias* and the River, she was rough. We lost too many young ones there, and it took a few days for the herd to become strong again."

"I'm sorry to hear it, Juan." A contemplative expression spread over Mr. O'Brien's face. "How did you fare when you passed through the farming country?"

"Not so good."

Anna turned at the strong voice from the end of the table on her left. Jacob O'Brien spoke for the first time that night. He leaned back in his chair, blue eyes relaxed as he gazed at his father. He'd shaved before the meal, revealing a strong jaw and chin. His face was tanned, but not nearly as chocolate as his Mexican companions. The skin where his beard had been was almost as tanned as the rest of his face.

"They weren't too keen on so much traffic coming through their pastures, especially when some of the cows knocked down a few fences."

That seemed to be all he was going to say on the topic, so another of the cowboys across the table jumped in. "A group of the farmers came at us with *las pistols*, but Jacob calmed them down with quick talking and gifts." The Mexican turned to Jacob and grinned.

"Gifts?" Mr. O'Brien quirked a brow.

"I gave them a few head of cattle for their trouble, then they seemed fine."

The same cowboy across the table continued, "After that, we stayed away from the fences and kept the cattle moving. By the time we reached Kansas, though, the herd was footsore and tired."

After the meal, Monty called orders to the men in Spanish while Aunt Lola helped Anna carry dishes into the kitchen. As Anna returned to the dining room, Jacob wrapped an arm around the older woman and planted a kiss in her strawberry grey hair. "It's awfully good to be home, Aunt Lola. You look more beautiful than I remember."

The older woman swatted him playfully. "Your eyes are blind from the sun. And it's the food you missed, not this old biddy," she teased.

Just then, Jacob's gaze stopped on Anna in the doorway, and he stepped back a bit. "The food was good, ma'am. I'm much obliged."

With that, he settled his hat on his wavy brown hair and strode past her. He soared a head taller than her as he moved by. She couldn't deny the fact that of all the compliments Anna had received on her cooking, none had warmed her stomach like this man's simple words.

CHAPTER 8

Jacob avoided the house as much as possible over the next few days. It wasn't that he didn't want to be home, but the pretty young woman in the kitchen made his stomach do flips. And it wasn't something he was used to. For so many years, the only woman he'd spent much time around was Aunt Lola. Unless the women he met at church on Sundays counted, but he didn't stay in their presence any longer than he had to. Some people called him a loner, he was sure. Truth was, he was more comfortable and alive with the cattle and cowboys than around strangers in town. Monty and his family were like brothers to Jacob, and ranching ran in his blood. The long days and hard work were part of the life.

And now, sitting atop his horse studying the herd, Jacob's chest surged with pride. Their herd size had gone down some since they'd taken a thousand head to Kansas, but most of what was left were cows due to calve in the spring, so their stock count would more than double.

Marshall stamped his hoof and flicked at a fly. He patted the horse on the shoulder. "Hey boy, you gettin' bored? How 'bout we go look for strays by the river?"

Jacob reined the horse alongside Monty and told the man his plans. Even though Jacob was part owner of the ranch and rode with the cowpunchers every day, Monty was still the foreman and was responsible for all the cowboys. Jacob respected the man's leadership and instincts and considered him a true friend.

As he neared the river, Jacob slowed the horse to a walk and peered through the thicker brush where the longhorns liked to hide. Bordering the woods were scrawny oaks and eucalyptus trees with cow-itch vine and more weeds than he could count growing up around and between them. He was so focused on scanning through the trees to his right, he almost missed the horse and rider on his left next to the river's edge.

"Hello," Miss Stewart's soft voice came from atop the Appaloosa mare he'd learned to ride on all those years ago. She appeared comfortable in the saddle, with the late morning sun illuminating her face.

Something in his chest tightened. "Howdy." He touched the brim of his hat and reined in Marshall. The last thing he wanted was to hang around this woman in such a secluded area, but he couldn't simply ignore her. They might live on a ranch in the middle of Texas, but Pa had taught him decent manners.

"You lost out here?" His voice was a bit brusquer than he'd intended, but his defenses rose in an effort to maintain his distance. She was a pretty thing to be sure, with those piercing brown eyes and long dark lashes hiding under the brim of her bonnet. Her worn brown dress didn't do much to disguise her slender waist or the fact that she curved in all the right places.

"I'm afraid you've caught me," she said with a sheepish grin. "This is my favorite spot by the river. I like to come here after morning chores any chance I get. I've never known a place so peaceful."

The shy smile she displayed softened Jacob's resolve a tiny bit. He nodded in acknowledgement and stared off across the river. "It's a nice spot. One of the prettiest on the Guadalupe."

"Is that the river's name? The Guadalupe?" She let the word roll across her tongue, as if tasting it for flavor. It came out in a rhythmic melody, like the sound the river made as it flowed over rocks a little further downstream.

He spoke before his mind realized what his mouth was doing. "I used to swim here when I was a boy. Ma would bring lunch and we'd have a picnic, just the two of us." So many times Jacob had gone back to those memories. The familiar ache tugged at his chest.

"It sounds like you had a wonderful mama." Miss Stewart's voice broke into his reflections. He glanced at her earnest expression, but there wasn't sympathy there, only understanding. She'd lost her mother, too. Could she help bear his burden? Jacob turned away from her intense gaze. Time to get this conversation back in a less *emotional* direction.

"So I hear your brother has the makings of a pretty good cowhand."

Her face brightened at his words. "Do you think so? Monty says he's learning faster than most, but he's just a boy still."

Jacob leveled her with a strong look. "He's fifteen years old. And in Texas, that's old enough to be a man and then some. The boys say he's doin' a fine job learnin' to rope, and he seems to have a way with the ornery cattle. His demeanor is calming so animals aren't afraid of him." *Much like you,* Jacob added to himself. "You should be real proud of him."

Anna's expression turned soft as he spoke and pride shone in her eyes. "He is good with animals, isn't he? Just like Papa was." The last part was spoken so softly he almost missed it.

"Your Pa is...gone?" He regretted the words as soon as they left his mouth. He didn't want to know anything about this woman. Not at all.

"He died fighting Sherman's army after they burned our home in Columbia." A touch of bitterness tinged her voice, and he could tell the wound was still raw. No wonder, though. After losing both parents and her home, she was an orphan.

He mumbled, "I'm sorry." Jacob had never been good with words, and his mind didn't seem to be ready to change that fact now. But Anna seemed to understand what he meant to say as she gazed at him with those liquid, amber-brown eyes.

Then, her demeanor changed as she squared her shoulders and raised her chin. "I'm glad Edward's doing well. He's always been a quick learner, and he'll work hard for you." Gathering her reins, Anna sighed. "I suppose it's time for me to head back. Today's laundry day." She gave him a wry grin.

He was about to let her go, then remembered the barking he'd heard that morning. "There's coyote in the area. Did you bring a gun?"

She raised a dark eyebrow at him. "No, I didn't think I'd need one."

He shot her a scowl. "You *always* need a gun out here. Ya never know what animals you'll come across. Men, too. With all the soldiers coming home from the east, you never know who you'll meet up with. And not all of them are honorable." A surge of protectiveness rose in him toward this woman—barely more than a girl—who had lost so much. "Even if you can't shoot a gun, you should at least carry it."

Her back stiffened. "Of course I can shoot a gun."

He ignored the look of indignation she shot him. "Then you'd better start carrying one. I'll ride back with you as far as the herd." Without looking at her, he turned Marshall and started in the direction of the cattle. His skin tingled from the daggers she was likely shooting at the back of his head, but he didn't stop. Stubborn woman. She couldn't see what was good for her if it bit her on the nose.

After a moment, the thud of Bandita's hooves sounded behind him. His tone had been harsh. Should he apologize? But he was just trying to protect her. He slowed Marshall enough to allow them to catch up. Anna rode beside him without speaking. Her posture in the saddle was excellent. She didn't ride side-saddle like most city girls but sat astride, the extra material in her dress covering her legs and draped across the mare's rump.

The silence was stiff between them, and at last he made an effort toward a truce.

"How do you like 'Dita?" he asked, nodding toward the Appaloosa mare.

Anna's shoulders relaxed, and some of the tension left her face. "She's wonderful." She reached down to rub the mare's neck. "She's so responsive to the touch and loves to move out as much as I do."

He bit back a grin. It seemed he'd found a topic she was enthusiastic about. He nodded. "She's the horse I grew up riding. She taught me how to cut calves, and we had more than a couple good runs. She's a fast one for sure."

Anna cut him a sideways look, a mischievous gleam in her eye. "This is usually the spot where we get to canter."

A grin tickled his jaw. "Well don't let me hold you back." But she was off before he finished speaking. Jacob gave Marshall his head and a hard squeeze, and the gelding responded with a forward leap, as eager to catch the mare as Jacob was. He allowed the grin to break loose.

Anna held Bandita to a steady canter, and he soon caught up. They stayed in an even lope until the herd of longhorn came into sight. Reining the horses back to a walk, Anna let out an exhilarated breath. "Boy, that felt good."

This captivating woman drew him despite the call of his work. But the other cowboys had already stopped to gawk at them with curious stares.

"Thank you for the escort, Mr. O'Brien. I'll bid you good day now."

"Mr. O'Brien is my pa. Ya might as well call me Jacob like everyone else does."

She hesitated, her eyes clouding so he couldn't read her expression. Was she too uppity to use his Christian name? She'd need to get over that, because on the ranch common sense ruled. They had more to worry about than whether or not it was proper for her to use his first name.

Finally, a weak smile touched her lips. "I suppose it wouldn't hurt. It will make things less confusing, to be sure." And with that she squeezed Bandita into a jog, calling over her shoulder, "Goodbye, Jacob."

He couldn't help but sit there and gaze after her. This woman was so different than anyone he'd ever met. She was a mixture of caring and spunk, innocence and strength. He didn't know quite what to think of her. He'd been so careful not to get himself wrapped up with anything that would detract from his work on the ranch. And if anything could be a distraction, a female would be.

~

At church the next Sunday, Anna sat in her usual seat between Aunt Lola and Edward. The only difference was Jacob's rich tenor voice that wafted to her from the older woman's other side as they sang the opening hymn:

When peace like a river attendeth my soul,
When sorrows like sea billows roll,
Whatever my lot, Thou hast taught me to say,
"It is well, it is well with my soul."

The words washed through Anna like a rain as she added her clear alto harmony. Throughout the sermon, she kept going back to the words of the hymn. *It is well with my soul, no matter what. Lord, please teach me to trust in You, so I can say in any circumstance it is well with my soul.*

After the service, Anna stood under a pecan tree in the church yard with her little clan of cowboys. Mr. O'Brien and Aunt Lola greeted an older couple from one of the ranches north of town. Juan recounted a story for Edward from a church he'd attended in Mexico. A hand touched Anna's arm. Turning, she expected Aunt Lola's wrinkled smile, but instead found a wide grin on the face of a little blonde slip of a woman, just a few years older than Anna.

"Hello," the woman began in a bubbly voice. "I hope you don't mind, but I just had to introduce myself. I'm Virginia Wallace. We live on the farm just past the Double Rocking B. I've seen you at church the last couple o' weeks and have been dyin' to meet you."

"I'm pleased to meet you, Mrs. Wallace. I'm Anna Stewart."

"Oh, call me Virginia. Or better yet, Ginny. And over there talking to Reverend Walker is my husband, Everett, with our little girl, Katie. She's a handful, that one, but such a joy, too." Ginny glowed with motherly pride as she talked of the girl.

"She does look precious." Anna smiled at the young mother. "How old is she?"

"She's three now but will be four by the time the new little one arrives." Ginny rubbed her slightly expanded mid-section, a hint of pink rising to her cheeks. "Should be sometime in January."

"Oh, that's wonderful." Anna touched the woman's arm.

Ginny grabbed Anna's hand in return and gave her a delighted smile. "Oh, I just know we're going to be good friends. It gets lonely out on the farm, so it'll be so nice havin' someone my age within riding distance. I hear you and your brother are working on the Double Rocking B?"

Anna laughed at the petite woman's exuberance. "Yes, I do the cooking there and Edward is one of the cowboys. It's a new venture for us both, but we've settled in."

"I'm so glad to hear it. Well, I need to run now. Everett'll be hungry and it's a long ride home. See you soon." As the little blonde magpie hurried off, Anna smiled to herself. It would be so nice to have a friend and neighbor like Ginny.

CHAPTER 9

The next few days flew by as Anna consumed herself with her work. She was determined to make her meals the best they could be—the highlight of the men's days. She scoured her memory for every dish her mother or neighborhood women had made. As her repertoire grew, Anna began experimenting with food mixtures and seasonings. Most of the men had grown up in Mexico, where the food was cooked with peppers and strong spices. The first time she fixed tamale pie for the men, they responded with such impassioned thankfulness that her heart grew two sizes.

The next day, Anna prepared Arroz con Pollo for supper. She had spent hours in the preparation, seasoning the tomato sauce to just the right flavor and hovering over the chicken so it boiled to the perfect tenderness. She hoped the men would find the taste satisfactory.

After Mr. O'Brien's prayer came the typical mad scramble to fill plates and scarf down food. As the men took their first bites, Anna held her breath and searched the faces around the table to catch their expressions. Many were so weather-worn they took on the appearance of dark, wrinkled leather, making them harder to read than an Indian chief.

Juan was the first to speak. In a hushed, reverent tone he declared, "Senorita, will you marry me?"

Every noise in the room ceased except for Anna's sharp gasp. The tough leather around Juan's eyes crinkled and his cheeks creased to reveal dimples as big as valleys. The dark brown skin made his coffee-darkened teeth appear a stark white. "The food you make is so magnificent. I only think to pay you the highest honor I know. You make magic en la cocina, Senorita."

There was a general murmur of agreement as the cowboys went back to devouring their food, but Anna's cheeks burned as hot as the fire she'd used to cook the meal. She glanced at Jacob. His deep blue eyes penetrated her. She couldn't read his expression, a mixture of approval and something else…it looked almost like jealousy but couldn't be. She wasn't sure what emotions she read there, but they held her captive for several seconds before she found the strength to look away.

Just then, a crash of thunder reverberated through the room. Anna must have jumped six inches from the surprise of it. She placed a hand over her racing heart.

"It's going to be a rough one this time," Paco announced in his lilting Mexican accent. "The wind, she was strong."

As if he had summoned it, a distant shriek of wind called from outside the sturdy walls. With that howl echoing through the room, the buoyant mood changed to a somber scene. The men went back to eating, heads down and food shoveling into their mouths as if this was to be their last meal.

Another crack of thunder broke just as a flash of light illuminated through the doorway into the kitchen. For once, Anna was thankful there weren't any windows in the dining hall. Storms had never bothered her before, but these cowboys gulped their food with pinched brows. Every thunder clap seemed to add urgency to their movements. They were more familiar with Texas storms than she was, so if they were worried, shouldn't she be concerned, too?

The meal finished soon after, and Monty dispatched the boys to help batten down the hatches of the house and barn, and settle the few livestock left in the corrals. He was giving orders to Jacob just like the rest of the men. But wasn't Jacob the boss's son? No time to ponder that now. She set to work clearing the table and washing dishes, moving quickly tonight instead of the steady pace she usually set for the nighttime ritual. Lightning continued to flash outside, and the howling of the wind took on an eerie wail, vibrating the glass window with forceful gusts.

When the dishes were washed and put away, Anna completed a quick wipe-down of the counters and table then scooped up the lantern and headed toward the den. By this point, her nerves were rattled enough that she was looking forward to human companionship.

As usual, Aunt Lola sewed in the rocking chair by the fire. Mr. O'Brien propped in the overstuffed chair beside her, leather-bound book in hand and wire-rimmed glasses perched on his nose. His face was intent on the page in his hand, lips quirked into a slight grin.

Anna settled into her usual seat on the settee and reached for her mending basket to work on Edward's pants with the large tear across one knee.

Mr. O'Brien looked up and removed his spectacles. "I tell you, I never do get tired of reading about the adventures of this Oliver Twist fella." He held up the book. "Do you read much, Miss Stewart?"

"I do love to read. I'm afraid all my books burned in Columbia, though. I only have my Bible and a Jane Austen novel that was a gift from my aunt."

The wrinkles between his brows puckered. "Well, books we have a'plenty." He waved in the direction of his office. "You're welcome to any in our library. And if there's something you'd like to read that we don't have, you let me know and I'll pick it up in town. I don't know how I'd have made it through life without my books." The twinkle reappeared in his eyes, and a kinship toward this man welled up in Anna. At the same time, her heart ached for her old leather-bound friends that had burned in the fire.

A sudden whoosh in the hallway signaled the opening of the front door. It sounded like the storm had blown inside. The noise was fierce but died down with the thud of the door closing. Boots clunking on the hardwood floor announced Jacob's presence before his tall frame appeared in the doorway.

"How is it out there, son?" Mr. O'Brien peered over his spectacles.

"Wind's pretty rough. I think we'll be okay as long as we don't get a tornado or a stampede out of the mix. The boys are setting a watch, just in case." Jacob collapsed in the wood arm chair by the fire, across from his father.

Anna imagined Edward sleeping out in the smaller bunkhouse, wind howling all around him. "Do you think it's safe for the men to be in the bunkhouse tonight? What if there's a tornado or lightning strike?"

Jacob snorted. "Safe enough. The bunkhouses are built of good, solid pine. If we get any tornadoes, this place'll go down as quick as any other building. Besides, those men have slept through a lot worse."

Not Edward. But she refrained from voicing it. Should she ask if Edward could be allowed to sleep in the main house tonight? Her brother would most likely be mortified, but at least he'd be alive.

Jacob eyed her with a hint of challenge, as if he could read her mind and planned to deny her request straight off. Her dander rose, but she clamped her mouth shut. At least Edward was in the same cabin as Juan. The older cowboy had weathered many storms in his years on the range. Hopefully, he could help Edward make it through this one.

~

Thursday morning dawned cool and clear, with a sunrise that lifted Anna's spirit. She'd planned a traditional breakfast this morning with flapjacks, eggs, bacon, and fresh, warm biscuits spread with strawberry preserves. She'd learned early on the men didn't take time to add niceties to their food before gulping it down. So now she applied condiments to the food before the cowboys arrived at the table, in hopes they might actually take time to enjoy the extra flavor.

She laid the serving dishes, piled high with food, strategically down the center of the long table, making sure a dish of each type of delicacy was within every man's reach.

Anna grew conscious of a presence in the doorway. She glanced up, and Jacob leaned against the door frame with his arms crossed, blue eyes following her movements. His dark brown hair must still be damp because it lay brushed sideways in controlled waves, only one unruly lock daring to touch his forehead. His blue plaid work shirt stretched across wide shoulders, the top two buttons open as if they couldn't contain his muscular frame. He didn't wear a vest like many of the cowboys, but his shirt fit snuggly enough to expose a trim waist and flat stomach. He was gorgeous. He really was. But he was her boss. And she had no business swooning over him. Loving meant opening herself up to the possibility of losing. No, she wasn't planning to attach herself to anyone else. She was only there to protect Edward and provide them both a home. She had to keep her focus on those two facts alone.

"Food smells good."

The words broke through Anna's thoughts, and she dropped her eyes to the plate of bacon in her hands. "I've almost finished setting everything out. Would you like a cup of coffee while you wait?" She peeked back up at him for a response. His square jaw made him look so strong and capable. Catching his nod, Anna scurried toward the kitchen, relieved to leave his scrutinizing gaze.

As she brought the steaming cup to him, Anna was careful to keep her eyes on the brew and hold it so her hand wouldn't brush his as he took possession. Just standing close to this man made her stomach do flips. He was her *employer,* after all. She needed to keep that in the forefront of her mind.

"I'm goin' to town today." His words brought her head up, shattering her intention to not make eye contact. "Thought you might have a list of things you want me to pick up. Or...maybe you'd like to go along?" He asked the question like he didn't want to. "I know it gets a bit lonely out here, and you may want to see your family. It's up to you."

Anna's heart did a little leap. She longed to see Aunt Laura and Uncle Walter again. They hadn't been at church last Sunday, and she wondered if they were ill. "Do you mean it? Oh, I would love to go. If it's not too much trouble."

He gave a quick nod. "We'll leave an hour after breakfast. Just meet me in the yard." Jacob turned to leave then looked back and raised his cup. "Thanks for the coffee." Then he was gone.

CHAPTER 10

After breakfast, Anna hurried through the mounds of dishes then took a careful inventory of the supplies she needed. These men went through food like water through a sieve, so her list was longer than she'd expected.

That done, Anna hurried upstairs to freshen her appearance. Staring in the mirror at her faded brown dress, she looked so plain and unattractive. Her only other dress was still covered in tomato sauce from yesterday. Perhaps she'd use some of their earnings to buy material for new clothing. That brought a smile to her lips. Yes, she could splurge just a little. She'd already planned to buy a cowboy hat for Edward, like the other men wore. That might stop their ribbing about the 'city' hat he wore with the skinny brim that didn't hardly keep the sun out of his eyes. Edward would need a pair of the leather chapparros and high-heeled boots soon, but she'd have to take things one at a time.

Since nothing could be done about her attire, Anna re-pinned her hair and secured the bonnet atop her brown tresses. She'd have to smile brightly to make up for the drab, faded appearance of her clothing.

Jacob sat in the wagon, arguing with himself while he waited for Anna to appear from the house. What had he been thinking, offering to let that woman come along? It was okay to look from a distance, but spending all day in her company was getting too close for comfort. She was a beauty, no doubt, and could perform miracles with food like he'd never before tasted. The men spent most of their days talking about what she had fixed for breakfast or making bets about what would be at the supper table. Jacob even hurried through his morning and evening chores so he could be one of the first to enter the dining hall. Although, for most of the men, the room held more draw than just the food. She was a fascinating creature, with her expressive hazel eyes and confident air.

Just then, the subject of his thoughts stepped onto the front porch, her straight posture accentuating the soft curves in her dress. Jacob gulped, trying to moisten his dry mouth. As she strode toward the wagon, his mind finally kicked into motion. He should be on the ground, ready to assist her. It'd been so long since he'd been around any female—except Aunt Lola who wouldn't hear of his 'coddling' by helping her into the wagon—his manners were getting sloppy.

Vaulting to the ground, he guided her into the seat with a hand under each elbow. His skin tingled from the contact on his palms. Forcing his insides to calm, Jacob marched around to the other side of the wagon and climbed aboard, settling himself with the reins in an easy motion. "All set?"

She turned a brilliant smile on him and declared, "I'm ready."

Jacob gritted his teeth against the butterflies her smile inspired in his mid-section. And when her thick skirts settled against his leg, the line in his jaw clenched a bit tighter.

He flicked the reins across the horses' backs. "Giddup." At

the end of the ranch drive, he turned the animals onto the main road and settled in for a long drive. If that woman talked the whole way…

But she didn't seem to be much of a magpie. After a long silence, she shared an anecdote from her work around the house. A little bit later she chuckled about something funny Aunt Lola had said. Anna seemed to hold a special tenderness for his feisty Aunt, and it was plain from their interactions the older woman shared the feeling. One thing for sure about Aunt Lola, she said what she meant and you always knew where you stood with her. Not like most women.

The verdict was still out on Anna. She appeared to be sweet and genuine and seemed to understand him in an uncanny sort of way. Time would tell, though, if there was more to her than met the eye.

The familiar sight of the concrete wall around Seguin had Anna bouncing in her seat. The air was thick with the scent of horses, chimney smoke, and a yeasty aroma from the cafeteria on the corner.

Jacob's manner was stiff when he helped her from the wagon in front of Stewart's Mercantile. "I've got a few other stops. Will it give you long enough if I come back in a couple hours?"

"That's perfect." She'd make every minute count.

As she stepped into the Mercantile, the familiar aroma hit her with a wave of homesickness. A mixture of leather polish, pickle juice, and baked goods. She stopped to take it all in and almost jumped when Uncle Walter's booming voice came from the direction of the counter.

"Anna, dear girl. What a pleasure to see you again." He strode around the counter, wiping his hands on an already-smudged work apron. He enveloped Anna in a quick bear hug then held her out at arm's length as if to make sure she was whole. "How are you, girl? We'd best go find your Aunt Laura, or she'll never forgive me for stealing even a second of her time with you."

Anna returned his grin. "I'm here for both business and pleasure, actually. I have a list of supplies we need to pick up today. Jacob will be returning in a couple of hours, so that should give you plenty of time to fill the order."

"By all means, put me to work." He reached for her list.

"I'll tell you what," she said in a conspiratorial whisper, "let me visit with Aunt Laura for a while then I'll come back down and help you put things together. And I was hoping to look through your dress goods for new material?"

"It's a deal. I wouldn't pass up help from a pretty young lady for anything." With a wink and a bow, he allowed her to pass behind the desk and through the door to the stairs leading up to the living quarters.

Aunt Laura squealed when she saw Anna and wrapped her in a tight embrace. They settled in at the sink, peeling potatoes while Anna filled her aunt in about the details of ranch life—especially cooking for such a large herd of cowpunchers. Even when they slipped into companionable quiet, pleasure wrapped around Anna's shoulders like a warm cloak. *Father, I can't thank you enough for putting this wonderful woman in my life. To be my aunt, but especially my friend.* When they made their way downstairs, Aunt Laura guided Anna straight toward the fabrics. "We have a gorgeous new hunter green muslin that would be the perfect thing to bring out the green flecks in your eyes."

Anna fingered the soft material, dress ideas swirling in her mind's eye. "I love it. And I could use these buttons for the bodice and this ribbon for the edging and…" Her words halted as a tall figure entered the store. Jacob. Even from a distance his presence made her breathing grow shallow.

His eyes searched the store until they found hers. "Anna." The sound of her name in his warm voice caught her off guard for a moment. Did he realize he'd used her Christian name? Urgency tinged his voice as he marched toward her. "There's a bad storm brewing from the direction of the ranch. We need to get going *now* if we have any hope to miss it."

Anna flew into motion at his words and was vaguely aware of her aunt and uncle doing the same. They loaded numerous crates and bags into the wagon, then Anna hugged her aunt as Jacob settled his bill with Uncle Walter. Jacob escorted Anna out of the shop with her elbow resting firmly in his strong hand. A warmth of security washed over her.

Jacob kept the team at a steady trot after they left town, which made the wagon jump and jostle until Anna thought she would be jolted right off the seat. She kept a white-knuckled grip on the wooden bench, determined to stay in place, but Jacob never slowed his pace. His blue eyes kept roaming to the dark, menacing clouds rolling into position overhead. The wind grew stronger as the road passed through open pasture land, and the temperature dropped by the minute.

About half an hour after they left Seguin, the rain started falling in huge drops. Still holding on to the seat, Anna squinted against the moisture blowing in her face.

"I think there's a small blanket under the seat." Jacob called over the noises of the wind and raindrops on the wagon.

Anna reached down between her legs and ran her hand along the wood until her fingers touched soft cotton. Without warning, one of the front wheels hit a deep rut, thrusting Anna head first over the footboard. A strong arm tightened around her waist, dragging her back up on the seat. She blinked and looked around to get her bearings, finding herself tucked next to Jacob's side.

"Are you okay?" He turned his face toward her ear so his words would be heard over the storm. The warmth of his breath on her face made Anna's skin tingle, and she wasn't sure if her rapidly beating heart was due to her near tumble over the edge of the wagon or from being tucked under Jacob's arm.

He was still looking at her with concern on his face. Anna nodded and yelled above the din, "I'm fine." Before she could disentangle herself from his protective grip, the sky opened up and chunks of ice the size of silver dollars began falling. Anna gasped and burrowed deeper into Jacob's side to escape the sting of ice pelting her skin through the thin cotton of her dress. The wagon lurched as the horses moved faster to get away from the cold assault. Jacob's arm tightened around her as he moved the reins into both hands for a better grip.

"What can I do?" she yelled, lifting her face toward his ear to be heard through the racket.

"Hold on," he called back. "There's no cover for a couple of miles, so we have to push on. And *pray*."

Anna obeyed on both counts. She clutched Jacob's side with both hands as she curled into his warm protection. *Lord, please guide the horses and keep them from bolting. Give Jacob strength and wisdom to get us home safely.*

CHAPTER 11

The hail lasted for about ten minutes, but it seemed an eternity. Jacob's shoulders tensed in preparation for the horses to bolt against the frightening phenomenon. Even after the sky stopped showering large masses of ice, the rain continued in torrents. Jacob was thoroughly soaked except for the side where Anna's warm body pressed against him. He tilted his head to rest on top of hers so the rain flowing from his hat brim didn't soak her hair. Anna's bonnet had been pushed off her head when she'd almost catapulted over the front of the wagon, and her hair still smelled a bit like honeysuckle. This ride should have been miserable in the ice and rain, but the warm bundle tucked under his arm made it almost comfortable.

As they finally entered the ranch yard, Anna shivered under his touch. She was such a slender thing and didn't have enough meat on her bones to serve as insulation. Three men bolted from the bunkhouse, pulling their coats on as they came. One grabbed the horses' bridles while the other two began unloading the supplies.

Anna had pulled away from Jacob when the wagon stopped and now sat huddled on the seat, arms wrapped around herself.

He wasted no time in jumping from the wagon, then reached up to lift Anna down. "Can you walk?"

"Yes, of c-course." Anna's teeth chattered so hard, it was difficult to make out her words. Her face was white, and she wobbled like she would collapse any second. Jacob kept a hand under her arm and called instructions to the men to care for the horses. Turning back to Anna, he led her toward the porch. She stumbled on the first step and he wrapped an arm around her waist to help her regain balance.

Aunt Lola met them at the door, her wrinkled brow creased in concern. "Bring the lass into the parlor. I have hot water on the stove for tea and a fire built to warm your bones. I'll go get towels for the both of ye."

Jacob did as his aunt instructed and settled Anna into the overstuffed chair closest to the fire, grabbing a quilt to wrap around her.

Anna sat with her arms hugging her body, shivers visibly convulsing her shoulders. Jacob kneeled to stoke the fire then turned back to her. What else could be done to make her more comfortable? Where was Aunt Lola with that hot tea? Anna needed to get warm from the inside out. And she needed to get out of these wet clothes.

"Aren't you c-c-cold?" Anna asked in a weak voice, her teeth chattering faster than the rattle on a snake's tail.

Jacob knelt in front of her, both to hear better and to see her at eye level. "I'm okay, but we need to get you warm so you don't catch a chill. Do you think you could make it upstairs to get out of these wet clothes?"

Anna nodded, biting her bottom lip. It didn't stop her teeth from chattering.

"Okay, then. Let's get you up." Jacob gently pulled Anna to her feet. He stayed right next to her as she took tentative steps.

"I'm f-fine," she said, as if trying to convince herself. "Just a little d-dizzy."

By the time she reached the stairway, Anna seemed to gain a little strength. On the third stair she started to sway. "Oh..." she breathed, and then she collapsed.

Jacob had kept his arms hovering nearby, so he was able to scoop her up before she fell. He carried her the rest of the way up the stairs.

Aunt Lola waited at the top for him and led the way to Anna's room. "You lay her on the bed there and then skedaddle. I'll take it from here." The older woman shooed him.

Jacob laid Anna down and gazed at her pale face. She looked so fragile, with dark circles under her long black lashes.

Aunt Lola patted a gnarled hand on his arm. "She'll be fine now. She's probably just overtired from everything she does around here then getting soaked through was the final straw. Why don't you go get yourself changed into dry clothes and get some hot coffee. Ya might as well bring Anna a cup of warm tea, too."

Aunt Lola seemed to understand he needed to feel useful. Jacob gave a quick nod and headed out the doorway.

When he ran back upstairs about fifteen minutes later carrying a mug of hot tea, Anna was sitting up in bed, propped on pillows. Aunt Lola was pulling quilts out of a trunk in the corner and stopped to wave him in. "Come on in. She's ready to drink something warm."

Anna's cheeks tinged pink as he approached the bed, and she dipped her chin, looking up at him through those beautiful black lashes.

"How're you feeling?" It was all Jacob could get out. Seeing Anna lying there in her dressing robe with skin still pale and her long brown hair flowing to her shoulders caused a strange lump to clog his throat. He swallowed, trying to clear the obstruction.

"I'm much better now." Anna's sweet voice sounded like an

angel. "I don't know what happened to me. Getting a little wet shouldn't have done all that."

Aunt Lola's "Hmmph" came from the trunk in the corner as she raised herself up to glare at Anna, wrinkled hands settled on her hips. "Missie, you've done more than get a little wet. I've been telling you for days now yer workin' too hard and yer gonna make yourself sick if you don't get some rest. Well now, I'm gonna see you get that rest, and that's all there is to it. You're to stay in that bed all day tomorrow. I'll bring your meals up to you and you can sleep or read the day away."

The feisty woman nodded as if the matter was settled, but Anna spoke up. "But I can't stay in bed tomorrow. The men need to eat, and it's the day to make bread again, not to mention the garden vegetables need to be canned. I won't work too hard, I promise, but I can't stay in bed." Anna spoke the last few words with finality and a stubborn set to her chin. The weak little angel who had lain in bed two minutes ago was gone, replaced with a fighter.

Jacob almost grinned, but one glance at Aunt Lola showed her Irish roots were kicking in, and she was looking forward to a good battle. He'd better step in before the boxers squared off. He hated to gang up against Anna, but it looked like she wasn't going to take care of herself, so someone else had better see to it.

"If Aunt Lola says you need to stay in bed, then that's exactly what you're going to do." He spoke in a stern voice, but he wasn't talking to an ornery cow. "Please." He added the last word with a touch of gentleness as Anna's eyes met his. A parade of emotions passed through them—first anger, then frustration, and finally resignation.

"Just for tomorrow then." Turning to Aunt Lola, she added, "And can you please bring me the mending stack so I can work on that while I sit here?"

Jacob did smile then. She was a bit hard-headed, to be sure.

Anna awoke several hours later to a gentle rap of knuckles on her bedroom door.

"It be me, lassie, bringin' stew to warm up yer bones." The strong Irish brogue came from the other side of the door as it creaked open. Aunt Lola's petite frame backed into the room, shoulders hunched under the weight of the tray.

"Thank you." Anna cleared her throat, trying to rid herself of the sleep-induced tickle. "I'm sorry you have to wait on me. I could get up and come to the table, at least."

"Nonsense. I told you ta stay in bed and I expect ya to mind me."

Anna gave a weak smile at the woman's mothering. She suspected Aunt Lola enjoyed the opportunity to play mother hen, but it irked Anna more than a bit to be sitting around while everyone else was working.

After the tray was arranged just right on the bed next to Anna, Aunt Lola stepped back to examine the scene. "There now. You just call down the stairs if ya need anything. I'll be cleanin' up a bit, so I won't mind the interruption."

Anna's "Thank you" was heartfelt, and she confirmed the words with an appreciative smile.

"And your brother was askin' about ye, of course. I told him I'd check and see if you were up ta havin' visitors tonight."

"Of course. I'd love to see Edward. Please tell him to come up anytime."

Aunt Lola nodded in confirmation. "I'll send him on up to sit with ya while ya eat." She turned toward the door but stopped, as if forgetting something. "Oh, I almost forgot. I put your fabric and trimmings on your dresser over there."

Anna's eyes followed the direction of Aunt Lola's finger and she glimpsed two packages wrapped in brown paper—one about the size of a hat-box and the other much smaller. "Those are mine? Where did they come from?"

Aunt Lola looked at her, curiosity clouding her eyes. "Ya brought them back with the supplies today. That's the prettiest dark green muslin I've seen in a long time. Will make a right lovely dress, it will."

Anna sank back against the pillows, warmth flowing through her. Aunt Laura must have cut and packed the dress supplies while they were loading the wagon. What a wonderfully thoughtful thing to do. Despite her exhaustion, Anna's heart soared at the thought of a new dress. She'd made do with so little for so long, but things were finally getting better.

True to her word, Aunt Lola sent Edward straight up to visit while Anna ate. He caught her up on the day's activities, and it appeared the storm had been the highlight.

"You shoulda' seen how nervous the longhorns got when the hail started coming down, Anna. Monty thought they would stampede for sure, but we were awful glad they stayed put." Anna smiled at the boy's excitement. He was even starting to sound like a Texan.

The next day, Anna slept in and enjoyed a leisurely breakfast in bed and began work on her dress straight away. She drew out several patterns before settling on one she liked, then started cutting the material. It seemed just short of criminal to slice through the soft muslin, but one glance at her sketch brought the end result back into focus.

After a couple of hours working on the dress, the pain across her forehead forced her to take a break from the exacting focus of the tiny stitches. Setting the fabric aside, she reached for her Bible on the bedside table and opened to the Old Testament. After flipping through several pages, she landed in the book of

Judges and her eyes caught sight of Gideon's name. She began reading, enthralled with his victory over the Midianites. She had forgotten how exciting the Old Testament stories were, and Gideon had always been a special favorite. She marveled again at the way he put so much trust into God's plan, even when it sounded like the craziest thing in the world to do. But God had kept His word, like He always did.

Her mind drifted to her own life. Things had seemed impossible after Papa died and she and Edward had to move from one neighbor to another. They hadn't really had a choice when they moved to Texas to stay with their Aunt and Uncle, but God had used that situation to bring them to a wonderful new home. On a cattle ranch, no less. And who knew what was in store for them next? *Father, please forgive me for not trusting You to guide us in the best path. Thank You for bringing us to this new home, and help me to keep my eyes focused on You.*

Just then, a knock sounded on the door. Time for lunch.

"Come in," she called. Placing her Bible on the bedside table, she looked up with a smile to greet Aunt Lola. But it wasn't the aged Irish woman in the doorway. It was Jacob. He was looking at her with those sky blue eyes and one brow quirked.

"How's our patient today?" He was wearing his work clothes, complete with leather vest and bandanna, and carrying her lunch tray.

Anna's jaw had slackened so she quickly closed it. "What are you doing here?"

A twinkle sparkled in his eyes. "This is where I live, remember? You must still be pretty tuckered out. Do ya think you should stay in bed another day?"

"No." Anna responded before she stopped to think. "I mean, what are you doing home in the middle of the day? Why aren't you out with the herd?"

Jacob shrugged. "Had some things to take care of here. I'll head back out in a bit." He brought the tray in and balanced it on the bed next to Anna. "In the meantime, Aunt Lola tells me the thing that will help you regain your strength besides resting, of course, is to eat everything on this plate."

Once he'd settled the food tray, Anna looked at him expectantly. He'd be heading off now to finish whatever it was that had brought him to the ranch during the middle of the day.

Instead, Jacob pulled the side chair over next to her bed and settled himself in it, long legs spread out in front of him, crossed at the ankles, and arms settled across his broad chest. The room seemed half as big with him in it.

When he looked up and caught her watching him, an impish grin raised one corner of his mouth. "Well, go ahead and eat."

"Are you going to sit there and watch me?" Anna asked, a touch of defiance in her voice to cover the butterflies that flitted in her abdomen.

"Yep. Have to make sure you build up your strength so you can come back to the kitchen. The boys are threatening to mutiny if they miss out on your cookin' another day."

Anna stared at Jacob for a second in disbelief then released the giggle that would not be suppressed. It wasn't her most lady-like moment, but something about Jacob's words and the stoic expression on his features was more than she could contain. Jacob's face broke into a grin at her reaction, revealing slight dimples when he smiled. Funny, she hadn't seen that before.

Regaining control of herself, she ate the beef stew and biscuits Aunt Lola had prepared on the tray. After two bites, though, she sat back and met Jacob's gaze. "So Aunt Lola's not feeding you enough?"

His neck turned a couple of shades red. "Well, she's feedin' us plenty. It's just, well… I don't think we ever knew how good food could taste until you started cookin' it. And the cowpunchers, well, I think we could stop payin' 'em and they'd still stay on just to eat the food. It's about all most of 'em talk about."

Anna grinned at his embarrassment. "Well, you can tell them I'll fix something extra good for breakfast tomorrow."

Jacob's face sobered. "How are you feeling? Really."

Anna's heart lightened at his concern. "I'm much better, I really am. I slept a couple of hours this morning and have been able to catch up on my Bible reading."

"What are you reading?" He leaned forward, glancing at the Bible on the bedside table.

"I'm in Judges, studying one of my favorites, Gideon."

He nodded, picked up the Bible and started thumbing through. "I always did like that story. Reminds me God can use anyone to accomplish His plan, even a farmer's son like Gideon or a rancher's son like me."

Anna was surprised at his honesty, but nodded. "It helps to remember He's in control of things, although I confess I still do my fair share of worrying."

Jacob looked at her, his gaze drilling. "And what do you worry about?"

His eyes were wide but intense. Anna's answer was easy. "Edward, mostly. I'm responsible for him now, and he's still just a boy. I worry about his safety, but I also want him to grow into a strong man of God. He doesn't have a father to teach him the things he'll need to know."

Jacob nodded and sat back in his chair, considering her words. At last he spoke. "Edward is a fine young man. He has a good head on his shoulders and spends time every day reading the Bible. With that foundation, he's on the right track. Monty and his family are Godly men, as well, so they'll help keep him out of trouble." He leaned forward in his chair and caught her gaze. "And I'll teach him everything I can—about cattle and ranching, about becoming a man, about learning from his Heavenly Father."

The familiar clamp tightened around Anna's chest, so much that she could only breathe a single word, "Why?"

Jacob inhaled a deep breath and then let it out. "I guess because I care."

She let his sentence hang in the air as she searched his eyes. Did he mean he cared about Edward or her?

Jacob's eyes dipped to her still half-full plate. "Now you'd better focus on your food." Rising, he turned toward the door. "Rest up, and I'll check on you again tonight." At the doorway, he glanced back at Anna as if to assure himself she was okay, then he was gone.

CHAPTER 12

Over the next week, things settled back to normal with just a few changes. One of the most interesting was a difference in the start of Anna's morning routine. From the first morning she went back to cooking, a pail of milk and a basket of eggs awaited her on the work counter when she entered the kitchen. The first day, she assumed Aunt Lola had milked the cow and gathered eggs to help her ease back into her daily chores.

But when she thanked the Irish woman, Aunt Lola said, "Ye be getting' your facts wrong, dearie. It wasn't me. Ya must have another little elf helpin' ya." That was all she would say on the topic, but her dark blue eyes sparkled like she knew a secret.

Could it be Edward trying to help out? There was no way it could have been one of the other cowboys. She'd learned early on these men would do almost anything necessary for the longhorns, suffering all manner of hardships and long nights in the line of duty. But it seemed they had a strong aversion to what they called "footwork"—milking the cow, slopping the pigs, feeding the chickens, and anything else they couldn't do from the back of a horse. Mr. O'Brien even hired a boy from a neighboring farm to cut their firewood every fall.

The second morning that Anna came into the kitchen to find her early morning chores completed, she couldn't believe it. After breakfast, she pulled Edward aside to ascertain if he was her secret helper. The boy looked at her in confusion. "Are you kiddin'? I'm tuckered out come time to hit the bunkhouse every night. It's all I can do to make it outta bed in time for breakfast. I'm not tryin' to get up any earlier."

So the mystery continued. By the fourth day, Anna was determined to find out who was doing her chores. Instead of going through her normal washing and dressing routine that morning, she slid on her grey dress, tied her hair back with a ribbon, and wrapped a shawl around her shoulders. She hurried downstairs to the quiet kitchen, lit a lamp, and headed outside in the chilly morning air. As she stepped into the barn, a soft tenor melody drifted from the milk cow's stall.

From this valley they say you are leaving,
I shall miss your bright eyes and sweet smile.
For they say you are taking the sunshine
That has brightened my pathway awhile.
Come and sit by my side if you love me
Do not hasten to bid me adieu,
But remember the Red River Valley
And the cowboy that loves you so true.

The song had a haunting sound, and Anna stood outside Stella's stall until the last note drifted off in the morning fog. The only noise that remained was the "ping, splash" of the milk in the bucket. She finally dared to peek through the open doorway. Jacob's broad shoulders hunched next to the brown and white cow. Warmth flooded her insides. Jacob had been the secret helper doing her morning chores—the chores no respectable cowboy would be caught doing. She couldn't stop the smile on her face as she stepped forward and murmured, "G'morning."

Jacob's shoulders straightened. "Morning." The flow of milk never slowed. His voice was husky and Anna's stomach did a little flip at the deep tambour.

She stepped forward and gingerly laid a hand on Jacob's shoulder, the muscles under his shirt tightening at her touch. "Thank you for doing my morning chores. You didn't have to."

Jacob's hands stopped milking and he slowly unfolded himself to a standing position. Without looking at Anna, he carried the milk bucket to the corner of the stall, then brushed his hands on his pants and turned around to face her. "It's no problem. You have plenty of work on your hands without doing the outside chores, too." He didn't quite meet her gaze.

She grinned. "You're one to talk about working too hard. You're up as early as I am and work most nights until after dark." Stepping toward him, she craned her neck forward and up to meet his gaze. "But I appreciate your help."

The way Jacob looked at her in that moment made it hard for Anna to breathe. His Adam's apple bobbed, and he reached out to finger one of the loose curls that lay on her shoulder, his eyes never leaving hers. "It's no trouble." His voice held an intimate tenor. "Now let's get you inside where it's warm."

~

After that morning, Jacob continued doing the outside chores, and Anna always met him at the door with a cup of warm coffee. Early morning became Jacob's favorite part of the day. Anna's warm greeting was better than the coffee he drank, sitting at the kitchen table while she cooked breakfast. They never spoke many words during this time, but the silence was comfortable, like a favorite shirt. She seemed to understand him without needing to muddy the air with small talk.

As he sat sipping coffee one Monday morning, Jacob couldn't keep his mind off the conversation he'd had after church with Jared Thomas from the Lazy T Ranch. It seemed several of the area ranchers were missing cattle from their herds. Jared's best estimate was about five hundred head missing from the area, but it was hard to tell, because most ranchers allowed their cattle to free range. Five hundred cattle was a lot. Cattle rustlers were pretty common in Texas, especially since so many soldiers, both Yanks and Rebels, were coming back from the war. Most of the time, the rustlers were just hungry men trying to catch a free meal or ten. It had been several years since they'd seen a band of cattle thieves that worked on a larger scale. He squinted, thinking back to the last time he'd seen the full Double Rocking B herd. Had they looked smaller recently? They hadn't done a head count since the fall round-up, but it sounded like it was high time to do just that.

"Do you want to tell me what's wrong?" Anna's soft southern accent came from the worktable where she had stopped slicing tomatoes and stood watching him, expectation in her eyes.

A small sigh escaped Jacob. He didn't want to burden Anna with his worries, yet she was so easy to talk to. "Found out at church yesterday some of the ranchers are missing cattle. Jared Thomas says they suspect rustlers, but it's too early to tell."

Anna went back to cutting tomatoes, a line forming on her forehead. "Do you think they've taken some of our cattle?"

Interesting she called the animals *our* cattle. She considered herself to be a part of the ranch, too.

"Not sure yet, but the boys and I will start counting them today. It's kinda hard to know for sure, though. We only had about a thousand head of heifers left after we made the drive to Kansas, but the boys have been branding the wild cattle that come on our land, so we should be close to thirteen hundred by now."

"Wild cattle?"

"Yep. There's always been a handful of loose beef running in Texas. But with all the ranchers leaving for the War these last few years, cattle got loose and owners died. The wild stock are as common as jackrabbits. Nowadays, folks consider them a natural resource if they come on your land."

Anna nodded, her brows pinched as she met his gaze. "Is there any way to find out who's doing the rustling?"

Jacob shook his head in frustration. "Jared said they've reported the missing cattle to Sheriff Brown, but there's not much he can do until someone catches sight of the men. Don't know how many there are, but it sounds like a gang of 'em if several ranches are being hit. They're likely gathering up a herd to drive north and sell."

Rising, he carried his empty mug to the bucket of water Anna kept in the sink for washing dishes. She continued her work at the counter, assembling sandwiches for the men's lunch packs, but she never took her eyes off him as he walked. He could feel her gaze piercing the back of his neck. He turned around to face her and leaned back against the sink. She wore a dark green dress this morning that drew out the same color in her eyes. It was amazing how they could change like that, wavering between brown and green.

His gaze met hers for a long moment and, for a second, he had an overwhelming urge to wrap her in his arms and kiss her soundly. The desire spooked him a bit, and Jacob gripped the edge of the sink to steady himself. It was time to leave before he did something he would regret. Finally, he offered his usual parting words, "Thanks for the coffee," and strode past Anna, not waiting for her response.

~

Edward whistled the tune to *Sweet Betsey from Pike* as his horse jogged through the brown grass. He'd been assigned as line rider today, so he and his horse patrolled the outer edge of the north pasture to make sure Double Rocking B cattle weren't drifting off the ranch's property line. It had taken a while before Monty let him ride line, since the job took him out of sight of the rest of the cowpunchers, and he'd need to be able to think on his feet if danger hit. The men all told him stories of the wild animals that roamed the area, from cougars to wolves to rattlesnakes. So far, Edward had only spotted tracks, but he would be on the lookout.

"If you run into trouble, Son, just fire a shot and we'll come a'runnin." These had been Monty's parting words before sending him off for the day's work. He hadn't found any trouble yet but hadn't seen any cattle either. Edward was finally getting used to the solitude on the range, although he got tired of talkin' to his horse sometimes.

Up ahead, a cow bellowed from a patch of trees. The underbrush was thick around the trees, so she was hidden, but the insistent bawling sounded like she was upset. The cow's long horns were probably stuck and needed a bit of help to get loose. Edward was learning to respect these crazy longhorns. He'd have to come up on her quietly so she didn't get riled. No matter what, he had to stay mounted on his horse. Jacob had drilled that rule into him until he heard it in his sleep. "A cowboy on foot is helpless. You'll lose every time around these longhorns, and you'll probably die in the process. Never, ever get off your horse for any reason."

As Edward entered the trees, a cow appeared through the branches. Sure enough, her horns were caught in the brush. From the trampled bushes and muddy ground around her, she'd been there a while, too. He opened the sheaf that held his hunting knife and prepared to cut the vines restraining the cow.

As he rode closer, the cow became almost frantic and started thrashing about. He backed his horse toward the edge of the trees, hoping to give her room to calm down.

Her flaying must have loosened the vines, though, for she finally twisted herself free. But instead of turning to run away from him, the half-crazed animal charged straight ahead, bellowing like an angry bull. Edward's horse spun underneath him as it prepared to outrun the frantic cow, but Edward wasn't prepared for the sudden change of direction. As his horse bolted forward, there was nothing but air beneath him until his back hit the ground with a thud. He rolled over onto his knees, gasping as he tried to suck in the air that had been knocked out of him.

Just when his lungs began to work again, he became conscious of a raging cow charging about fifteen feet away. One glance told him she was preparing to take out on him all her frustration at being caught in the brush for hours or days. The sharp tips of her dangerous horns would probably be the death of him today.

Edward lunged to his feet and sprinted toward the tree line, but the cow had the advantage of momentum. When she was about five feet away, Edward closed his eyes, but never stopped running. And then a whoosh clapped through the air. A ghostly scream from the cow. The ground shook beneath him. Edward didn't stop to look back until he made it to the other side of a stout tree. The sight that greeted him when he turned made his jaw drop.

Jacob sat atop his horse with a tight rope stretched between his saddle horn and the wild cow, now lying prone on the ground with a rope around her belly and front legs. The cow looked to be in shock and was breathing heavily.

"Get on your horse!" Jacob yelled, never taking his eyes from the longhorn. Edward scrambled away from the tree and jogged toward his horse grazing about fifty yards away.

Once he was securely mounted, Edward called, "Okay, I'm on."

"Draw your rifle and aim at this cow, but stay where you are. I'm gonna ride forward to loosen the rope, but if she charges again, you shoot."

His hands shook as he drew his Winchester and rested the stock in the crook of his shoulder. The men shot often when they hunted, but he'd never needed the rifle for protection before. He'd do whatever was necessary to defend Jacob, though.

"Okay, I'm ready," he called.

Keeping his eyes on the cow, Jacob eased his horse forward, loosening the rope. The animal continued to lay on the ground, breathing hard but no longer bellowing. When Jacob's horse was within five feet of the cow, he pulled out his hunting knife and cut the rope then backed his horse away from the animal. When he had backed about ten feet, he turned Marshall and jogged away from the cow, waving for Edward to do the same.

When they were a respectable distance away, Jacob stopped. "I don't think she knows she's free. She's not hurt or she'd be bawlin'. Just scared and thinks she's still tied up."

At last the animal started to struggle again, loosening the short rope, and scrambled to her feet. After standing unsteadily for a moment, she took a tentative step then trotted off in the opposite direction.

Edward let out a breath and Jacob finally looked at him. "You all right?"

Edward nodded, still a bit shaken from his near-death experience. "I'm all right. You saved my life, though."

Jacob grinned at him. "I reckon someone had to, since ya went and got yourself in a fix. C'mon, let's get back to the herd for now."

Edward shook his head in wonder as they rode. "How'd you

throw that cow with just one rope? I thought it took two men to throw a full-grown cow."

"Yep, it does when you rope their horns and back legs. That's the way we normally do it because it's easier on the cow. The only way to throw a cow by yourself is to land a blocker loop over the hump. The top of the loop settles over the withers, and the bottom catches the front legs while they run and usually makes 'em take a tumble. It's a hard throw and pretty rough on the cow, so a good cowpuncher doesn't use it unless he has to."

"I reckon you had to this time, huh?" Edward shot him a grin.

"Yep, your sister woulda skinned me alive if I brought you home all bloody and full o' holes. She probably wouldn't let me eat for a week, and that's something I couldn't abide." At the mention of Anna, Jacob added with a serious tone, "What d'ya say we keep this to ourselves and not tell your sister? There was no harm done, and I'd hate to make her worry."

"Yeah, she already worries enough for both of us." Edward scowled. "She's worse than a mama hen sometimes."

Jacob laughed. "Well it appears from your little incident today that you need someone to worry about you every now and then."

~

That night the boys were extra noisy at dinner. Juan had given her a recipe for pork carnitas, and Anna had spent all afternoon making them. She'd worked hard to get the seasoning just right while not cooking the meat so long it became tough. Their praise now justified the effort.

In between bites, several of the Mexicans were swapping stories about crazy longhorns they'd encountered over the years. Anna listened with amazement at the tales the men told. Some of them seemed a bit far-fetched, like the time Juan watched a cow stomp a cougar to death to protect her young calf. She glanced at Jacob, expecting to see the usual twinkle in his blue eyes as the men teased Juan about his wild account. Instead, Jacob's jaw was tight and he seemed to be eyeing Edward with an expression Anna couldn't read.

Just then one of the men spoke to Edward, "You know a bit about loco cows yourself now, Little Brother, don'tcha?"

Before Edward could answer, Jacob responded in a deep voice that came out almost in a growl. "Let the boy eat, Paco. Can't you see he's still growing?"

The man who'd asked the question looked at Jacob in surprise, but he didn't question the boss when he'd been given an order. And Jacob's words had definitely sounded like an order.

Anna glanced back and forth between Edward, whose red face was focused on the beans he was busy pushing around his plate, and Jacob, who also seemed quite interested in the pork he was loading into a fried tortilla. She had the sinking suspicion something had happened, or almost happened, to put Edward in danger—and she *would* find out what. Anna knew better than to question either man in front of the whole crew, but the moment she got Edward or Jacob alone, she'd have the truth. Every detail of it.

~

As Jacob finished his last apple tart, he chanced one more peek at the stony look in Anna's eyes and the firm set to her jaw. Yep, she was mad. And she hadn't even heard the story yet. He let out an internal sigh. Apple tarts were usually one of his favorites, but he couldn't taste the flavor this time with those pretty brown eyes shooting daggers at him.

As the men stood and headed toward the bunkhouse, Jacob

rose with a mental groan. Edward glanced at him with a question in his eyes.

"Go on out to the bunkhouse with the rest of the men. I'll see you in the morning." *And I'll handle your sister.*

While the room cleared, Jacob stood near his chair, shifting from one foot to the other. Anna stomped back and forth from the dining room to the kitchen, carrying dirty dishes. For a moment it crossed his mind to help her, but she looked mad enough to throttle anything that got in her way. He needed to find a way to calm her down. And she didn't even know what had happened yet.

She didn't stop, just kept charging around the table, stacking dirty plates on her arm. Jacob finally walked up behind her.

"Anna."

Still no response or any sign she'd heard him. Jacob gingerly touched her shoulder. Her muscles were solid tension beneath his fingers. He turned her to face him, then took the stack of dirty plates from her hands and placed them on the table. When he moved back to face her, the hurt in Anna's eyes made his chest ache.

Jacob stroked a finger down her temple, pushing an errant strand of hair behind her perfectly-shaped ear. She shivered as his fingers moved over her skin, and he had to fight the urge to wrap her in his arms and press his lips to hers. Jacob's eyes moved to those beautiful lips. They probably tasted like the apple tart she'd just eaten.

"Jacob." Her voice broke through his thoughts.

"Yes."

"Will you tell me what happened with Edward?"

He looked in her eyes again, read the fear and uncertainty there, then let out a long breath and ran a hand through his unruly hair. "All right. Come sit down in the kitchen and I'll tell you everything."

And he did. Jacob didn't spend a lot of time on the

dangerous parts, and he focused on the fact that Edward was unhurt, but he did tell her everything. When he finished the story, Anna paced to the kitchen window and stood very still, staring out into the darkness. He couldn't gauge what she was thinking. She just stood there staring, but he held his tongue. She needed time to process this, to work it out in her mind.

At last, she turned to face him. "I'm glad you were there."

Jacob nodded and slipped over next to her. "I am too. I hadn't planned to be there. I was riding bog and saw a group of fresh tracks going away from the herd. After I had trailed them for a ways, I heard that crazy cow bellowing and headed toward the noise." Jacob focused a penetrating gaze on Anna. "It was God looking out for Edward, Anna. If I hadn't been there, God would've used something else to keep him safe."

Her chin quivered a bit as she soaked in his words. "I know." Her voice was so quiet he almost missed it.

When she looked up at him again with those luminous brown eyes, he couldn't stop himself. He pulled Anna into his arms and gently kneaded circles in her back, wishing he could rub away the pain and fear in those windows to her soul. Anna clung to him as if she never wanted to let go. And the feeling was mutual.

At last, she seemed to gather her strength and stepped back shyly. "Thanks for telling me. I need to finish clearing the table."

Jacob nodded, not sure what else to say. She disappeared through the doorway to the dining room. Letting out a long breath, he turned toward the back door. He needed some air.

CHAPTER 13

As October progressed into November and the weather began to cool, things seemed to slow down a bit around the ranch. With no more work in the garden and all the wild fruits and berries gone until spring, Anna spent more time helping Aunt Lola with the housework, but the older woman wouldn't let her do much.

"Now, Anna, if you make me slow down, my bones will get old. I've given you the kitchen and the washin', but the rest of the cleanin' is mine to do. You're tryin' to make me die before my time, ye are."

So Anna contented herself with her domain in the kitchen and dining room, as well as the laundry and a few of the heavier chores Aunt Lola would relinquish. The bit of free time left to her was usually spent reading or exploring the surrounding countryside on Bandita. Her favorite ride was still to the banks of the Guadalupe, where she would often go with a book or to spend quiet time with the Lord.

"You're going to ride all the way to the Wallaces' by yourself?"

Anna kept her focus on the eggs she cracked for breakfast, but her lips twitched at the protective tone in Jacob's voice. He sat in the kitchen drinking coffee on this cold mid-November morning, his brow wrinkled and mouth pursed. He was such a good man.

"Theirs is the next farm over, right? I didn't see them at church on Sunday, and Mrs. Thomas said the doctor's put Ginny on bed rest." She flashed him her best pleading smile. "That has to be awfully hard with a farm to manage and a three-year-old running around. I was hoping you could give me directions?"

She tried to appear nonchalant but caught herself holding her breath. Anna had so enjoyed getting to know Ginny at Sunday services, and this was her chance to be there for her friend in a time of need.

Jacob was quiet as she whipped the hotcake batter. At last, he sighed. "It's not hard to find. Just head west and follow the tree line until it ends. Ride to the top of the hill there, and you'll see their house in the distance."

She glanced over at him from the griddle where the hotcakes sizzled next to strips of bacon and gave him an optimistic smile. "Sounds easy enough. I'll be fine."

Jacob's brow still furrowed. "Take a gun with you. We have the herd in the west pasture, so the men won't be too far away. Shoot once in the air if you need anything at all." His brow creased in concern. "Do you know how to shoot a gun?"

Anna almost giggled at the way he sounded like a mother hen clucking at her chick. "I already told you I can shoot. It's been a while since I've had to, but Papa always believed girls needed to learn how to take care of themselves just like the boys did. He taught us both how to ride, shoot, and swim."

Jacob blew out a breath, finally conceding. "Okay, then. But be careful."

Anna had a sudden giddy urge to run over and hug him, but she contained her impulse and settled for a grin that tugged her cheeks and bubbled over into her heart.

As soon as her chores were done for the morning, she packed her saddle bags with breads and canned goods for Virginia's family then headed to the barn to saddle Bandita. When she pulled her saddle from its spot on a rail attached to the barn wall, something heavy hung from the back. Anna's heart squeezed. Jacob had secured a rifle in its scabbard to one of the ties on her saddle. Warmth ran through her at his actions. Pulling out the Winchester, she rubbed a hand over its smooth metal barrel. She certainly didn't plan to use this, but it was so nice to be cared for.

The ride to Ginny's was blessedly peaceful, although it took longer than Anna expected. As she rode into the farm yard, a brown and white collie dog bounded out of the barn toward her, barking and tail wagging like a flag in the Independence Day parade.

"Hey there, girl," Anna crooned as she dismounted and reached out to pet the dog. The animal sniffed her hand for a few seconds then submitted willingly to a bit of rubbing behind her ears.

"You'll never get rid of her if you do that," Everett Wallace called in a teasing voice as he strode across the yard from the direction of the barn.

"She's a sweetie. What's her name?"

"We call her Rachel. She came with Virginia when we got married, kinda like a dowry." He said the last comment with a rueful raise of his thick eyebrows.

Anna laughed at his expression as she untied her saddle bags. "Well, every bride does need a dog."

Everett chuckled, too, and lifted the bags off of Anna's horse.

He had an easy-going, pleasant temperament that was a perfect blend to Ginny's vibrant personality. No wonder Ginny always got starry-eyed when she spoke of her husband. They were the ideal match for each other.

"Ginny will be thrilled to see you. Katie's probably still taking a nap since it's so quiet inside, so maybe you'll have a chance to talk before the whirlwind wakes up."

Anna glanced back at him, her voice turning serious. "Does the doctor feel Ginny's getting better?"

"Yep, he says she and the baby should be fine as long as she stays in the bed. Should be able to carry him all the way until January."

Anna raised a brow. "Him? The doc told you it's a boy?"

A sheepish smile came over Everett's face. "A man can hope, can't he?"

Anna laughed as she followed him up the porch and into the house. She found Ginny lying on a sofa in the parlor, reading a book. When Anna poked her head into the room, Ginny threw down the book and exclaimed, "Anna. Oh, my dear friend, I am *so* glad you've come. Sit down in this chair and tell me everything you've been up to."

Anna chuckled at her friend's exuberance. "All right, but first you have to tell me what happened to you and how you're handling bed rest."

By the end of an hour, Anna was caught up on Ginny's condition and the struggles of running a home from the couch, but Anna was relieved to find her friend still in good spirits.

"Everett's been such a help through everything. He's patient with Katie, even though I know this has been hard on him, too." With a wave of her hand, Ginny continued with a devious twinkle in her eye. "Enough about me, though. I want to hear all about how things are going at the Double Rocking B. How is your tall, blue-eyed cowboy doing?"

Heat crawled up Anna's neck, probably turning her cheeks

the color of Ginny's bright red shirtwaist. She sat back in her chair and played with her thumbs. "He's not *my* cowboy. He's my boss, for goodness sakes."

"Pshaw." Ginny dismissed the words with a wave of her hand. "Anyone can see the two of you act like love-struck school kids when you're around each other."

"We do not." Anna was taken aback by the thought.

Ginny leaned forward, propped on her elbow. "Are you trying to tell me you're not attracted to him?"

"Well, of course I'm attracted to him." This time the heat went all the way down to her toes. "But any girl would be. I just cook his food, that's all."

Ginny lay back with a knowing grin. "You're lying to yourself, Anna Stewart, and you know it as well as I do. Has he kissed you yet?"

Anna gasped and drew back. "No."

"Oh, he will, don't you worry. And when he does I want to hear all about it."

CHAPTER 14

As November progressed, Anna planned a special Thanksgiving meal for her cowboys. The men had all been on the lookout for wild turkeys for the dinner, but the only thing they found was a herd of deer. So Anna killed a few chickens and served roast chicken and smoked venison with truffle gravy. Since Thanksgiving was an American holiday, she skipped the tacos and made traditional Thanksgiving foods, like sweet potato casserole, bread pudding, cranberry sauce, apple pie, and even plum pudding that she brought flaming to the table amidst a round of cheers from the men.

The memory of that happy occasion brought a smile to Anna's lips as she scrubbed bed sheets in the kitchen one cold December day. Today was laundry day for the family's clothing, but it was also the monthly day she washed the linens from the beds in the main house. Mr. O'Brien slept in the large bedroom on the first floor, while Jacob, Aunt Lola, and Anna each used a room on the second floor. With Aunt Lola doing most of the housework, Anna was thankful she rarely had to venture into the O'Brien men's rooms. The rest of the cowpunchers, including Edward, slept in the bunkhouse and were responsible for their own washing. She had a feeling their bedding was *not* laundered once a month, if ever. Maybe she should offer her services.

Anna added some extra elbow grease as she scrubbed a large stain on Jacob's shirt. She studied the spot. Was that turpentine or carbolic acid? How in the world had he gotten the stuff on the *back* of his shirt?

So many emotions flooded her when she washed this man's clothes. She hated to immerse them in the water that would remove the smell she had come to associate with him, a mixture of man and sweat and horse and cow all wrapped into one very masculine scent. And sometimes a few stronger odors added in for good measure. Anna bit her lip to stop a grin.

She performed a very wifely duty for this man by washing, drying, and folding each of his garments. Her stomach tingled. Of course, she was performing the same service for his father and aunt, but there was something different about handling the clothing that had touched Jacob's person.

Ginny's words came back to her. Did Jacob have any feelings for her? Or was Ginny's reaction just female imaginings? He still did her early chores and stopped in for coffee every morning. Anna treasured those times and tucked them away to remember throughout the day. Sometimes they would talk about the cattle, or the men, or of the latest news from town. And sometimes they would not talk, and Jacob would simply watch her prepare breakfast and pack lunches for the men. Anna's respect for him grew daily as she observed his wisdom and the deep faith that penetrated everything he did.

Anna sat back from scrubbing and stared down at the shirt in her hands. Was it more than respect she held for Jacob? He certainly made her stomach flutter when he turned those sky-blue eyes on her. Yes, it would be fair to say she was infatuated with him, although she'd worked hard to keep feelings of that nature at bay. He was her employer, and this was a good home for Edward and for her. It was important she not mess this up. Jacob seemed to enjoy her company, but that wasn't too surprising since he didn't have much opportunity to spend time around female company. The kind he wasn't related to, that is. Of course, he didn't pay much attention to any of the single ladies at church on Sunday. Anna sighed. She wasn't likely to find answers by studying the buttons on his shirt, and it didn't really bear thinking about.

She set aside that shirt and reached for another at the same time she reached for a new question. Hopefully one for which she could actually find an answer. *What am I going to give for Christmas presents this year?* This would be their first year without Papa or their home in Columbia, and it probably wouldn't be easy for Edward. She fought back the ache that rushed her spirit. She couldn't focus on the circumstances. Her focus had to be on making this special for Edward. And for their new friends. She planned to add as much festivity as possible to the occasion by putting together a small gift for each of the men and Aunt Lola. But what should she give? She could use a bit of money from her earnings, but that money was precious. It was for their future.

As Anna finished scrubbing the next shirt, her mind ran through various gift ideas. But everything was either too expensive or too intricate to make them all before Christmas day, just two weeks away. As she picked up the next item in the basket, one of Mr. O'Brien's bandannas, she examined it for stains. The cloth was frayed around the edges. And that gave her an idea…

Christmas Day dawned clear and cold, and Jacob sat at the kitchen table with a cup of coffee as the sun rose through the small window. Anna was in her element, already scurrying about the kitchen, peeling potatoes, steaming the plum pudding, and rolling out pastry dough for the pies.

"You're gonna wear a hole in the floor if you keep flyin' around the kitchen like that."

She glanced up with a nervous smile. Then her face turned to a questioning look as she sniffed the air. "My casseroles," she gasped, spinning around to the oven. Grasping a corner of her apron in each hand, she jerked open the oven door and peered in at the two huge pans full of bubbling yellow *something.* A wave of tantalizing smells drifted over to Jacob. The aroma was more than he could resist, pulling him to his feet and toward the root of the fragrance.

He peered over her shoulder as Anna set the first pan on a warming pad. "Mmmm... I hope you're not planning to make us wait 'til Christmas dinner to eat those."

She shot him a teasing grin as she moved back to the oven to remove the second pan. "Papa always told me good things come to those who wait."

Something about Anna's words drew his gaze to her lips, which formed a cute little pout while she focused on the casseroles. Protruding like that, their smooth surface was flawless. How warm and soft would they feel if he lowered his mouth to hers? He jerked his eyes away to outside the window. That rabbit trail was sure to lead toward trouble. His concentration needed to stay with the ranch and the cattle. Getting mixed up with a female was sure to be a distraction. With the talk of cattle thieves in the area, now was definitely not the time to let his attention wander.

Jacob turned back to Anna. She sprinkled loose cheese on the casseroles then stepped back to eye them. She looked so cute with her forehead puckered in concentration.

"Can I help with something?"

Anna glanced up at him as if she just realized he were still in the room. He wished he could forget *her* presence that easily.

"Would you mind carrying these casseroles into the dining room and set them on the table?"

As he moved forward to lift the first pan, an idea struck him and he turned to the woman. "Anna?"

"Yes?" She looked up from the bread dough she was kneading, a hint of white dust on her cheek making his gut tighten a little.

"I was thinking of going for a ride down to the river after dinner today. If you don't have any plans, I'd be glad for you to come along." He cleared his throat. Why did he feel more nervous than a wrangler breaking a new horse?

Her eyes widened and her brows rose. Was that excitement? "I'd love to. I'm afraid it might take me an hour or two to get things cleaned up from the meal, but I'll be ready as soon as I can, if you don't mind waiting for me." Her eyes dipped back to the dough oozing between her tightly-squeezed fingers. "Of course, if you'd rather not wait, I understand."

Reaching forward to brush the white smear from her cheek, he couldn't help his answer. "Someone once told me good things come to those who wait."

With a chuckle at the red creeping into her face, Jacob picked up a casserole and headed toward the dining room, his mood lighter than it had been in a long time. It was going to be a good Christmas, after all.

~

The meal turned out to be everything Anna had hoped for. She'd managed not to burn anything, and the men offered their usual compliments on her talent with flavorings. Jacob seemed to especially like the yeast rolls smothered with warm apple butter, and she made a mental note of his choice.

As they dug into dessert, the men discussed their plans for

the afternoon, including a rousing checkers competition. Anna grinned as Edward promised to "take home the pot quicker than any of ya can count the checkers ya lose." He was sounding more and more like a cowboy.

"Well, Little Brother," Jacob announced, using the nickname the boys had assigned to Edward, "I reckon you'll get your chance to prove it right after you and Bo finish cleanin' up the kitchen." Anna turned to Jacob, her mouth dropping open. Out of the corner of her eye, she noticed Edward and Bo did the same.

"Clean the kitchen?" Edward's voice cracked a bit, probably from disbelief. He would never disobey an order from Jacob, but she had to admit the assignment surprised her as well. Most cowboys considered work in the house to be beneath them.

"Yep, I reckon' your sister deserves the afternoon off since it's Christmas and all."

Edward's head bobbed in assent, even as his eyes dropped down to the custard on his plate. Disappointment shrouded his features.

But her heart leapt at the idea of not having to scrub pans after the meal. Maybe a little Christmas spirit could lighten his mood.

"Well," Anna said, as she rose. She picked up a stack of small parcels from the sideboard, each wrapped in brown paper and tied with red ribbon. "I have a little something for each of you to celebrate the day."

She moved around the table, handing out packages according to the name she had inscribed next to the ribbon on each. "It's not much, but I wanted you to have a little something special. You've all come to mean so much to Edward and me over the last few months."

Aunt Lola patted her hand as Anna placed the little bundle into the older woman's grip.

"You're a special one, Anna Stewart. I think we're gonna keep you around."

Anna squeezed the older woman's hand, emotion clogging her throat at the tears that glimmered in the dark blue eyes.

When she made it back to her seat, Anna glanced around. The men looked expectantly at her. "Well, open them." She almost laughed at the way they tore into the paper. These rough cowboys were just overgrown boys after all.

Anna peeked over at Jacob to catch his expression as he peeled the paper from the blue flannel bandanna, the same color as his sky blue eyes. He fingered the soft cloth and rubbed his thumb across the letters *JOB* she had so painstakingly embroidered. Why had she given him such a silly gift? What did a cowboy care about a piece of cloth? He wouldn't know she had gone to two different stores to find flannel just the right color and had redone the stitches three times so the letters in his initials would be perfectly angled. When he looked up, though, Anna didn't see scorn in his eyes, only appreciation…and something else.

"It's not much." she whispered, almost afraid to speak as the intensity of his gaze deepened.

"It's perfect." A smile played on his lips. Yes, perfect.

The "Thank you's" and "Muchas gracias, Seniorita's" tore Anna's attention away from Jacob as she settled into the warm spirit of Christmas giving.

The next round of gifts came from Mr. O'Brien and included a bag of peppermint sticks and a five-dollar gold piece for each of them. Anna flashed him an appreciative smile. Gold pieces were not easy to come by since the War, especially in the Southern states.

After the meal, Jacob held Anna's chair while she stood then touched her elbow as he leaned forward to speak softly in her ear. "If you're ready, I'll saddle the horses while you get your coat."

Anna nodded, not meeting his eyes. "I'll be right back."

As she hurried upstairs to gather her cloak and gloves, a tickle built in her stomach.

In the front yard a few minutes later, Anna rested her left boot in Jacob's cupped hands and he boosted her onto Bandita's back. As she settled the reins in her gloved hands, a motion on the front porch caught her eye.

Monty settled in a rocking chair and eyed them with a speculative grin. "You two checkin' on the cattle or just headin' out to enjoy the warm weather?" he asked in a teasing Mexican accent.

Heat rushed up her neck, but Jacob didn't seem a bit embarrassed by the remark. "We're tired of hanging around a bunch of grubby cowpokes and thought we'd get some fresh air." Mounting his own horse, Jacob called over his shoulder, "Good luck in the checker match, amigo." Then he motioned for Anna to precede him, and they started off. Monty's deep chuckle drifted after them.

CHAPTER 15

Anna settled into the ride as they skirted around the edge of the herd, and Jacob pointed out a few of the most ornery cattle that had caused particular trouble at one time or another.

"See that cow with a full white face and the really long horns? Last year she lost a calf in the birthing. She had a full bag of milk, and Vegas needed to milk her so it wouldn't spoil and cause infection. You should have seen the ruckus she caused. He got the job done but had so many bruises, he couldn't sit straight in the saddle for days."

Anna laughed until tears sprang to her eyes. It was captivating the way Jacob's face lit up as he talked of the cattle and the men. The ranch was so much a part of him, and passion radiated from his voice as he spoke. She couldn't help a bit of envy at the way he seemed to know what he wanted from life. He'd been settled in one place since childhood, pursuing his dreams.

When they made it to the river and dismounted, Jacob tied the horses to a large pecan tree about twenty feet from the river while Anna strolled toward the water's edge. She loosened her bonnet, allowing it to dangle by the strings as she relished the warmth of the sun on her face. A pair of Cardinals danced on the bare branch of a small tree down the bank. The sun glinted off the surface of the gently flowing water, giving the illusion of warmth. But she had a feeling it was ice cold from the winter nights.

Jacob joined her, and Anna was thankful he didn't speak to disturb the beauty around them. After a few long moments, he bent down and picked up a branch from the ground then pushed the dry leaves away as if searching for something. She looked over his shoulder, curious. He rose and moved along the river's edge, following the current but staring at the ground as he walked. His brow was puckered a bit, like he was trying to figure out a puzzle.

"What's wrong?" Anna finally asked. But Jacob just continued plodding downstream. Anna followed at a distance. What was he doing? And why was he ignoring her? They were almost out of sight from where they'd started when Jacob squatted to examine the ground, then peered across the river. Hundreds of hoof prints molded the muddy patch of ground at the water's edge. They were not the rounded prints of horses, but the two smaller oval prints of a cow—and there were lots of them.

"Is this where our cattle come to drink?" she asked cautiously, still not sure what to make of Jacob's behavior.

"Not usually. There are a few tracks from horses, too, and one of the horses is wearing a bar shoe that doesn't match what our animals wear." He sighed, rising to stand next to her. "These prints don't look like the cows just came to the water's edge to drink. It looks like they walked right out into the river. My guess is they were driven into the river and came out somewhere downstream on the other side."

Anna stared at Jacob in horror, not liking the implication of his words. "Do you think it was the rustlers the other ranchers are talking about? How many do you think they took?"

"It's hard to say for sure, but it looks that way. There are enough tracks to be about fifty head but hard to tell for sure there, too. I guess we'll be adding a night watch for the herd."

Anna studied Jacob's expression. He had a hard set to his chin and a worried look in his blue eyes. Losing fifty cows was not good for the ranch, but he was probably worried about the threat of losing even more. Still, the thought of their men running into a gang of bandits in the dark made her stomach queasy. "Who would you send out for the night watch?" Some of the older cow hands might welcome the solitude.

"We'll all take turns, two each night."

The nausea in Anna's stomach threatened to bring back the plum pudding she'd eaten for dessert. "Everyone? You, too? But what if you run into the thieves and they have guns?" Then another frightening thought occurred to her. "But surely not Edward, right?"

Jacob read the near panic in Anna's eyes and tread carefully. He turned to face her and laid a hand on each of her shoulders. "Anna, night watch is part of a cowboy's life. We don't usually stay with the cattle when we're around the ranch, but if there's a threat to them, it has to be done. We all carry guns and stay in pairs, so there's not really much danger. Edward will be fine. He's a man now and a smart one at that. He knows how to handle himself, and I'll make sure he knows to head back for reinforcements at the first sign of trouble. In fact, I'll make sure I have night duty the same time as him so I can keep an eye out for him."

As he spoke the last words, tears pooled in Anna's brown eyes. When one of them broke through the dam and rolled down her cheek, Jacob couldn't help himself any longer. He pulled her against his chest and stroked her back. She felt so good against him, like coming home. After a minute, Anna's shoulders relaxed and she drew a deep shuddering breath then took a little step back, putting space between them. Jacob loosened his arms around her but didn't let her go completely, sliding his hands to Anna's elbows. He immediately missed her warmth against his chest.

Anna focused her gaze on his chin, not meeting his eyes.

"Anna, look at me."

She raised her gaze until it locked with his, those brown orbs stirring strong emotion within him. "No matter what happens, God will be with us." He stroked her cheek. So soft, but still a little damp from her tears. "And if I can do anything about it, nothing will ever hurt you again."

"Jacob..."

His name on her lips was more than he could stand. Jacob leaned down and covered her lips with his own. Her kiss was every bit as sweet as he'd imagined, and he pulled her closer, sliding his hands around her waist. Anna reached her arms to his shoulders, touching the nape of his neck and adding fuel to his desire. He deepened the kiss, kneading her back and pulling her even closer. Craving flooded his body. Anna moved a hand down to his chest, clutching his shirt. Jacob wasn't sure if she was pushing him away or pulling him closer, but the movement was enough to help him reclaim some of his senses. He took one last sweet taste then ended the kiss, bringing his forehead to rest against Anna's. He stood there for a moment to catch both his breath and his self-control. Anna seemed to be doing much the same.

"Jacob..."

"Hmmm..." He moved back a few inches to see her face and cupped her cheek with his palm. Wow, she was beautiful. *Lord,*

I'm still not sure why You brought this incredible woman into my life, but please help me not to blow it.

"Do you think we'd better head back now? The others might start missing us, and I need to get supper started soon."

Jacob groaned and pulled Anna's head back to his chest. "I don't know how you can think of food after that Christmas dinner we had." Giving her one last gentle squeeze, he finally released her. "But I guess we'd better get back to the house, though. Knowing your brother, he'll be ready to eat a side of beef by the time we get there."

Anna laughed, creating a warmth that spread through Jacob's chest. "He's still a growing boy."

CHAPTER 16

Over the next few weeks, the men took turns guarding the stock at night. Worry was Anna's companion during the darkness, especially when Jacob and Edward were on duty. But as time progressed and the men experienced no trouble, her fears began to fade.

Anna handed Jacob a cup of coffee in exchange for the basket of eggs one morning after he had come in from milking. The white liquid had a thin sheet of ice over the top when he set the bucket on the counter, confirming Anna's suspicion that it was extra cold outside that morning.

"Temperature's dropping." Jacob rubbed his hands together and blew between them, creating a bit of heat in his fingers. "It looks like there's a storm coming."

"Are the men going to stay in today until after the storm is over?" Not much snow fell in South Carolina, but Texas storms might be worse than the mild snowfalls she had experienced. After all, everything was bigger in Texas.

"Nope. Need to move the stock to cover under the trees in the north pasture. One of the men will head out to the line shack, too, so we can keep someone close to the cattle if things get bad."

Anna looked up from stirring oats over the cookstove. "The line shack?"

"It's a shed out on the northern corner of the property. That area has the best cover when the snow storms hit. The men take turns living there for a week at a time during snow season. That way, someone is always close by to open up water holes and help with early calving."

Anna didn't like the sound of that, but she was learning these cowboys were a tough breed. They could handle anything that came at them and then some. And, too, they all trusted in the Lord to keep them safe. That helped her to bite back the concern she wanted to voice. "Who will stay in the line shack first?"

Jacob took another swig of coffee then set the cup down and shrugged his shoulders. "That'll be up to Monty. But I do know you'll probably want to get food provisions ready for whoever goes. Mostly beans and cornmeal, but enough to last at least three weeks."

A snowstorm did hit that day, and Anna was amazed at the fury it unleashed. After two hours of snowfall so thick she couldn't see more than four foot out the window, it finally slowed to a light misting. She'd planned a hot stew for dinner that night and was relieved when the men came in not long after their usual time, stomping off snow on the front porch and shedding ice-covered coats in the front hall.

The snow definitely made things harder around the ranch, and they were all relieved when it melted in a couple of days. But a week later another storm hit, bringing with it almost a foot of frozen precipitation that lasted for a week. This pattern continued through the middle of February and Mr. O'Brien said this was the most snow they'd experienced in at least fifteen years.

Each evening, the cowpunchers would drag themselves in for supper, exhausted from trudging through the snow or mud, pulling cattle out of drifts, breaking through thick ice to create water holes, and who knew what else. The men continued to take turns staying in the line shack, rotating each Monday. Anna was relieved neither Edward nor Jacob had been required to perform this particular role yet. It still amazed her that even though Jacob was part owner of the ranch, he worked side by side with the cowpunchers and took orders from the foreman like any other hired hand.

"Do you want to tell me what's wrong?" Anna set down the knife and potato she'd been peeling and focused her attention on Jacob. He'd been sitting at the kitchen table all morning, coffee untouched, with his brow furrowed and his mind somewhere far away from the cozy kitchen they were in. She'd studied him curiously at first but couldn't stand the suspense any longer.

Jacob's brows rose at her question. "Why do you think something's wrong?"

Did he think she was that dense? His innocence would have been endearing if she wasn't so worried about what was bothering him. "Because you've been sitting there for twenty minutes stewing over something. Are more cattle missing?"

He shook his head. "It's too hard to tell with the snow and all the cattle taking shelter. I know we've lost a few from the weather, but we haven't seen any more sign of rustlers. We won't be able to get a good head count until spring round-up and branding."

"So..." Anna prompted.

"So, what?"

Anna let out an exasperated sigh. "So are you gonna tell me what you've been stewing about?"

Jacob breathed his own sigh. "I've been *stewing* because I'm headed to the line shack today."

Anna dropped her knife on the counter with a clatter. "You?"

"Yep, I was just thinkin' how I'm gonna have to make my own coffee in the mornings." His blue eyes turned to her with the hint of a twinkle.

Heat rose to her cheeks, but then the full meaning of his words began to sink in. Jacob would be gone for a week? No early morning time with him all to herself, drinking coffee and talking while she cooked breakfast. No more sitting next to him at the dinner table. She had come to enjoy and depend on his presence. He was a good friend, but it was something more than friendship. But, how much more? He hadn't touched her since that kiss by the river on Christmas Day. Had she dreamed the whole wonderful event?

"Are you gonna miss me?"

At Jacob's words, the heat rushed past Anna's neck and flamed in her cheeks. She dipped her chin and focused on peeling the potato in her hand.

Jacob released a husky chuckle, and his figure loomed in the corner of her vision as he rose from his chair and moved to stand next to her. Furiously peeling the poor potato, Anna didn't dare look up or even breathe. Her insides were too jumbled with him standing so close.

After what must have been an eternity with Jacob standing near, Anna's nerves were stretched tighter than a banjo string, and her hands flew around the tiny nub that was left of the potato. He finally reached out and placed his large work-roughened hand over both of hers, stilling them instantly. She chanced a cautious peek at his face and froze at the intensity in those deep blue eyes. She was putty in his hands as Jacob extracted the knife from her grip and turned Anna to face him.

"You haven't answered my question." His deep voice broke through the fog swirling in Anna's brain. "Are you going to miss me?" He reached out a hand to cup Anna's cheek. "Because I know I'll miss you."

Anna's stomach was a ball of nerves. "Is it me you're going to miss or my coffee and food?"

Jacob took a step toward her, eliminating all but a few inches of distance between them. "You. I'll definitely be missin' you." He moved his hands to Anna's shoulders, trailing them down her arms to rest on her elbows. Her skin tingled everywhere his fingers grazed. He pulled her to him, and her eyelids fluttered closed as his lips came down to touch her own. His kiss was sweet and yet his mouth melded to hers with an intensity she had only dreamed about. Anna's heart responded in kind as her hands reached out to caress him, one coming to rest on his heart and the other stretching around his neck to tug him closer. Closer. She couldn't get enough of this man she had come to—

"Uhh-hmm..."

A throat cleared in the doorway. Anna jumped back. Her face was surely the color of the chili peppers she had set out to use for dinner that night. Monty stood in the doorway, grinning like a cat with a cornered mouse.

"What do you need?" Jacob's voice was low, almost a growl.

Monty didn't seem fazed by his less than enthusiastic welcome. "Sorry to interrupt." He sauntered into the room, hands in his pockets. "I needed to fill you in on a couple of things before you head to the shack today."

Jacob sighed and ran a hand through his curly brown locks. "All right, have a seat." He motioned toward the chair then turned to Anna with an apologetic look.

She could barely meet his gaze, heat still searing her cheeks.

As Jacob sat down across from Monty at the kitchen table, Anna set a second cup in front of Monty and poured steaming coffee into both mugs. She kept her head down, trying to be as invisible as possible.

While the men talked about supplies, cattle, and grazing areas, Anna forced her attention onto finishing breakfast. As she sliced potatoes into the skillet, the heat flooded her chest again from their kiss. Was it love she felt for this man? Or just a strong attraction? Who couldn't be attracted to such a tall, muscled cowboy with gorgeous blue eyes set in a perfectly proportioned face? But her feelings ran deeper than attraction. She respected his wisdom and deep faith, and over the months of coffee and conversation, she'd come to value his friendship. In fact, she was as close to Jacob as she was to her own brother. These were definitely the right ingredients for love.

Jacob heaved the ax over his shoulder and brought it down hard on the ice in the creek. *Crack*! A layer of the frozen stuff splintered, leaving another solid sheet underneath. He raised the ax back over his shoulder, welcoming the groan of his muscles at the effort. After five long days and nights staying in the line shack, he was glad for anything to distract his mind from the thoughts and images of Anna that had lodged themselves in his brain. *Crack*! This time he broke through the last layer of ice, and water poured into the frozen hole.

The lowing of the cattle behind him grew stronger as they smelled the water and charged forward. He grabbed the ax and jumped out of the way as horns clattered and animals vied for position in front of the small water hole. Standing off to the side, Jacob wiped the perspiration from his forehead with the back of an arm then repositioned his hat. Even in the freezing cold, he'd worked up a sweat. Glancing up at the grey sky, he tried to gauge how low the clouds were. Texas storms could be harder to predict than a bronco's next buck, but if he didn't miss his guess, they were in for more snow.

And he was right. Snow fell for two days solid, covering everything in sight and making it almost impossible to leave the shack. They had built a stall onto one side for a horse with a door in between so he could feed and water Marshall without having to traipse out in the snow. With almost four feet of the white stuff, the animals couldn't move around much and were likely to stay holed up in the trees.

Jacob stayed in the little building, thankful he'd brought extra supplies with him. He'd never had a problem with eating beans and cornbread at every meal, but after Anna's food for the last few months, it was hard to stomach the gritty stuff day after day. If it hadn't been for his Bible and a few other books they kept in the shack, Jacob might have gone mad from being left alone with all his thoughts.

Finally, four days after the snow began, the sun came out and temperatures started to rise a bit. As Jacob saddled Marshall, the gelding stomped impatiently. "I know it, boy. I'm ready to get out of here, too." He patted the horse's shoulder before reaching to tie his bedroll and slicker behind the seat of the saddle.

Marshall had been with him since the horse was a two-year-old. Most cowboys left the horse breaking to the ranch wrangler, but Jacob had always preferred to train his riding horses himself, building a bond with the animal and preparing them thoroughly for any situation. Marshall's intelligence was evident right away, and Jacob worked with the horse each day. First, teaching him to lead and tie, then getting him used to all kinds of noises and scary objects, including gunshots and barking dogs. Eventually, he trained the horse to ride, rope, and out-think even the most ornery longhorn. Jacob still rotated his riding horse daily to give each of them a rest, but Marshall was by far his favorite.

After a long day pulling out cattle from snow drifts and breaking layers of ice, Jacob was more than relieved to turn Marshall toward the ranch house. It was Bo's turn to stay at the line shack, and Jacob was plenty happy to pass the torch. He couldn't wait to fill his stomach with something warm and tasty, anything but beans and cornbread. And he would see Anna. In the flesh, although he'd seen her in his mind's eye every night as he lay on the cot in the shack, trying in vain to sleep.

A faint breeze ruffled his hair and Jacob caught a whiff of stale body odor. Ducking his head for another sniff, he wrinkled his nose in disgust. He smelled worse than a pig after a rainstorm. There was no way he could show up at supper looking and smelling as rank as he did, but there wasn't enough time for a bath. He'd have to settle for a wipe down and a change of clothes. Jacob ran a hand over his face, the coarse hairs way beyond stubble by this point. A little overgrowth on his face had never bothered him before.

~

Anna stared at the doorway from her seat at the far end of the table as the men around the room dove into their Irish stew and yeast rolls. Monty had said Jacob came back tonight with the men, but he hadn't shown up for supper yet. Should she be worried? But maybe he was just tired and went to bed early. Should she send up a tray for him?

As she glanced toward the door again, Monty caught her eye with a reassuring grin. "He'll be here soon, Senorita. He's probably just cleaning up a bit. Smelled like a scared skunk by the time we finished today."

She wasn't too pleased with his comparing Jacob to a skunk, but before she could set the man straight, Jacob appeared in the doorway. He looked *wonderful* and *whole*…if a little haggard. His deep blue eyes met Anna's as he moved around the table to sit in his usual chair at the end, right next to her. She gave him a shy smile, the butterflies in her stomach doing double-time at his sudden nearness.

"Welcome home," she whispered, hoping the others couldn't hear or wouldn't notice. Jacob flashed one of his brilliant smiles at her, the kind that made her heart miss a beat.

"Jacob! Glad you made it home, son." Mr. O'Brien's greeting boomed across the table, stealing Jacob's attention. While he answered the questions that flew at him from around the table, Anna busied herself filling Jacob's bowl with stew and passing the yeast rolls and apple butter.

"How many head do ya think we lost in that last storm, boss?"

"Did the creek freeze through or could ya hack a bit o' water out of it?"

"Sure was a cold one this time. One of them newspaper men from town said it got down to ten degrees one night last week."

When Anna placed the bowl of hot stew in front of him, Jacob shot her a smile full of gratitude, then dug in as if he hadn't eaten in weeks, which was probably not far from the truth. At least not a decent meal. His large frame bent over the bowl while he ate, but the men kept volleying questions like snowballs. He shrugged, nodded, or shook his head to most of the inquiries, and gave one- or two-word answers to those that required them.

When the cowhands had eaten their fill, including almost four whole peach and apple pies, they stood and ambled out of the room, heading in the general direction of the bunkhouse. Anna, too, rose and stacked dishes in preparation for clearing the table. Jacob was one of the last to stand, and her heart picked up a bit of speed. Was he waiting to spend a quiet moment with her? As she made her way around the table with a stack of plates, Mr. O'Brien strode toward his son and clapped him on the shoulder.

"Well, boy, glad you could make it back for your birthday. It would have been awfully lonely for all of us to have you spend it out at the line shack."

Anna's head jerked up. Her eyes zeroed in on both men, trying to gauge if she'd heard correctly. Was today Jacob's birthday? Why had no one told her? She would have made a cake and maybe even bought him a gift. But a gift would have been too forward. Wouldn't it? At least she would have liked to know about it. Now it was after dark and much too late to do anything special to celebrate.

As the dining room emptied, Anna's mind whirled. She gathered a stack of dirty plates and proceeded toward the kitchen, lowering them into the clean water she'd brought in before supper for the washing. She turned to head back toward the dining hall for another stack of dishes. But as she stepped through the doorway, she ran squarely into Jacob who was balancing a rather precarious stack of bowls. He shifted the dishes in an effort to free his left hand to catch Anna but only succeeded in tilting the stack further toward the right.

Anna righted herself and stood, jaw open in momentary horror, as the entire stack of ironstone dishes continued their sideways momentum. Everything moved in slow motion. Anna forced her shock aside and sprang into action, catapulting forward to catch the bowls. Her efforts didn't help much, though, because the entire stack landed with a crash on the hardwood floor.

"No..." The word came out like a moan as Anna dropped to her knees and examined the white dishes for damage. Each bowl was made of shiny white ironstone with wide, fluted edges and delicate leaf prints pressed into the sides. She had long admired their simple beauty and was always so careful when handling them. Now they lay scattered across the floor, covered in soup broth and leftover chunks of potatoes.

"Are you hurt?" Jacob's voice was thick with concern, or maybe a touch of fear, as he dropped down beside her.

Anna didn't stop to think about it. Her arms had padded the landing of a few bowls, but the violent crash had broken many. A chunk of ironstone slid several feet away. "The beautiful dishes..." she moaned under her breath as she began stacking each item she found undamaged. So far, four were not broken. Five. Six. Remnants of broth moistened the floor and clung to the bowls, spreading onto Anna's hands as she handled them. Seven.

"Anna, you're bleeding."

She glanced down at both hands. A smear of blood coated the inside of her right thumb. Her heart sank. That meant another dish broken. She turned a bowl over in her hand. A chip was missing from the circular base. Before she could examine it closer, Jacob pulled the pottery from her grip.

"I need to see it." She grabbed for the dish.

He held it out of her reach with one hand and with the other, grasped Anna's arm to examine the injury.

"It's just a little cut, but I need to see how badly that bowl is broken. Maybe I can glue it back together."

"I'm not worried about the bowl, Anna." Jacob's voice sounded as if he were trying hard to rein in his patience like a runaway horse. "We need to see how bad you're hurt and make sure there aren't any shards still in your hand."

Anna tamped down her frustration and finally stopped fighting his overpowering strength. She sat back on her heels to allow him to peer at her thumb. It only stung a little, nothing to stop the presses for.

"I don't think it's very deep, but we need to get it cleaned up."

"It's not deep at all, and I'll take care of it when I'm done here." She didn't mean to sound as annoyed as she really was, but the words slipped out. Aunt Lola had told her these dishes first belonged to Mr. O'Brien's wife, Jacob's mother, and Anna wanted desperately to see if she could repair the damage.

At her words, Jacob stilled and the sudden lack of motion made Anna stop as well. He raised his sky-blue eyes to meet hers. Their expression changed several times, from hurt to anger to sympathy. Anna found herself captivated, as always, by their intensity. His Adam's apple bobbed.

She held her breath. "I'm sorry," she whispered.

He nodded, his gaze touching her lips before it skittered back up to her eyes. He still held her injured hand, cradling it in both of his own.

Anna's mouth was dry, but the silence seemed to beg for words to fill it. "I didn't know today was your birthday. I would have baked a cake."

His eyes twinkled. His gaze dropped to her mouth again and he leaned forward, bringing his lips down to hers. So strong, so gentle. It wasn't a deep kiss or a long one, but it held such sweetness that Anna almost followed him when he pulled away.

Jacob's right hand came up to cup her cheek, his rough fingers stroking it gently. His eyes roamed her face, as if cataloging its features. "I've missed you."

"I'm so glad you're home."

His eyes smiled. "Not half as glad as I am."

He held her gaze for another long moment then leaned back and reached for another bowl to add to the stack between them.

Anna blinked and scanned the area then started to help him. "I'm so sorry about your Ma's dishes. I know these were special to her."

Jacob glanced up and let out a little chuckle.

Anna eyed him. "Why are you laughing?"

"Because we've broken so many of these dishes, and Ma would get so upset each time. Finally Pa sent off and bought a complete second set so every time a dish broke, we could replace it and keep this collection complete."

Anna absorbed his words. What a smart man Mr. O'Brien was. She couldn't hold back a giggle of her own. "You mean there's another set of this same pattern here somewhere?"

"Half a set. We broke an awful lot before Ma taught us big, rough cowpokes how to be civilized. I'll show you where we keep them in a bit." He reached for a chunk of broken dish that had slid several feet away.

Anna's conscience pricked. "You don't need to be down here helping me clean up. You've just come back from two hard weeks at the line shack and you should be in the den relaxing."

He shook his head, his square chin forming a stubborn set. "If I'd have been more careful to start with, they wouldn't be scattered all over the floor." Stacking the last of the pieces, he rose and extended a hand to help Anna stand. When she came to her feet, he continued the tug and pulled her straight into his chest, wrapping both arms around her waist. He gave her a sly grin. "Besides, this beats talkin' to myself in a cold little cabin any day."

Anna burrowed into his strong arms and nestled her head under his chin. It was so wonderful to have him home, safe and sound. She could stay like this forever, listening to his heartbeat.

CHAPTER 17

As the snow finally melted and the sun began making a more regular appearance overhead, new signs of life popped up everywhere. The grass showed green patches scattered among the brown, and tiny shoots of new growth sprouted on most of the trees. Jacob and his men spent every daylight hour with the cattle, now that calving season had officially begun. Anna stayed quite busy herself, as she and Aunt Lola gave the house a thorough cleaning and airing. She longed to take Bandita out for a nice long canter, but that would have to wait. There was work to be done.

Edward rode his horse along the river trail, scanning the tree line for cattle as he listened for their low mooing. Monty had assigned him as a line rider along the river that day, searching for cows beginning to calf. When the birthing was imminent, the expectant cow would usually separate from the herd to find a quiet place to deliver. Most times, the cow would labor successfully without help from the cowpunchers, but if the calf was breeched or the cow carried twins, things could go south pretty quickly without a pair of strong arms to help the mama cow along.

Before coming to the ranch, the only thing he'd witnessed give birth was their neighbor's hound dog, Bessie. This year, though, he'd already helped with at least a dozen calvings. Jacob had taught him how to tell if the calf was facing the wrong way inside the mama, and how to reach in and turn the baby so its front hooves and nose faced first. It was a tricky process and had to be done at just the right time in between the mama's pushes. Edward still wasn't sure he was ready to do it himself, but Monty seemed to think he could. He'd give it his best.

So far, he'd been riding the river's edge for about half an hour and hadn't spotted any longhorns in the area, but he'd follow orders anyway and ride all the way to where Two-Fork creek split off from the Guadalupe.

Just then, a low moo drifted from the woods to his right. The trees were much thicker here, but he plunged into the brush, dodging branches and hanging onto his hat so it wouldn't be knocked off.

As he progressed deeper into the woods, the cattle noises grew louder, but they didn't sound like a cow struggling to calf. Was it a whole herd of cows? But that didn't make any sense. If a group of cattle were napping in the trees, they didn't make a lot of noise, just an occasional stomping or tail swishing.

Edward pushed forward and finally broke through the woods into a little clearing. A huge group of cattle milled around the large open space, lowing uneasily. At first Edward wasn't sure what was keeping animals in the area until he saw a small group of cowboys circling the outer edge of the herd.

Cowboys? This didn't make sense, either. The men all had the dark features of Monty and his family, but none of them looked familiar. He hadn't crossed over Two-Fork creek, so he had to be still on Double Rocking B land. Why were strangers here rounding up cattle? He peered at the closest cows. These animals had the Double Rocking B brand. The confusion began to clear in Edward's mind as understanding dawned.

A rifle cocked behind him. Edward spun around in the saddle and faced hard black eyes underneath a wide-brimmed hat. They glared at him from behind the double barrels of a Winchester.

"Move and your life is over, gringo." The words spoken in a strong Mexican accent made Edward's blood run cold. He'd found the cattle thieves.

Edward opened his mouth to retort but was stopped short when a rope settled around his shoulders and pulled tight. The rope jerked him backward, and he flew through the air, hitting the ground with a thud. A loud grunt pierced the air, but his mind focused on trying to draw breath into his empty lungs. It came in short gulps at first. When he was able to draw a full breath, he realized he was being dragged across muddy, manure-covered ground. Finally, he came to a stop.

Mexican voices called to each other in quick short bursts. Edward's brain struggled to catch up and couldn't understand the words. A short, stocky man who stank of tobacco knelt at his side and began binding his wrists with a coarse rope. Edward fought, but with the lariat still tight around his upper arms, he couldn't gain any leverage. The solid punch of a boot heel in his back forced Edward's head to the ground, stilling his efforts to resist. The Mexican mumbled something under his breath.

Edward took the opportunity to scan his surroundings, cataloguing the area. It was hard to tell from his vantage point on the ground, but there must be at least seventy or eighty head of cattle. Four men rode horses around the herd, and three others were mounted and deep in discussion about a stone's throw away. He strained to pick up a few words from their conversation, but they spoke so fast and quietly, he could only distinguish the words "gringo" and "caballo".

When Edward's hands were bound, his captor rose to stand next to him, arms crossed and legs planted solidly like an Arabian sultan. One of the men, who gave most of the commands, yelled a quick order to Edward's guard, who jumped into action.

Someone yanked a rag over Edward's mouth. It tasted of sweat and wretched body odor. Another cloth covered his eyes, and the knot in his chest threatened to smother him. They had bound his hands and gagged him, but the loss of his sight meant he couldn't detect a blow coming. Couldn't gather important information about the bandits. Couldn't see his chance for escape...

~

Jacob reined in his horse to stand next to Monty's mount and rested both arms on the saddle horn. They sat in companionable stillness for a few moments, the cattle grazing nearby. At last, Jacob broke the silence. "The outriders find any new calves this mornin'?"

"Paco and Bo each found a couple. Haven't seen Little Brother yet."

Jacob shot a look at his friend. "He left when the others did?"

Monty nodded.

"Which way'd he go?"

"The river trail south to the creek."

Jacob glanced up at the sun almost directly overhead. The boy should have been back two hours ago. He must have come across a struggling cow trying to deliver. It hadn't taken Edward long to pick-up on what to do during the calvings he'd helped with so far, but sometimes the longhorns got extra ornery after they'd been laboring for a while. Jacob couldn't say he blamed them, but it never hurt to have an extra set of hands available at a time like that.

"If it's all right with you, think I'll head out that way myself. Just in case he needs back-up."

Monty nodded. "Wouldn't hurt."

Jacob loped his mount over the sandy soil until they reached the river then slowed to a steady jog. He couldn't explain the urgency that tightened his gut. Edward was a smart young cowboy and knew when to call for help, but something didn't feel right about this one.

After keeping a steady jog for almost an hour, Jacob reached Two-Fork creek with no sign of cattle or of the young cowboy. The water here was only about eight feet wide and hummed cheerfully as it hurried along with the extra volume of the spring rains. It was oblivious to the fist-sized knot that had formed in Jacob's gut.

He turned his horse northwest to take the shorter route back to the herd. Surely Edward had made it back by now. As he jogged his mount over the uneven terrain, a half dozen large birds circled the sky just ahead and toward the west. Turkey vultures. The presence of the ugly, meat-eating birds always signaled death. Had one of the cows died trying to give birth? A new sense of unease prodded him to turn his horse off the trail and move toward the circling birds.

He rode through a patch of trees which opened to a large meadow. Urging his horse into a canter, Jacob scanned the tree line surrounding the area. They were mostly shortleaf pine trees, with a few oaks and maples mixed in the group. A large rock poked up from the ground near one of the oak trees, almost directly under where the vultures soared.

For a second, it looked like the rock moved. Reining his horse to a jog, he reached for the rifle that was always strapped to his saddle. If someone was hiding behind the boulder, Jacob would be an easy target out in the middle of the open pasture.

As he cautiously moved closer, however, the shape shifted again. The image cleared. It wasn't a rock, but a man sitting against the tree. Every nerve in his body stood on edge. Was the man friend or foe? Was he riding into a trap?

A soft call drifted to Jacob's ears and he reined in his horse to listen. The noise was so faint he almost missed it. "Hmmpphhh..."

In an instant Jacob had his horse in a dead run, closing in on the distance between him and the weak figure propped against the tree. *Edward.*

CHAPTER 18

Anna pulled the last loaf of bread from the oven and almost dropped it on the warming pad. *Ouch.* The fabric on her apron was wearing too thin to shield her from the heat of the pan. She mentally added material to the list of things to buy on her next trip to town as she ran a knife around the outside edge of the bread, loosening it from the baking tin. The front door slammed, and male voices drifted through the house. Anna stopped moving and strained her ears. Mr. O'Brien had gone to town this morning to take care of ranch business. He must have returned with a guest. Anna brushed the flour from her hands and moved the coffee pot to the front of the stove. A visitor would need refreshments.

Just as she was arranging cookies on a plate, the voices rose and her own name echoed in a familiar tone. Jacob. Why was Jacob back in the middle of the day, calling for her? A warm flutter tickled Anna's stomach. Had he come in from the range just to see her? As quickly as it came, the flutter hardened into a knot of dread. Was he hurt?

Anna dropped the plate on the work table with a clatter,

picked up her skirts in both fists, and sprinted out of the kitchen and down the hallway. Just before she reached the door to the parlor, she almost ran into Jacob. He caught her with a firm hand on both of her upper arms. Anna's eyes scanned his body, checking for blood or breaks. Legs, arms, chest. Her gaze trailed to his face and found it whole, if a bit dirt-streaked. A wave of relief washed over her that left her weak, with legs unable to bear her own weight. She sank into Jacob, needing to touch him. To hear his heartbeat as her cheek rested against his chest.

"You're okay..."

For a few seconds he held her, and she relished his strength. But all too soon, Jacob disentangled himself and gripped her at arm's length. The firm set of his jaw and worried look in his eyes ignited a burning sensation, like pin pricks in Anna's chest.

"Edward found the cattle thieves. They roughed him up a little and left him tied, but *he's okay*."

The burning sensation exploded into a blaze inside her at Jacob's words. She struggled to move past him. She had to get inside the parlor to see Edward, but Jacob grasped her shoulders firmly.

"Anna."

The sharp insistence in his voice made her stop struggling and turn back to face him.

"He's *okay*. Just a little worn out, but nothing a cup of coffee and a good meal won't fix."

Anna nodded, but his words hadn't penetrated her mind. She needed to see Edward. She had to verify for herself whether he was hurt or not.

Jacob finally released her, and Anna surged past him. There, in the overstuffed chair near the fireplace, sat her little brother. Edward gave her a weak grin as Anna knelt down in front of him.

"Hey, sis. Did you hear I found the cattle thieves?" Mud was caked along the left side of his body, including his face and hair.

Anna inspected every inch but found no evidence of blood. She stroked his hand. "So I heard. Did they hurt you?"

"Nah, they just tied me to a tree and left me there, but they got away with a bunch of cattle."

Anna's pulse throbbed in her temples. "How many were there? Did you recognize them?"

"I saw eight men and they were all Mexican, but I'd never seen any of 'em before." Edward leaned back in the chair and yawned, pulling his hand from his sister's grasp. "Sure am hungry, though. Is that fresh bread I smell?"

"It is. C'mon to the kitchen and I'll fix you a slice with butter and peach preserves while you tell me everything that happened. Maybe you can finish off the apple pie from last night, too."

Anna rose to her feet and assisted Edward as he brought his gangly limbs to a standing position. When they turned toward the kitchen, Jacob leaned against the door frame, watching them. She couldn't read the expression in his eyes, but they clouded a darker blue than normal.

When she reached him, Anna rested a hand on his arm. "You must be exhausted, too. Come and get a bite to eat. You'll feel better with something warm in you."

The right side of his lip quirked just a bit. "I don't doubt that. I need to get back out to help the men, though. Bo went to town to get the sheriff and Pa. The rest of the boys started tracking the thieves and cattle they took. I need to get out there soon."

Anna nodded. She wouldn't be able to hold him back. It didn't stop the bile churning in her stomach, though. "Let me pack you something to take then."

He gave a single nod. "Guess I wouldn't turn that down. I'll put Edward's horse away while you get it together."

A few minutes later, Anna met Jacob on the front porch with a flask of coffee and a cloth full of ham sandwiches and several apple fritters she'd prepared for supper that night. As she handed the bundle to him, Jacob offered a stiff smile, but it didn't disguise the extra firm set to his jaw. He was worried about the missing cattle. "Any idea how many they got away with?"

He shook his head, his lips forming a thin line. "Edward said he thought he saw seventy or eighty head. Could be more."

"Do you think you'll find them?"

"Hard to say." His eyes turned to stare across the pasture in the direction of the Guadalupe River. "The land to the south on the other side of the river has so many wild cattle roaming, it'll be hard to track our herd. Lots of trees, too, so it wouldn't be hard to find another spot to hide for a few days before they move on out of the county. We'll do our best, though."

"Jacob…"

He brought his gaze back to meet hers.

"Please be careful."

For a moment, his eyes darkened, then he pulled her close and his lips swooped down to cover hers with an intensity that stole Anna's breath. The kiss spoke his frustration, anger, and worry better than any words could have communicated. Anna responded to his kiss, infusing it with strength and encouragement and…love. Yes, in that moment, beyond a shadow of a doubt, her head and her heart finally agreed. She loved this man.

Much too soon, Jacob pulled back, his hand moving up her arm to cup her face. He stared at Anna for a long moment as if memorizing her features, then he released her. Without a word, he reached down to pick up the bundle of food from where he'd dropped it on the porch, strode down the steps, and mounted his horse. After one last look at Anna, he turned his horse and jogged out of the yard.

So many emotions filled her chest as he loped across the pasture and out of sight. With a prayer on her lips, Anna finally turned back toward the house. Jacob would have to rest in God's hands. Edward needed her now.

That night, the men came dragging in an hour after dark, worn out and irritable. The nights were still chilly, so she'd made a huge pot of chili and spicy cornbread with butter and honey, along with apple fritters and donuts for dessert. When Mr. O'Brien said the blessing, he added a special thanks for Edward's safety and a petition for the missing cattle to be found.

Anna reached under the table to squeeze Jacob's hand. He had to be discouraged, and she wanted to impart what little comfort she could offer. He turned his hand to grip hers, and the feel of his large, work-roughened hand sent a warmth up her arm. After they all said "Amen," Anna opened her eyes and snuck a peek at Jacob. He caught her glance and winked then squeezed and released her hand under the table. The heat crept all the way up to the tips of her ears as she focused on spreading the napkin in her lap.

Anna was thankful conversation began around them, and she soon became engrossed in the discussion herself.

"So ye found the spot they were holdin' the cattle?" Aunt Lola's rich brogue filled the room as she addressed her cousin.

"Yes, we found the area. Looked like they'd camped there for a while, probably gathering up the cattle over a week or so. We followed the tracks as far as the river where the creeks split off and the main branch runs shallow for a ways. Couldn't pick up the tracks again before it got dark. They most likely kept the herd walking in the river or one of the creeks for as long as they could. The sheriff said he would send men back out to track them tomorrow."

Monty looked up from his bowl of stew. "Hope it doesn't rain tonight."

CHAPTER 19

After she scrubbed the dishes and cleaned the kitchen, Anna was too restless to join the rest of the family in the den like normal. Her emotions were still in a jumble from the happenings of the day, and what she needed most was quiet time with her Heavenly Father.

Grabbing her cape from a peg by the front door, she slipped outside into the cool night air. Clouds shielded the stars overhead, making the darkness thicker than usual. A damp breeze sent a shiver through her, and Anna pulled the cape tighter around her shoulders.

Standing on the porch by the rail, she replayed Jacob's departure from earlier that day. The old familiar vise squeezed her chest. So much could happen to him out there. It brought back memories of the fear that had gripped her when Edward recounted how the bandits had roughed him up and left him tied to a tree. Abandoned there. Weak, bound, gagged, and blindfolded. He could have easily been attacked by a bear, coyote, or cougar. Edward might well have died if Jacob hadn't found him. The what if's tormented Anna.

Lord, please don't take Edward from me. First Mama, then our home and Papa. I just don't think I could stand to lose Edward, too. An image of Jacob's blue eyes and strong chin flashed through Anna's mind. *Please keep both of my boys safe.*

The door behind her creaked, and the warm glow of a lantern spilled onto the porch. Anna turned to find Jacob easing the front door closed. He strode across the porch toward the stairs but stopped short when his eyes met hers.

"Hello," she offered softly, suddenly shy in his presence. *My goodness, but he's tall.*

"It's a bit cold out for stargazing." Jacob's voice was deep, almost husky, in the stillness of the night. He set the lantern down on the porch and strolled toward the rail.

Very aware of his large frame next to her, Anna faced the night sky. "I wish there were stars to gaze at. Just clouds tonight, though."

"Clouds are good for thinking, too." His voice was low and trailed off at the end as if lost in thought himself.

Anna let out a sigh. "I guess either one works for praying."

"You worried about Edward?"

How could he read her thoughts so accurately? Anna bit her lip. "Do you think they'll come back?"

He turned to face the cloudy sky, too, and was quiet for a few moments. "It's hard to say. The sheriff said they've been hitting one ranch at a time. They steal about a hundred head then move on to another ranch. Hopefully they got enough of ours and won't be back." He glanced at Anna and held her gaze. "But whether they come back or not, God is in control."

Anna pivoted to face him squarely, a lump clogging her chest. "But that's what I'm struggling with. I know in my head God is in control, that he's taking care of us. But actually placing Edward in God's hands, to do with as He wills? What if God doesn't keep him safe? Edward is everything I have left. If anything happened to him, I'm not sure I could stand it." Her voice cracked at the last words and moisture burned in her eyes.

Jacob pulled her into his arms. The tender touch was too much for her raw emotions, and a sob escaped. As tears broke through her barriers, Jacob's strong hands rubbed her back, gently stroking the pain away.

After a few minutes, Anna managed to staunch the flow. With a sniffle, she straightened, giving Jacob a weak smile. "I'm sorry. I don't usually break down like this."

When she tried to step back, though, his muscular arms wouldn't let her go. "You have nothing to apologize for." His voice was strong, yet gentle.

Anna tried to secure her smile. "Well, thanks for the hug, then." His arms felt so good, still holding her close.

His blue eyes twinkled in the lantern light as he tapped a forefinger to her nose. "Anytime."

Finally releasing her, Jacob picked up the lantern. "Well, I came out to check on a couple of the mares that are due to foal. The babies usually come at night, and we try to keep an eye on 'em in case they have trouble." He spun back, a question on his face. "Do you want to come?"

A flicker of interest bubbled inside Anna. "I'd love to."

Just before they entered the barn, Jacob stopped walking and cautioned, "Stay as quiet as you can until we see if they're in labor or not. Most mares are very private when they give birth and some will actually stop the foaling process if they see people. After the waters break, though, that baby's coming no matter what."

Anna nodded, absorbing his words. Other than their neighbor's dog when she was little, she had never witnessed anything give birth. She sent up a little prayer that she would get to see one of these foals being born. Edward had described the excitement of each of the calvings he'd watched over the last few weeks, and she couldn't help a twinge of jealousy over his experiences.

She crept into the barn behind Jacob, the musty combination

of horse, hay, and leather flooding her senses. She followed him as quietly as her long skirts would allow until they reached a stall midway down the row. He turned the lantern wick down so it emitted only a soft glow of light. She peaked over Jacob's shoulder through the wood beams into the stall. He slipped a hand around Anna's waist and moved her in front of him. Now she had an unobstructed view.

Inside the stall, a large chestnut horse with very swollen sides stood. The mare's neck and flanks gleamed a darker brown from perspiration, and she hung her head low in a painful stance. The mare's attitude suddenly changed. Her skin tightened and she swung her large head around to nip at her belly. She pawed the straw on the stall floor and turned around in small circles several times.

"She's having a contraction," Jacob whispered.

Anna didn't dare speak, but her heart pinched at the mare's pain. The poor creature looked miserable. After pawing the ground and circling several more times, the horse finally laid down, an effort that sounded a bit like a tree falling. The mare lay propped on her side, breathing hard. Then with a whoosh, a flood of water escaped from under her tail.

Jacob touched Anna's elbow, keeping his voice low. "It shouldn't be long now. I'm gonna get the foaling bucket and blankets."

Anna could only nod, eyes focused on the horse so she didn't miss anything. The mare seemed to be resting for a moment, though. She became aware of another presence at her side. It was Manuel, the ranch's wrangler who usually cared for the horses. Relief washed over her. The man had a vast amount of knowledge when it came to the animals. If anything went wrong, he would know what to do.

The mare began breathing hard again. She lay flat on her side, tail raised, muscles rippling along her sides.

"There's the first hoof." Manuel pointed toward the mare's

tail where Anna glimpsed a little white bubble barely visible. He slipped into the stall to crouch in the corner, but Anna's attention stayed focused on that little bubble. When the mare gave another push, the bubble became bigger and a dark color appeared underneath the semi-translucent film.

With each push, the mare would groan and more of the bubble appeared, until it took on the shape of a miniature head. Manuel stepped forward and broke the end of the bubble, pulling it away from the little face. Anna sucked in her breath at the tiny, delicate features.

As the mare continued to strain, the head with cute floppy ears and part of a neck, along with the two front legs surfaced. The baby still kept its eyes closed, and only the barely flaring nostrils announced it to be alive.

"Manuel, it's not moving," Anna whispered. Was the foal not strong enough?

"He's doing fine. They don't usually open their eyes until everything's out of the Mama. If it moved now, he might kick her insides and do some damage. As long as he's breathing, everything's going along just right."

Anna released the breath she'd been holding and watched in rapt attention as the mare's next push brought out the foal's shoulders and most of the torso. That left only the rear feet still inside. The foal's eyes opened then, and it raised its delicate little head to look around in bewilderment.

The mare lay still for a few moments then gave a final grunt and rose to her feet. The motion caused the baby to pull free, and it lay quietly on the stall floor until its mama came to nuzzle its neck. She licked the foal's body free of the white film that still covered in spots. The mare worked her tongue back toward the little head, finally finding the baby's muzzle. Mama and baby touched noses, and the mother gave a soft little nicker. The action was so sweet, Anna felt like she was intruding on a private moment.

She took a step back from the rail and hit a solid form behind her. Spinning around, Anna stared into Jacob's blue eyes, the shadows from the lantern making them appear darker than usual. He caught her shoulders then lightly ran his fingers down the back of her arms, sending shivers coursing through her body.

"Cold?" he asked in a husky whisper. The intensity in his gaze made it hard to breathe, let alone speak, but she couldn't tear her eyes away. Instead, she shook her head slightly.

"Pretty neat, isn't it?" The twinkle appeared in his eyes and the corners of his lips rose to reveal slight dimples. *My goodness, but he's handsome.*

Jacob quirked a brow. He was expecting an answer. She blinked, remembering the miracle of the birth she'd just witnessed, the joy of new life. "It's amazing."

CHAPTER 20

As March rolled into April, the spring rains came in a steady torrent. For two weeks straight, the deluge fell for at least a part of every day. The mud made things harder and messier for the cowpunchers, and each night the men would drag themselves into the dining hall, covered in the brown gunk. At least the temperature had warmed, so the rain produced rich green grass across the pastures.

When May arrived and the downpours became less frequent, the countryside opened up in a vast array of color. The woods were full of greenery, with pink cherry blossoms and white dogwood flowers mixed throughout. The pastures were covered in yellow, pink, and white wildflowers, and Anna took every possible opportunity for a ride on Bandita. The mare seemed to enjoy the outings as much as Anna and would toss her head continually until Anna loosened the reins and allowed the horse to stretch out for a run.

The highlight of Anna's day was still the early mornings when Jacob stopped in for coffee after milking the cow and gathering eggs. He would bring her up to speed on the happenings with the herd, and he was quickly becoming a master storyteller as he recounted the episodes the cowboys experienced on the range.

This particular morning was no different as Anna wielded the round biscuit-cutter in the floury sourdough mixture on the worktable. Jacob had just finished telling of Edward's growing skill with the lariat, when he stopped to take the last gulp of his second cup of coffee. He set the empty mug on the table and leaned back in the chair, but Anna didn't move to refill it. He held himself to a two cup maximum before breakfast.

"Well," Jacob spoke as if contemplating his words, "branding starts next week."

Anna quirked a brow. "What does that mean?"

"We always do our own branding on the ranch the week before the community round-up. Most of the other ranchers don't have enough hands to keep their cattle from roaming like we do, so every spring all the ranchers round-up the cattle in one spot, brand the calves, and drive the steers to Kansas. Since we keep the Double Rocking B cattle on our land, we brand the new calves before the main round-up. We still participate in the town event, though, just in case some of our cattle have strayed. It helps us stay in good standing with the community, too."

Anna worked in silence for a moment, processing the information. At last she looked up. "Does that mean our boys will be going on the cattle drive, too?"

He shook his head. "Not yet. We don't do a spring drive like most of the other ranchers. Since they already have their cattle rounded up, they go ahead and drive them to market. I like to wait until the fall, though, when the young ones are stronger and they've had a chance to gain weight over the summer."

Anna was once again amazed at the wisdom of this man. "So you'll start the branding on Monday?"

"Yep." He leaned forward in his chair. "Hopin' to get it done by Wednesday. Everyone'll have a job for the branding. Aunt Lola usually comes out with the wagon to handle the food and medicine. She's gettin' up in years to be sleepin' on the hard ground." His eyes roamed down to stare at his hands. "I was hoping maybe you could take her spot this year?" He looked up at Anna with a bit of pleading on his face, almost like a boy begging for a second piece of dessert.

A surge ran through her chest. "I'd love to. What will I be doing?"

His shoulders relaxed. "We work from sun up to sun down and sleep out with the herd to keep the finished cows separated from those we haven't touched yet. You'll be cookin' and makin' sure the boys have the supplies they need, as well as doctoring any scrapes they come up with."

Anna took a deep breath. "I probably need to get more supplies then."

He nodded. "I was plannin' to go to town on Saturday to get a few things we'll need. You and Aunt Lola can come too, if you'd like. She can show you what she takes."

The branding was different than anything Anna had imagined. The men set up camp on the northern end of the property and quickly developed a system: The calf was roped and brought first to the man in charge of the branding iron, then another cowboy would step forward with a knife to mark the cow's ear, another method of determining ownership on the range. After the calves were marked, the male calves were castrated. A final cowboy was stationed nearby with a bucket of foul-smelling medicine to dab any open wounds the cattle might have.

The process was a loud, miserable event with the painful bleating of the calves almost as awful as the aroma of singed hide that filled the air. At least the cowboys weren't rough with the animals, just matter-of-fact in their handling. Monty said each of these tasks had to be done to properly identify and care for the cattle, but they were still painful to witness and probably even harder to perform. The cowboys rotated jobs frequently.

Anna's role was much less miserable, cooking meals and bringing the men fresh water, rags, and medicine. The cowboys ate in shifts, and she did her best to make the food as appetizing as possible. She relied heavily on the canned goods she'd bought in town, as well as those she and Aunt Lola had put up in the fall. Of course, she made sure to provide something extra tasty for dessert like peach cobbler in the Dutch oven or apple tarts in the frying pan. She was a little bit limited without her stove, but after the first time she burned the flapjacks, she started to get the hang of how to improvise over the open fire.

Aunt Lola had warned Anna she would also be in charge of the camp medicine box, doctoring any wounds the men received from the long sharp horns of the cantankerous cattle. She'd often cared for Edward's scrapes growing up and the times Papa had burned himself in the candle shop. But should she be doctoring grown men not in her family? That was a bit unnerving. Before the War, such a thing would have been unheard of, but now most people thought it acceptable. Women had doctored men in war hospitals all over the country, and the harsh realities of the Texas plains often loosened society's strictures by sheer force of necessity.

During the first day of branding, the wounds were few and fairly mild. Donato had sliced the top layers of skin on his arm while trying to mark the ear of a feisty overgrown calf. Paco had been kicked by another calf during the castration process when the frightened animal managed to get a hind leg loose from the tie string. But these casualties served to heighten Anna's awareness of the dangers inherent in ranching. She kept a watchful eye on Edward throughout the day but was thankful he stayed safely in the saddle as a roper.

By the second day, Anna was getting used to the sights and

sounds of the branding camp. After finishing the breakfast dishes, she grabbed her Bible from the tent the men had rigged for her and sank down on the back side of the wagon to read, propping herself against the large metal wheel.

From this vantage point, she could see the cattle grazing peacefully in the herd that had not yet been branded. She couldn't help but feel sorry for the innocent calves playing around the edge of the group. They had no idea what trials they were about to experience. Funny how people were often like those calves, going along about their own business, never knowing what calamity was about to befall them until it changed their lives.

As she sat in the sunshine, unopened Bible still in hand, Monty appeared on horseback in the distance, riding toward the edge of the herd with his rope coiled and loop ready to throw. His arm was quick and his aim true as he landed the noose around a calf. He guided his horse back out of sight toward the branding station, calf begrudgingly in tow. The little guy had been so busy exploring new patches of grass, it never saw the rope coming and didn't have any choice in the matter.

Anna's life had unfolded much like the roping of that little calf. So many times she had been hit, out of the blue, by a life-changing event. By now, she was so gun-shy and always seemed to be fearing the worst. Always worrying about the next catastrophe.

She flipped open her Bible, hoping to find encouragement in the Psalms. She skimmed a well-worn page, not sure what she was looking for. Her eyes settled on a verse the Pastor had used in his sermon a few weeks ago. *I will lift up mine eyes unto the hills, from whence cometh my help. My help cometh from the Lord, which made Heaven and Earth.*

The words hit her like a ton of bricks. *Father, I'm so sorry for not trusting in You for help. I know You know the future and want the best for us. Please help me to place it in Your hands.*

Anna sat with her eyes closed, warm spring sunshine washing down on her face as an even more comforting peace soothed her soul. "Thank you, Father," she whispered. At last, she opened her eyes to continue reading in Psalms chapter one hundred twenty-one.

A commotion sounded from the direction of the men working on the other side of the wagons. The fierce bellow of a cow pierced the air followed by shouts from the cowboys. Anna jumped to her feet and peered over the top of the wagon. A calf scrambled to its mama, lariat still looped around its neck. The men gathered around something on the ground. Dread crept into Anna's stomach as she placed her Bible on the tail of the wagon and hiked her skirts, preparing to hurry to where the men were standing. Edward split off from the group and ran in her direction.

"Get the medicine kit!" he called over the distance.

CHAPTER 21

The knot in Anna's stomach tightened as she pulled the crate out of the back of the wagon. She skimmed the contents and threw clean rags into the box to replace those she'd used yesterday, then picked up the container and moved as fast as her thick skirts would allow. Edward met her and took the crate, allowing them both to move more quickly.

"What happened?" Her breath came in gasps.

"It's Miguel. A cow charged his horse. The horse threw him and the cow got him good in the side. He's bleedin' somethin' fierce."

The men parted like the Red Sea to allow Anna access to the man writhing on the ground. Poor Miguel lay with his hands covering his side but not stopping the blood that oozed over his fingers and onto the dirt. For a second, bile rose in Anna's throat. She forced it down with a swallow, then knelt next to the man and reached for a rag from her medicine chest.

Working quickly, she peeled away the bloody shirt, exposing a hole about the size of a silver dollar. She placed a clean rag over the opening, but the moment she touched it, Miguel cried out in an agonized tone. Anna wanted to cry with him but kept herself focused on her work. Glancing around, she motioned for Jacob to kneel on the other side of the man.

"Place your hand over this rag and hold pressure on the wound. Not too hard but steady. I need to get carbolic acid ready to clean the area."

Jacob's face was grim, but he did as she asked. Anna found the glass bottle and poured some of the strong-smelling liquid onto another cloth. A neighbor who had worked in the war hospital explained how important it was to get the wounds clean. The woman had told stories about men losing legs or arms from infections, and the doctors suspected dirt as being one of the main causes for the infections.

After saturating the clean rag with carbolic acid, Anna eased the bloody cloth from Miguel's side and gently wiped the wound, squeezing a bit of the liquid into the hole. The man groaned, his hands clasping a stick, knuckles white.

"Get a clean rag to apply pressure again." She spoke the order to Jacob while glancing at Miguel's face. His normally brown skin was white, and he labored when he breathed. Was his lack of color from the pain or from losing so much blood? At least the horn had punctured his right side, so it wasn't too close to the heart.

While Jacob held a clean rag to the wound, Anna sifted through the contents of her box, finally finding the roll of white bandages Aunt Lola had recommended she bring. *Ya never know what you might need out with all those crazy cows.* The woman had spoken with a knowing look.

Anna eyed the man lying on the ground. "We need to wrap this bandage around him to keep the gauze on his wound." Leaning closer, she looked into the white face. "Miguel, do you think you can sit up?" He nodded once, but didn't look very convincing. Some of his ribs must be broken. One of Edward's boyhood friends had cracked two ribs when he fell from a tree and experienced much pain while they healed.

With Jacob on one side and Monty on the other, they helped Miguel sit up, while Anna wrapped the bandage around his abdomen several times. She wasn't sure how tight to make it. The flow of blood seemed to increase when they sat him up, and they needed to stop the bleeding. She certainly didn't want to restrict his breathing, though. He seemed to be having enough trouble as it was. She tied it as tight as she dared then instructed the men to lay him back down.

Anna sat back on her heels and looked the man over. What else should she do? "He needs to stay still for a while until that bleeding stops." They couldn't very well leave him lying out in the middle of the pasture with cows grazing all around. She turned to Jacob. "We need to get him back to the wagon where he can rest and be more protected. Do you think the men could carry him on a blanket?"

He nodded. "We'll take care of it." After calling a few commands to the boys standing around, he helped Anna to her feet and picked up the crate of medical supplies. "You'd best go get a place ready for him."

Anna glimpsed Miguel again, who was lying quietly now, although still very pale. "Just be careful when you move him. He's in a lot of pain and I think he might have some broken ribs. We wouldn't want them to puncture his lungs."

Jacob tugged her arm. "We'll be careful."

Over the course of the afternoon, Miguel dozed fitfully, but he was able to keep down water and a little bit of potato broth. When Anna recommended one of the men ride to town for the doctor, Miguel spoke up for the first time, ardently refusing to allow the man to check him.

Monty shook his head. "He's too hard-headed to do anything good for him. He's awake and breathing, so I reckon he'll be all right. You fixed him up as good as anyone could."

Anna wasn't so sure, but she held her tongue. If Miguel took a turn for the worse, she would make Jacob send for help. For now, the bleeding had stopped and a little bit of color was showing in the man's face.

By the next day, Miguel was begging to get up and move around, but Anna wouldn't hear of it. She put a fresh bandage on the wound, which started a little bit of bleeding again. The wound needed much more time to heal before the cowpuncher was active again.

~

On Wednesday afternoon, the branding was finally complete, and Jacob was worn out. He finished tying down his bedroll onto Marshall's saddle and stopped to look around. The other hands appeared to be just as beat as he was, dragging themselves through the work necessary to clean up camp and pack the wagon.

"The boys'll be glad we finished up early today. Looks like they wore themselves out." Monty strode up next to Jacob, his reins in one hand and a bedroll in the other.

Jacob nodded. "Yep. Did we get a final count on the cattle?"

"'Round about twenty-three hundred, I think." Monty's brow furrowed a bit.

Jacob nodded, pinching his lips as he did a mental calculation. "That's a bit less than I'd estimated. We must have lost more than we thought in the snow…or from rustlers."

They stood in companionable silence for a minute while the hands made quick work of the campsite. Anna scurried around, directing the packing of the dishes, supplies, and bedding into the wagon. She seemed to be everywhere at once, moving twice as fast as the men. Did she never tire?

As if reading his mind, Monty spoke up. "She's quite a gal, ain't she." It was a statement, not a question, spoken in an almost reverent tone. "She can cook like the Lord himself, doctor a bloody wound, work all day and into the night, and still looks fresh as an angel."

Jacob stiffened. Hearing his own thoughts come from Monty's lips didn't sit well. He glared at his friend. "Stay away from her."

Monty raised a brow, one corner of his mouth twitching. "And why exactly should I do that? She's not spoken for yet. Leastways not as far as I've heard."

Jacob was being goaded, but that didn't help his rising temper any. "She's off limits."

"Really? Appears to me she's single, no one payin' court to her. Maybe she's looking for a good, honest cowboy to love. If you plan to claim her, you better git to it before someone else does."

Jacob's hand balled into a fist, but before he could start swinging, Monty clapped him on the back and sauntered away.

Jacob was left standing with his mind whirling. Did he plan to claim her? The ranch had always been his priority. A cowboy's life was hard and lonely, with long nights on the range and not much time left for a wife or a family. He'd always shied away from females, knowing they would only hold him back and mess up his focus from what was really important.

Anna was different, though. She was part of the ranch. Helpful. Supportive. But was he ready to make her his wife?

CHAPTER 22

The next week, Anna watched with a lump in her throat as Jacob and three of the other men left to help with the community round-up and branding. The first evening the men were gone, Mr. O'Brien filled the void left by Jacob's absence by regaling the women with stories of the times he'd joined in on the round-up.

Sitting back in his overstuffed chair with a mug of coffee, his eyes searched the distance. "Yep, all us local ranchers used to gather south of the Guadalupe River at Gus Konde's place. Each daybreak, the men saddled up and fanned out, pushing through the brush, herding cattle to the agreed holding pen. The calf that followed a cow was branded accordingly. Yearling strays that had escaped the branding iron or wild, full-grown longhorns would be divided equally among the cowboys making the round-up. The boys called 'em Mavericks." A twinkle touched his gaze as he winked at Anna. "I liked to call 'em walking twenty-dollar gold pieces."

Each day Jacob was gone, Edward took over the morning milking. And while Anna enjoyed seeing her brother's tousled hair and sleepy face first thing each morning, they didn't make her insides flutter like Jacob's blue eyes and strong chin covered by a day's growth of stubble.

The men had been gone for five days, and Aunt Lola predicted they'd be back today or tomorrow. This was the perfect time to make a cinnamon cake using the precious white flour that was so expensive in town. She usually reserved it for a special event or an occasional Sunday dinner. But having the men home would be a special occasion. Anna hummed as she measured out the cinnamon.

She'd missed Jacob more than she thought possible. Over the past couple of months, he never failed to show up for coffee in the mornings, but other than the occasional hand on her elbow as he helped her in or out of the wagon, he never touched her. And he hadn't kissed her since the day Edward had been tied and left for dead by the cattle thieves. It was as if he were keeping his distance on purpose. Did he feel nothing for her? He'd shown he was attracted to her physically. It was magnetic any time they were near each other. Maybe that's all it was, just physical attraction. Maybe he felt no stronger emotions and wanted to keep her from getting hurt.

Anna swallowed the lump in her throat. It was awful, this unrequited love. Maybe she should leave the ranch. But what about Edward? This seemed to be the perfect place for him. Could she leave Edward here alone? She didn't really want to leave. Even if Jacob never loved her, she still enjoyed his company. He had become a treasured friend.

A commotion drifted in from the yard. Anna poured the cake batter into a pan, placed it into the oven, and wiped her hands on a towel. Male voices called to each other, along with the whinny of a horse and the barking of a dog. A dog? The Double Rocking B didn't have any dogs, a fact she had lamented on more than one occasion. Aunt Lola seemed to have a grudge against the animals, so none were allowed on the property.

She strode through the house and stopped inside the front

door, touching a hand to her hair. A few stubborn baby tendrils always loosened around her face, but everything else seemed to be in place. She glanced down at her apron. She hadn't done the laundry yet this week, so she'd reused the same apron from yesterday. It was looking a bit battle weary, covered with smudged fingerprints and spackles of food. Oh well, not much she could do about it now.

Squaring her shoulders, Anna pulled open the door. The yard was full of their ranch hands, most of them dismounted and in various stages of unsaddling horses. Anna's eyes were drawn to Jacob emerging from the barn, saddle bags in one hand and bedroll in the other. A yellow dog jogged at his side, tongue hanging out in a jolly expression. Every few steps, the dog would lick Jacob's hand. The second time it happened, Anna glanced at Jacob's face to gauge his expression. It held a look of amusement, not the annoyance she'd expected. She couldn't help but grin. He was such a good man.

As man and dog approached the house, Anna stepped to the edge of the porch and offered a warm smile. "Welcome home."

Jacob stopped at the bottom of the steps and removed his hat, uncovering his tousled brown hair that could stand a trim. The dog kept charging up the stairs and bounded right to Anna, rubbing against her skirts to demand attention. She complied, bending down to stroke the animal's golden head. The dog gave her a look of adoration, tongue lolling to the side in a contented pant.

"I think she likes you."

Anna looked up at Jacob, still caressing the dog's soft coat. "What's her name?"

"Abigail. One of the ranchers on the other side of town was trying to make her into a cattle dog. She'd always bark at the worst times and almost caused a stampede once. I offered to take her off his hands so he didn't shoot her." Jacob shook his head. "She's still just an overgrown pup, but I think she'll be fine once she mellows out some. May not make a good cattle dog, but not too bad around the house."

Anna gave the dog a final pat and rose to her feet. "Do you think Aunt Lola will mind?"

Jacob shrugged, trudging up the stairs. His shoulders slumped and dark skin under his eyes cast a grayish tint over their normal blue. "I'm not sure. I hope she'll understand."

Jacob stopped on the porch just a few feet from Anna, and his nearness triggered butterflies in her stomach. In an effort to keep her emotions under control, she avoided his gaze, looking instead at the dog that had sprawled itself at her feet. "How did the round-up go?"

"All right, I guess. We brought home about two hundred head. The rest of the ranchers headed out with their herds on the trail toward the market towns. It's awful nice to be home, though." Anna peeked up. A teasing grin spread cross his face. "Looking forward to eating something other than beans, cornbread, and hardtack."

Anna couldn't hide her own smile. "Come in and have some fresh coffee and a snack. Supper'll be ready soon, but I have Irish apple pie left that'll hold you over."

"Sounds like heaven itself." He rubbed a hand over his jaw. The stubble there had grown thick enough to almost be considered a beard. "Think I should get cleaned up first. You don't want a mangy saddle-bum sitting at your table."

Anna almost said, "You look good to me," but stopped herself just in time. Although, warmth rose to her cheeks anyway. As if he could read her thoughts, Jacob took a step forward and caught Anna's gaze with a look that held more than a little heat. Her stomach flipped at the intensity in his eyes.

After a moment, he grinned and tapped a finger to the tip of her nose. "Looking forward to that pie." He winked then turned to disappear inside the house.

When he was gone, Anna let out a wistful sigh, and glanced

down at the dog still lying at her feet. "Well, Abigail, we'd better go finish the food. The boys are home." With a light heart and a spring in her step, Anna headed toward the kitchen.

The dog turned out to be a favorite with everyone. Aunt Lola pretended to be affronted and ignored the animal at first, but Anna sometimes caught the two together in the afternoons. The hardy Irish woman would stroke the dog's soft fur and murmur sweet nothings while Abigail sat and gazed at her with undying devotion.

Abigail was a sweet animal, to be sure. She became a part of the household, bounding from one cowhand to the next when they came in for meals. She always made her way back to Anna when they sat down and would lie between Jacob and Anna's chairs. Her loyalty was most likely due to the fact that Anna fed her the kitchen scraps. It was nice to have such a devoted companion, even if a little bribery was involved.

The arrival of June brought with it the oppressive heat and humidity for which Texas was known. The scorching sun forced Anna to do gardening during the morning hours before the heat became overwhelming. She enjoyed tending the variety of vegetables and herbs, and often Aunt Lola would come out to help with the picking. Anna was amazed at the wealth of knowledge she held, not just about anything related to the plants and their needs and growing habits, but also about life itself. The woman held a strong faith that shone through in her outlook on all parts of life.

On Saturdays, Anna always skipped her time in the garden in favor of a nice long ride on Bandita. They would usually share an exhilarating canter to the river, where Bandita grazed while Anna picked blackberries and huckleberries from the many plants that grew in the fertile soil. That made them move more slowly on the ride home so the berries wouldn't sustain injuries. Her efforts always resulted in a blackberry pie or cobbler on Sunday afternoons, and the men were quick to voice their appreciation.

On one such Sunday afternoon, Mr. O'Brien set his fork down after finishing off a second large portion of pie. Leaning back with a hand over his growing girth, he spoke across the table. "Anna, dear, I must commend you on your efforts. At the end of every meal, I decide I've finally found my favorite dish. Then you up and make something even better the next time. I don't know how you do it, but I am surely thankful. You're a rare treasure, to be sure." The last words were spoken with a wink and a proud smile that reminded her of the way Papa used to look at her when she'd help him in the candle shop. The memory tightened Anna's heart, but at least it didn't evoke tears this time.

"I heard Jared Thomas speaking to the Mayor after church today," Mr. O'Brien continued, capturing the attention of everyone at the table. "It seems the town is planning to expand the Independence Day celebration this year, in hopes it'll foster more of a sense of unity and national pride in the people."

A snort came from one of the men on the left side of the table. Several of the cowboys stared down at their hands with furrowed brows and pinched lips, so she couldn't tell from whom it had come.

After a moment of uncomfortable silence, Aunt Lola spoke up. "I know there's still a lot of grievin' people from the war, but I, for one, think it's high time we all got together for some fun. Just friends and neighbors enjoyin' each other's company." Several heads bobbed around the table in agreement.

Mr. O'Brien nodded. "It does sound like they're planning a day full of fun. In addition to the regular picnic, we'll have a shooting match, horse race, pie baking competition, and then a dance that night."

That statement finally brought a few grins, and the bantering began as the men one-upped each other to decide who would win the shooting match or the horse race. Bo finally settled things when he announced with a suave grin, "Ya'll can win all the fancy ribbons ya want, but I'll be havin' more fun dancin' with all the prettiest gals in Guadalupe County." He ducked the elbows and playful punches that issued from all directions. "Don't worry, boys, I'll let the rest of ya'll have a girl or two when I'm not dancin' with 'em."

CHAPTER 23

As her excitement over the Independence Day celebration grew, Anna finally convinced herself a new dress would be the perfect way to celebrate. At the mercantile, she found a yellow muslin, the color of the yellow roses that had climbed the rail of their porch stairs in Columbia. Anna had already sketched a design for the dress, but her sewing now began in earnest. The gown needed to be practical enough for everyday use, as she only had three dresses, and her gray one was so thin she could see through the material if she held it up to the light. It really needed to be read its last rites.

Anna planned to make sure the new dress was long enough to wear both of her petticoats underneath, giving some of the fullness she used to wear back in South Carolina. Sometimes, she still longed for just one of her fashionable gowns that had burned in the fire. With Papa being only a candlemaker, she never dressed in the height of fashion like the daughters of the plantation owners. But they'd lived very respectably, and Papa let her make two new dresses each year. She'd also become quite adept at making over her old dresses to keep up with the current styles.

Out here in Texas, though, style didn't seem to be a concern to most people. If the dark colors and simple lines were any indication, the local ladies only worried about practicality. But Aunt Laura had been saving copies of Godey's for Anna, so she had a few ideas for the design.

Despite her sewing project, the next couple of weeks seemed to drag by in the stifling heat. She dreaded cooking on the wood stove because of the warmth it added to the kitchen, and she discovered creative ways to serve cold meals to the men.

But as the day of the celebration drew near, she focused her efforts on putting together an amazing menu for the picnic. She and Aunt Lola killed several of the young roosters to make fried chicken, a rare delicacy but one both Jacob and his pa seemed to appreciate. She planned to prepare a mixture of Mexican and American foods, including potato salad, baked squash covered with cheese, buttered carrots, corn on the cob, sourdough bread with apple butter, bell peppers stuffed with beef and tomatoes, tamales filled with a variety of meats, chess pie, pound cake with a sweet glaze, and several kinds of fruit tarts. It was quite a variety of foods, but she wanted to have at least one favorite dish for each of the men.

Dawn of July Fourth, Anna scurried around the kitchen, sprinkling grated cheese over the tamales, shifting pans on the stove, and packing last minute supplies.

Aunt Lola drifted into the room with a couple of the cowhands and planted a wrinkled hand on each hip. "Now what be goin' on in here?"

Anna didn't stop moving as she answered. "The carrots are cooling now, the peppers are about ready to come out of the oven, and I'm just waiting for the cheese to melt on the tamales. I need to slice the bread still and …"

"Out." Aunt Lola shooed, pushing Anna toward the door. "I'll take care o' the bread and the rest of it looks fine. These boys'll load the food while you go make yourself presentable." She didn't allow Anna to turn back but pushed her right into the hallway.

Miguel tipped his hat as Anna passed. "You go on, Miss Stewart. We'll take care of this."

It didn't seem she had a choice, but the yellow gown upstairs softened the sting of her exile from the kitchen. Anna released a martyr's sigh for anyone who might be listening then headed toward the staircase.

Once in her room, Anna slipped out of her old gray dress, layered both of her petticoats, and pulled the new gown over her head. The shiny muslin almost looked like silk and fit perfectly as it tucked in at the waist and flared into a full skirt, drawn up at the bottom on each side to reveal an under layer of the same material. She'd sewn white ribbon around the collar, sleeves, and bottom edges for just the right amount of contrast. She twisted more of the white ribbon into her hair and tied it in a bow at the nape of her neck. Stepping back to examine herself in the mirror over the bureau, she smiled at her reflection. She'd forgotten how much fun it was to dress up.

Abigail barked outside, and Anna reached for the vanilla scent Aunt Laura had given her, dabbed a bit behind her ears, and hurried down the stairs. She grabbed her bonnet from the coat rack in the hall and stepped outside.

Mr. O'Brien sat on the seat of the loaded wagon, and Jacob helped Aunt Lola onto the bench beside him. The rest of the cowboys were already mounted on horses. Anna stopped on the porch to tie on her bonnet. Why hadn't she made one to match her new dress?

After finishing with his aunt, Jacob turned around and stared as Anna approached the wagon. He reached to boost her into the wagon, but held her on the ground for an extra moment before lifting. The pause was enough for her to lose herself in his gaze and the strength of his hands at her waist. In the morning sun, his eyes appeared bluer than normal as he lifted her onto the seat.

When she was safely on the wagon seat, Jacob stepped back and touched a finger to the brim of his hat in salute, the corners of his mouth quirking into a grin. A shiver ran through her as Mr. O'Brien urged the team into a walk. This was going to be a wonderful day.

When they arrived at the picnic area, the men spread out on blankets in the grass. Plates in front of them were heaped high with their favorite delicacies, which soon disappeared. Anna sat on the corner of the blanket next to Aunt Lola, enjoying the light breeze on her face. This mismatched collection of Irishmen and Mexicans from the Double Rocking B truly seemed to be her family now.

Edward ended a story, and Manuel burst into laughter and gave the boy a playful slap on the back. Edward's shoulders had filled out some, and he had lost most of his gangly, boyish look. *My goodness, he's starting to look more like a man than a boy*. Anna gulped at the sobering thought.

"Care to take a walk?" Anna glanced up to Jacob's outstretched hand. "I hear the pie judging is getting ready to start. And you should be on hand to accept your ribbon." His face and voice were matter of fact, but the wink he flashed conveyed his teasing.

Heat flushed her cheeks, adding to the swelter of the sun. "I can't imagine my simple little blackberry pie would win a ribbon with so many accomplished women here. But I would love to stretch my legs a bit." She placed her hand in Jacob's and allowed him to assist her to her feet.

They strolled toward the schoolhouse yard where a row of tables under a large pecan tree had been covered with numerous pie dishes. Three men sidestepped down the row, tasting each dessert and making notes on pieces of paper.

Anna recognized the salt-and-pepper beard and lean figure

of Reverend Wallace. Jacob pointed out the other two men as Sheriff B.A. Brown and Sam Wright, the county clerk. Several clusters of onlookers stood in groups a little distance away from the judges. When Anna and Jacob approached, Mrs. Wallace waltzed over and gave Anna a welcoming hug.

"It looks to be a tough competition this year," the matronly woman explained, turning back toward the men. "They've already sampled the pies once and are making a second round now."

"If they need a tie-breaker, I'll be happy to step in." Anna turned toward the voice and received a sheepish grin from a stocky man, one hand on his suspender strap and the other patting his already-full mid-section.

"You know the rules, G.W.," Mrs. Wallace chided in a lightly scolding tone. "The wives of the judges aren't allowed to enter a pie in the competition. And since your Emmaline has won the last two years, there's not much chance you'll ever get to be a judge."

G.W.'s smile widened as he draped an arm around the plump woman beside him. "My gal sure can cook, can't she?" His 'gal' rewarded the comment by smiling at him as if he were a knight who had just rescued her from a fire-breathing dragon.

Anna smiled at the pair. How sweet to watch two people in love. She sneaked a glance at Jacob and caught his gaze on her. Heat crept into her face, so she turned her focus back to the pies.

The three judges huddled together and discussed the paper in Reverend Wallace's hand. They finally separated, and the Reverend spoke in the deep voice he used for his sermons.

"Ladies and Gentleman, after much deliberation, we have selected the winners of the pie competition. With so many delectable entries this year, we've chosen to award the top five pies." He cleared his throat and glanced down at the paper in his hand. "First place goes to the rhubarb pie made by Mrs. Emmaline Strait."

"I knew it." G.W. slid an arm around his wife's shoulders.

"And second place goes to the blackberry pie made by Miss Anna Stewart."

Anna squealed before she could stop herself then slapped a hand over her mouth. At a touch on her elbow, she turned to a broad smile on Jacob's face and a twinkle flashing in his clear blue eyes. He leaned forward and whispered, "I never had a doubt, did you? I'm only surprised you didn't take first."

Jacob stayed by her side for most of the afternoon. He introduced her to so many people, the names and faces soon blurred in her mind.

"I had no idea you were so well-known in this town," she teased as they headed for a shade tree to escape the blistering sun.

Jacob shrugged. "That's what happens when you grow up in a place, I guess. When I was little, Seguin only had a couple of roads. Now it's a great big town and it's the county seat for Guadalupe County." He sighed, leaning against the tree with his hands in his pockets. He cut a handsome form, from his wavy brown hair playing in the slight breeze, to his dark green cotton shirt, to his snug fitting brown pants and heeled cowboy boots. "I guess change comes whether we want it to or not. I kind of miss the old days, though. Things were wilder back then but simpler, too."

Anna's eyes wandered toward the houses and cement buildings comprising the town of Seguin. Her mind brought back images of the busy streets of Columbia, with its constant flow of wagons, peddlers, and other traffic.

"I lived in Columbia my entire life before the fire. It was always busy, never a quiet little town like Seguin. On Saturdays, Papa would take us on rides through the countryside." Her tone grew wistful. "I used to envy the people who lived in the grand plantation homes. Things seemed so much calmer there. I've never known a place as peaceful as the ranch, though."

"Do you miss Columbia?"

"No." Her voice softened. "I miss Papa, but I don't miss the city."

Jacob's reply was cut off by an announcer calling from the direction of the hill to introduce the start of the shooting match. He straightened and offered his arm. "May I escort you, ma'am?" He winked.

Monty placed second in the shooting match, losing to Sheriff Brown. As the onlookers applauded, excitement rose in Anna's stomach, threatening to bubble over.

"I can't be letting anyone outshoot the lawman in the county, now can I?" The Sheriff shrugged and accepted the new spur straps offered as the prize.

The horse race was held in a large open area near the river, and at the sound of a pistol signaling the start, Anna cheered with the rest of the crowd. The riders were to circle the area twice, and as they neared the finish line a pack of three horses pulled away from the rest of the animals. Manuel's red shirt appeared in the group that crossed the line first, but she couldn't tell who had been ahead.

The announcer's voice boomed above the murmurs of the crowd. "And the first place rider is Manuel Jinjosa from the Double Rocking B." The spectators roared, with a few hoots mixed in, probably from their own cowboys.

As the announcer continued broadcasting where the contestants placed, Anna shouted with the rest of the group. The excitement was contagious and drowned out the announcer's voice. Then her breath caught at an unmistakable name.

"...Edward Stewart from the Double Rocking B."

Was that sixth place he'd just announced? A surge of pride welled in Anna's chest, and even as she continued to cheer, she couldn't hold back the tear that rolled down her cheek. An arm rested on her shoulders, and she spun to find a gentle smile curve across Jacob's face. With people still cheering around them, he didn't say a word, just wiped away the tear. In that moment, words weren't needed between them. The look in his eyes showed he understood.

CHAPTER 24

The women of the town had put together a chili supper for all in attendance, and Anna was thankful, for once, to not be responsible for the cooking. After the meal, she sat on her corner of the picnic blanket with both her real and adopted families scattered around. Uncle Walter and Aunt Laura joined them for the evening meal, adding extra flavor to the conversation. The sky was beginning to show deep oranges and purples in preparation for sunset. The day had been more fun than Anna imagined, but she was almost worn out.

Mr. O'Brien seemed to read her thoughts as he set down his bowl, wiped his mouth, and said, "Well, I hope ya'll aren't too tuckered out yet. There's still a whole night of dancin' ahead of us."

"I'm ready," Bo piped up, earning a playful shove from Juan.

As if on cue, the strains of the fiddle drifted from the open area in front of the schoolhouse. "I guess that's our sign," Mr. O'Brien announced, rising to his feet. He approached Aunt Lola and, with a bow, offered his hand to help her rise. "Might I escort ye, bonnie lass?" He broke into the Irish brogue so easily, it was obvious it came naturally to him.

He winked at Anna and leaned closer as if sharing a secret. "I should be so lucky to escort the two loveliest ladies to the dance, but I'm afraid with all these strapping young men around, I would be hung and quartered if I did. So, to save my own life, I'll step aside and give the others a chance."

Warmth rose up Anna's neck, and she dropped her gaze down to the blanket. Within seconds, a pair of worn brown boots stepped into the edge of her vision. Anna slowly raised her eyes, expecting Jacob. Instead, Monty stood before her with a sheepish grin. "May I have the honor of the first dance, Miss Stewart?"

Anna's heart warmed at the boyish hopefulness on his leathery cowboy face. Placing her gloved hand in his, she turned on her southern charm. "Why, I would be honored, Mr. Dominguez."

He seemed to grow three inches taller as he tucked her hand into his elbow and they strolled toward the sound of the music.

While they ambled, Monty chuckled. "Imagine me getting the first dance with the prettiest Senorita in town. The boys are gonna hold this one against me. Of course, I knew if I didn't jump on it, I'd not get another chance."

Jacob leaned against the pecan tree while the swirling skirts on the dance floor spun and turned to the caller's direction. He usually enjoyed a good square dance. He wasn't a great dancer, but he'd had a bit of practice, and it was always fun to grab a girl and dive into the fray. Tonight, though, he didn't feel much like dancing. The girl he had planned to step out with was twirling and spinning with Miguel. She'd already danced with every other cowboy from the Double Rocking B and three from the Lazy T, too. Why, some of them hadn't even gotten a full dance in before an interloper would butt in and take over. She was like a prize bull being passed around from one ranch to another.

Jacob had tried all night to be a gentleman, but every time he'd started to get close enough to ask for a dance, ten men stood in line in front of him.

"You plan to stand here and brood all night or you gonna dance with that gal?"

He turned to see a familiar head of salty red hair and blue eyes that were shooting sparks at him.

"It's nice to see you, too, Aunt Lola." He responded with as much of a grin as he could muster, then turned back, pretending to watch the dancers. Maybe if he ignored the question, she'd give up and leave him be.

She gave a "Hmphh" and scooted next to him, studying the dancers. Finally, she broke the silence. "Well?"

He let out a long sigh. "She's got a long line of partners, just waitin' to jump at the chance. She's certainly not waitin' around for me. And I'd just as soon stay here anyhow."

"Well, I'll be." Aunt Lola spun around to face him, hands fisted on her hips. "Jacob O'Brien, you know as well as I do you'd rather be dancin' with that little gal than breathin'. And if I don't miss my guess, she feels exactly the same. Now you better get up the courage God gave ya and quit skulkin' in the bushes. Just go out there and git her!" With that, she grabbed Jacob's arm with a bony hand and gave him a little push.

The speech caught Jacob a bit off guard, and he stood there staring at Aunt Lola for a moment. How should he respond? It wasn't courage he lacked but opportunity. But maybe courage really was his problem. He glanced toward the dance floor where Anna promenaded down the row in a lively Virginia reel. She was stunning in that yellow dress, and he'd never seen her look as happy as she did today. A twinge of jealousy struck Jacob as he turned his attention toward the lanky cowboy who twirled her around. Time to put an end to this. Squaring his shoulders, he pushed away from the tree and headed toward the lady in the yellow dress.

Jacob reached Anna just as she and her partner were preparing for another promenade. He grabbed her elbow and she glanced up at him, wide-eyed.

He tipped his hat to Anna then turned to face the blustering cowboy across from her. "Mind if I break in?"

"As a matter of fact—"

Jacob didn't wait to hear the end of it but grabbed Anna's elbow and steered her toward the edge of the dance floor. When they reached the line of onlookers, Anna turned to face him with a weak smile.

Jacob shot her a grin. "You're an awfully hard person to catch, Miss Stewart."

"I was wondering where you've been hiding all night," she retorted, matching his smile.

The music changed and the square dance caller stepped back to the front of the dance floor. Jacob offered his elbow. "May I have the honor of a dance?"

Anna hesitated, a look of indecision on her face. Jacob's gut tightened. *She'll dance with any roughneck that can stand upright but not with me?*

"I was kind of hoping we could sit one out?" Uncertainty mixed with hope in her expression. "My feet are killing me."

Jacob's heart sank a bit, but he tried to play it off. Raising an eyebrow, he teased, "Wore you out did they? C'mon, let's get a drink of lemonade, then we'll find an empty bench."

She looked at him with such gratitude, as if he'd just saved her from a charging bear.

After stopping at the refreshment table, Jacob steered Anna toward open seats in the far corner of the dance area. She sank down with an exhausted sigh, which sent a stab of guilt to his conscience. The poor thing was worn out, and he was whining about not getting to dance with her.

They were sitting close to the band, so the music was too loud for conversation. He enjoyed the silence with her, though. That's the way it always was with Anna. Over the months they'd spent sharing coffee in the mornings, they'd developed an understanding on a deeper level. Many times she would finish his thought, even if he hadn't actually stated it out loud. It was uncanny but part of what made it so comfortable to be in her presence.

The fiddles finally slowed on the last bars of "Rose of Alabamy," and the caller announced the final song of the night, "The Yellow Rose of Texas." Jacob raised an eyebrow at Anna. Her shy smile made his heart flip.

He led her to the center of the floor then pulled her into a waltz as they moved with the music. He'd never been particularly good at the slower dances and usually avoided them, but moving around the floor with his arm around this woman was the most natural thing in the world. In that moment, Jacob knew the truth. God had placed her in his life for a reason. She was exactly what he needed, and he was tired of fighting God's will in favor of his own futile plans. It was time to do something about it.

CHAPTER 25

Anna shuffled into the kitchen the next morning and yawned. They'd arrived home late the night before, but Monty had already given the boys fair warning he expected them back in the saddle at the usual time, no excuses accepted. And *that* meant Anna had to have breakfast on the table at the usual time. She groaned as she stoked the coals in the stove. After more than the usual amount of kindling, blowing, and coaxing, the wood finally caught fire, and she poured water into the coffee pots.

As she reached for the pots, her hand froze in mid-air. A yellow rose lay in front of the containers, and underneath it was a small slip of paper. Her exhaustion miraculously cleared. The words were written in a large, even script: *For the sweetest Rose in Texas.* It wasn't signed, but there was no question the note was from Jacob. The waltz they'd shared the night before, the feel of his arm around her waist, guiding her with the music, it had seemed like the most natural thing in the world.

Anna sighed. This was torture, being so close to Jacob day in and day out and him not returning her love. She glanced down at the rose on the stove then at the note in her hands. Was he starting to feel something for her? It had sure seemed like it last night. Maybe yesterday was the prodding he'd needed.

A whistled tune echoed from outside. Anna jumped into action. She hadn't even started the coffee yet, and she was already late this morning. The door opened behind her and boots strode across the floor as she filled the metal containers with water. A clunk echoed in the quiet room as Jacob heaved the heavy milk bucket onto the counter.

"G'morning," she called, but kept preparing the coffee with her back turned away from him. How was she supposed to thank him for the rose and the note? Should she just come out and say she loved it? Or wait for him to bring it up?

When the coffee was prepared, she placed the pots on the front of the stove and turned around, clutching the rose behind her back. Jacob stood next to the counter, studying her. His face was unreadable.

"I'm sorry I don't have the coffee made yet, but it'll be ready soon." A playful tone crept into her voice. "I got a little side tracked when I reached for the coffee pots."

He quirked a brow. "Really? If I'd thought it would interfere with my coffee, I might have held off on the present."

She cocked her head with a smile and pulled the rose from behind her back, holding it to her nose. "Thank you. This is one of the nicest gifts I've ever received."

He shrugged and looked down at the floor. His boot scraped against the wood. He resembled a nervous schoolboy, and Anna couldn't resist the impulse. Three steps brought her in front of him and she stood on her tip toes to plant a soft kiss on his cheek. Jacob's head popped up and his brows arched, then his blue eyes darkened.

"If you're going to thank me, Anna, you might as well do it right." The words were husky, and he wrapped his arms around her waist then gently covered her lips with his own. His kiss was sweet, tender, and only lasted for a few moments. He separated from her, only to rest his forehead against hers. His hand cupped her face, thumb stroking her cheek with a tenderness that made her chest ache. Anna couldn't think with him so close, couldn't breathe. Surely he could hear her heart beating like a drum. He was so close.

"Anna."

"Hmmm..."

"Would you do me the honor...of allowing me to court you?"

Anna leaned her head back so she could gaze into his eyes. Did he mean that? Had he said what she thought he'd said? "Really?"

The corners of his mouth quirked as he tapped her nose. "Really." He paused, as if thinking how to word his thoughts. "I never thought I'd marry. Always focused on the ranch and the cattle. It's not a life many women can handle." He pulled her back to him and tucked her head under his chin, rubbing her back with a possessive touch. "But I think I've realized it's not all that important without the right woman by my side."

They stood there for several moments, Anna relishing his strong arms around her. At last, Jacob leaned back and tipped her chin up. "Well, are you going to keep me in suspense?"

Anna grinned up at him. "Jacob O'Brien, I would enjoy being courted by you."

~

Later that afternoon, Anna left the Wallace farm with a spring in her step. She'd been concerned about not seeing Ginny and her family at the celebration yesterday, so she paid them a quick visit to make sure all was well. It turned out they'd only been suffering from a passing stomach ailment. The entire family was much improved today and regaining strength. Anna had enjoyed playing with new baby, Lilly, while she shared her news with Ginny.

Anna couldn't fight back the smile that spread across her face as Bandita jogged along. *Jacob asked to court me.* It still seemed surreal.

She kept the mare in a steady jog, too wrapped up in her thoughts to canter like they usually did. After a while, Bandita seemed to be frustrated with the slow pace and tossed her head, jerking on the reins. The disruption was enough to pull Anna from her reverie and she patted the mare's shoulder.

"Easy, girl. Are we moving too slow for ya?" As if in response, the mare bobbed her nose, and Anna couldn't help but smile. She glanced around, searching for a familiar landmark. All around her was open pasture, except for a tree line far ahead and to the right. Anna nibbled her lower lip. It didn't look like the woods she usually followed. Maybe she'd gone too far west and ended up on the other side of those trees. She aimed Bandita toward the east side of the woods and pushed her into a lope.

They rode for a while before Anna pulled the mare back to a walk to let her rest. She followed the tree line on her right, but things were still not familiar.

"I think we just need to go through this patch of woods and we'll be on our normal trail," Anna said, half to herself and half to her horse. She turned the mare toward the trees and they made their way through the pines, oaks, and walnuts, weaving as they went to clear low limbs and vines. Anna possessed a good sense of direction and did her best to keep going in a fairly straight line. The woods weren't very large here, so they should break through onto pasture land soon.

After a few minutes, a noise drifted across the breeze. The low mooing of cattle? She reined in Bandita and cocked her head to listen. Yes, it was definitely cattle. She must be close to the pasture where the ranch hands would be. She pushed on, turning a bit to the left toward the sound of the animals. Pretty soon, light shone through the trees ahead and a wave of relief washed over Anna.

As she broke through the tree line, Anna found herself on the edge of the herd of longhorns. She scanned the clearing for the men. If she was honest with herself, she was really looking for one particular tall, blue-eyed cowboy. But his familiar figure wasn't there. In fact, none of the figures were familiar. Confusion muddied her thoughts, and her mind struggled to make sense of where she might be. The cowboys all had dark features like Monty and his family, but she couldn't see them very well from a distance. A thread of unease crept into Anna's stomach. *Who were these men?*

Anna lifted her reins to turn Bandita back toward the trees but a rope settled around her shoulders and pulled tight. An abrupt stop and a yank, and she flew through the air. She hit the ground with a thud. A loud grunt pierced the air, but her mind focused on trying to draw breath into her empty lungs. It came in short gulps at first. When she was finally able to inhale a full breath, a man leered over Anna. A boulder-sized knot formed in her stomach.

CHAPTER 26

Jacob trudged toward the barn, his mount limping along behind him. Poor thing just had a stone bruise, but it had been a long walk back from the east pasture and the horse hobbled slower the farther they walked. It was still early afternoon, so he planned to catch a new mount and head back out. He'd stop in and see Anna for a minute, though. Maybe get a few cinnamon cookies if she had any left.

Jacob removed his hat and placed it on the hall tree then turned to greet Aunt Lola. He planted a kiss on her weathered cheek and peered down the hall toward the back of the house.

"Is Anna in the kitchen?"

"No, lad. I thought maybe you rode back home with her."

"Me? I came back because my horse is lame. Where'd she go?"

"She went avisitin' to the Wallace farm. Been gone since late mornin' so I 'spect her back any time now."

Jacob grabbed his hat and headed back out the door. Something didn't feel right. The chill bumps on his arms weren't there because it was cold in Texas in July. He'd just head out toward the Wallace farm and check into things.

An hour later, Jacob sat atop Marshall and scanned the horizon. He'd been over the trail to the Wallace's, but Everett said Anna had left there two hours ago. There was no sign of turkey vultures in the sky to signal a dead or distressed creature. Where should he start looking now? *Lord, where is she? I can't shake the feelin' that something's not right. Please keep her in Your hand, Lord. Keep her safe. And help me find her.*

An image of the Guadalupe River flickered through Jacob's mind. That was her favorite spot, but it was unlike Anna to be gone all day. Of course, she knew the cattle were being pastured near the river, so maybe she had gone to find the men. That sounded like a good place to start, so Jacob urged Marshall into a canter moving toward the southeast. He followed the tree line for a while then finally found the old shortcut through the woods. The trail was a bit overgrown, so they had to slow to a walk. After an eternity, daylight shone through the trees ahead.

Just then, voices drifted from behind Jacob. He halted Marshall and focused his attention in the direction of the sound. In the distance, cattle lowed, along with male voices calling to each other in Spanish. The little hairs on his neck prickled. The cattle and cowpunchers belonging to the Double Rocking B were still about a half mile to the east. Any men here most likely did not belong. He eased toward the sounds then dismounted and tied Marshall when he was getting close. He moved in on foot and crept to the edge of a clearing.

Exactly what he'd expected. About fifty head of cattle munched grass or milled around, while a few men sat on horseback around the outskirts of the herd. Jacob counted six dark-skinned cowboys but found no sign of Anna. Panic welled in his chest, but he smashed it down like the lid on a Dutch oven.

He needed help, more men. And he needed to find Anna. Each of the cattle thieves before him carried a revolver on both hips along with a rifle in the scabbard strapped to their saddles. Jacob's own six-shot revolver was not enough bullet power to take on all the men. Even if he retrieved his rifle from his saddle, he would need back-up.

Slipping back through the woods, Jacob mounted Marshall and urged the animal through the trees faster than he would have if he'd been thinking straight. The minute they reached open pasture, he pushed Marshall into a gallop, heading straight for the area where the rest of his men worked.

Monty loped out to meet Jacob.

"Bandits..." he panted, trying to catch enough air to speak. "I think they have Anna. Send Edward for the sheriff. The rest... mount up...come with me."

"Bo knows the way to town from here. Knows where to find the sheriff, too." Monty's voice was calm, fueling the fury in Jacob's chest.

"Send Edward." He spat the words.

"Bo's a better choice." Monty's voice held an edge now, but Jacob didn't care.

"Monty, if that boy gets anywhere near this mess, so help me, I'll..." He didn't finish his sentence. What would he do? He sure couldn't face Anna. "We're wastin' time. Send Edward for the sheriff, gather the boys, and come now." He ground out each word like he was flattening them into the dirt.

Monty raised his voice then, fighting back like a true brother. "Edward's a man now. You know that better than any of us. We need a strategy here, and Bo's the best one to go for the sheriff. Edward will be fine. You've taught him well."

That last line leveled Jacob like a blow to his gut. He had been teaching Edward how to be strong, think like a man. Didn't he always tell Anna she needed to let Edward grow up and let God take care of him?

He leveled his gaze on Monty, who returned it with a calm strength. "All right then."

Monty gave a nod, then spun his horse and cantered back toward the men, releasing a long whistle. The men must have been watching, because they immediately jogged their animals near, careful to skirt around the herd. Moving too quickly would only spook the cattle.

Monty barked a few commands, and the men began loading rifles. Bo tore off in the direction of town. Within minutes, although it seemed like hours to Jacob, they were all moving at a quick canter back the way he had come.

~

Anna twisted her arm, trying again to get at the knot that held her wrists tight. She only succeeded in scraping a layer of skin on the rough bark of the tree that held her prisoner. Perspiration ran in slow beads down her face and soaked into the filthy rag they had used as a gag. In the scuffle, she'd lost her bonnet, and already the skin on her forehead and cheeks flamed from the hot sun. It felt like she'd been tied out here for days, but this was still better than what that foul-smelling low-life who'd tied her up had alluded to happening after the men returned to camp for the night. A shiver ran down Anna's spine despite the scorching heat of the day. She had to figure out how to get away from here.

She had no idea where she was, but it was definitely not a place she'd been before. The men had secured her to one of the trees where it appeared they'd been camping, in the woods not far from the clearing where the cattle grazed. Eight bedrolls lay around the cold ashes of a campfire. A skillet and coffee pot sat next to the fire ring, but otherwise the place was empty. The thugs must keep their food and supplies packed in their saddle bags. Snippets of male voices called to each other, but they spoke Spanish and the words were too quick for her to catch any of the phrases she'd learned.

God, please help me! Anna struggled against the rope around her wrists again, trying in vain to loosen it even a little. *What time I am afraid, I will put my trust in Thee.* The verse dropped into Anna's mind, leaving calming ripples that spread throughout her body. That verse was in Psalms if she remembered correctly.

Cast your burden on the Lord and He shall sustain you; He shall never permit the righteous to be moved. Anna had not yet cast this burden on the Lord. She had no idea how she could get out of this terrible situation...but God could do it. There was no doubt. If He could help Gideon and his three hundred men destroy an army of hundreds of thousands of warriors, He could certainly save Anna from a few thieving renegades. A peace like never before settled over her, and she almost smiled. "Thank you, Lord," she whispered the simple prayer but meant the words with every fiber of her being.

More time passed, and the sun continued beating down, but Anna found it bearable. All she could do for now was watch and wait.

A shot ripped the air and Anna jumped. Men shouted and more revolver shots fired. Anna craned her neck, but the thin layer of trees blocked her view. She tried to call out, but the gag stopped all but a faint moan. The thud of heavy boots running through the leaves rose above the din of bullets and she tensed, not sure whether it would be friend or foe. A dark Mexican sprinted from tree to tree. Every few seconds, he would turn and aim his rifle at something behind him. He looked like the same man who had appeared to be in charge earlier.

Following about thirty feet behind, another man darted through the woods at a faster clip, shooting as he ran toward them. His gait was a bit gangly, and reality washed over her like the thaw from an iceberg. Edward.

Anna tried to scream at her brother, but the gag swallowed her words. *Run, Edward! Get far away from here.* Everything seemed to move in slow motion now. Her breath stopped as her brother approached, ducking low to avoid the rifle shots aimed right at him. Panic rose in her like a wild animal, and Anna wrestled against her bindings. She had to get to Edward. Get him out of this place. Get him to safety. *Oh, God. Where are you?*

Cast your burden on the Lord. The verse came back to her, but Anna fought against it, still pulling at her ropes. Edward dropped out of sight through the trees, and Anna's stomach dropped with him. *No!* His head reappeared, and she began to breathe again.

But the salvation of the righteous is from the Lord; he is their strength in the time of trouble. With that verse, a trickle of the peace that had come earlier washed over Anna. *God, I can't do this. You have to save my brother!* Panic threatened to overpower her again.

I will trust in the shadow of your wings. Another verse, but she had no idea where it had come from.

You have to help me, God. Help Edward. I can't do anything. Her shoulders slumped, and Anna was barely conscious of the tears rolling down her cheeks. She was broken. Had nothing left to give. There was nothing she could do.

The bandit was just a few feet away from her now, and one final lunge would bring him within arm's reach. As the man left the cover of his tree, Anna curled into as much of a ball as she could manage while restrained. The sound of gunshots was all around her now, and she kept her eyes squeezed shut, preparing for the sharp pain of metal piercing her flesh.

A scream rent the air. A crash beside her. Then the closest gunfire stopped, although it still raged in the distance. She forced her eyes open. The Mexican lay moaning on the ground while holding his lower leg. Blood oozed from the wound.

Edward ran the last few feet to the man, picked up the revolver that had dropped to the ground, and tucked it into his belt. He then stepped backward away from the wounded man until he reached Anna. He never turned away from the outlaw but bent down to loosen first the tie around her mouth then around her arms.

"Are you okay?" he asked, even before the gag was loose.

Anna still couldn't speak, even after the cloth was removed from her face. She nodded hard but kept her eyes on the man still moaning on the ground. At last, Edward finished with the rope.

"Stay here for a minute." Edward picked up the heavy cord that had been tied around her wrists and bent down to secure the man's hands behind his back. The bandit let out a painful groan, but her brother didn't flinch. He tested the knot he'd made, added an extra loop, then turned back to Anna, leaving the man still curled on the ground.

"Can you stand up?"

"Yes," Anna croaked. Her throat was so dry it hurt to speak.

"Come on, then." Her little brother, now her protector, grabbed both of her hands and hauled her up. She swayed a bit, so he positioned a hand under each of her elbows to hold her steady. She wasn't sure if her light-headedness was coming from the fact that she'd been tied in the sun all day without water, or from the sight of the blood oozing out of the man's leg not five feet away from them. She became conscious of the bullets still being fired from several directions. They were getting closer.

"We need to get out of here." Edward's voice was low, urgent. "We're going to run, so stay with me."

He grabbed her wrist and moved forward several steps, then looked back as if to make sure she was coming.

"I'm right behind you." She spoke with as much confidence as she could muster. The gunfire continued to close in. How many more bullets could the men have?

Anna ran behind her brother, one hand clutching his in a death grip, the other holding up her skirts to keep from tripping. Branches tore at her face and arms, but she kept moving forward blindly. A strong force slammed into her left thigh, leaving a sharp sting. Anna kept running. She didn't have a choice. Edward forged ahead like a stampeding cow, pulling her with him as he went. The stinging sensation became sharper until it radiated throughout her leg like a swarm of angry bees attacking. At last, the pain took over and her leg crumpled, taking Anna down with a gasp. Edward was at her side in an instant, his body crouched over her like a shield.

"What's wrong?" he called above the din.

"My leg."

Edward took one look at the blood stain that was beginning to show through Anna's dress where she clutched her thigh, then scooped her up in his arms and continued running.

At last they made it to the horses, and Anna was barely aware of Edward shouting to someone as he placed her on the saddle. Someone climbed up behind her. The awful bouncing ride began, but strong arms held her tight, keeping her upright. The pain was taking so much energy now, sapping the last of her strength. She tried to focus on the house ahead in the distance, but the edges of her vision were so hazy. The haze grew larger and larger. Finally, it turned into blessed darkness.

CHAPTER 27

Her leg throbbed like someone was trying to cut it off at the thigh. Anna sucked in her breath even before she opened her eyes.

"I think she's waking up, Doc."

The voice was familiar and so comfortable. The sound made the pain in her leg a little less intense. Anna carefully opened her eyes, afraid to move anything more than her eyelids. Faces crowded around her bed, a man she didn't know on her right, Edward, Aunt Lola, Jacob...

Her mouth was cotton and her throat craved water. "Drink..."

Jacob placed one hand behind her head to assist as she took several sips. It soothed like food to a starving man, but the effort was exhausting. She sank back against the pillow.

"What...happened?" she managed to croak.

The man on her right answered, "It seems you got in the way of a bullet, young lady. It passed through the outer edge of your leg cleanly, so it should heal fine if you give it the chance. Might be painful for a while, though."

Anna turned toward the man as he spoke. He was of medium

build with salt-and-pepper hair and round-rimmed glasses that made him look scholarly. As if he could read her mind, he smiled. "I'm Doctor Steiner. It's a pleasure to meet you, Miss Stewart, but unfortunate to be under these circumstances."

She offered a weak smile. "Thank you."

The doctor turned to Aunt Lola, who was hovering at the foot of the bed. "I've sanitized the wound and will leave you laudanum to give her for the pain. You'll need to change the dressing once a day for the first week. I'll be out again to check on her in a few days."

The older woman nodded. "Don't you be afearin', Doc. We'll take good care of our girl."

"I have no doubt." He nodded and pulled a small glass bottle from his bag. "One spoonful if the pain gets bad. I've already injected a dose, so she shouldn't need any more for a while."

He turned back to Anna. "Stay in bed for a full week, then you can move around a little bit with walking sticks. You'll need to use them to help you walk for at least two weeks after that."

Jacob nodded. "We'll make sure she gets plenty of rest and doesn't overdo things."

Doctor Steiner looked satisfied and reached out to shake Jacob's hand. "I guess I'll be on my way then."

"You'll be needin' a snack for the road, I'm a'thinkin'," Aunt Lola said, leading the doctor out the bedroom door. "I'll cut ye a slice of pound cake."

When the pair left, Edward edged closer to Anna, opposite from where Jacob stood like a guard on sentry next to the bed. Edward's eyes held a hint of worry but also a new maturity that had not been there before. "Are you gonna be okay, sis?"

Despite her exhaustion, Edward's question sent a warmth through her chest. She reached out to touch her brother's hand. "I'll be fine, thanks to you. I can't believe you saved me."

He dropped his head and scuffed at the floor, red touching his cheeks. It made him look like the overgrown boy she was accustomed to. Still, his broad shoulders and muscled forearms foretold the man he was becoming.

She had to speak before she lost her nerve. "Jacob was right."

Edward's head shot up, and his eyes drifted to Jacob before meeting her own.

"I do need to let you grow up and become the man God has planned for you." She squeezed his callused hand. "I'm proud of you, little brother."

He didn't hold her gaze long, and she could tell she'd embarrassed him. It had needed to be said, though.

"Why don't you head downstairs now? I'll just rest for a bit." Even as she spoke, her eyes drifted closed.

Jacob poked his head through Anna's open doorway the next morning. "G'morning. Edward said you were awake. Are you hungry?"

Anna was propped up on pillows and gave him a smile that seemed to require real effort. "Come on in."

He maneuvered through the doorway holding a tray filled with steamed oats, bacon, and tea. "Aunt Lola sent this up for you. I'm afraid she has her hands full making food for the men, so I volunteered to bring it up." He gave her a wink.

"I'm sorry she has to do my work, too."

"Don't be feelin' sorry for her. I think she likes the challenge."

Jacob set the tray down on the edge of the bed and tucked his large frame into the chair next to Anna. The room seemed small and confining, and he tugged at his collar. He would much rather be outside where he could have room to breathe and stretch his legs.

Anna raised a brow. She must have noticed his discomfort. "You don't have to stay and watch me eat. I know you need to get out in the pasture with the men." Her skin was still pale except for the pink that spread across her cheeks and nose from the harsh sun while she'd been tied to the tree.

A wave of protectiveness washed over him. "I'm not going anywhere for now. You eat up so you can get your strength back."

Her eyes widened a bit, but she obeyed and managed a few bites before sinking back onto the pillows.

She turned to him with questions in her eyes. "You never told me what happened yesterday. Did they catch the cattle thieves? I remember seeing one of them wounded on the ground. Is he okay? Was anyone else hurt?"

The muscles in Jacob's jaw tightened. "They caught 'em all. Sheriff Brown has them locked up for now until the judge comes back from San Antonio to hang 'em."

Anna's hazel eyes widened even more. "You think they'll be hung?"

"I'm sure of it. This is the same band that stole our cattle and tied up Edward last winter. With that and what they did to you yesterday, they'll be lucky if a lynch mob doesn't take them out before the judge does."

Her body shuddered.

Jacob stroked a finger over the lines on Anna's hand. "You're safe now." He looked up into her eyes, and the haunted look he found there tightened his chest. "I will never let anything like that happen to you again as long as I live." He raised her fingers to his lips and gently kissed them. If only he could erase the awful memories that would likely haunt her for weeks to come.

Anna drew a shaky breath. "When I was out there, tied to the tree waiting for them to come back and do who knows what, I prayed."

Jacob kissed her fingers again and murmured, "I'm sure you did."

Anna continued, "I prayed and God reminded me of several

verses from Psalms where he talks about saving us from evil. He gave me this overwhelming feeling of peace." The corners of her mouth turned up in the beginnings of a smile. "Then he sent my little brother to save me."

"He's not so little anymore."

Her long lashes dipped as she blinked then looked back up at him. "No, you were right. Thank you."

"For what?"

"For helping him grow up."

A surge of warmth sluiced through him. He loved this woman with everything inside him. It was way past time to tell her so and make her his own. He almost opened his mouth right then to tell her, but one look at her lying injured in the bed stopped him. Not here. Not like this. He needed to give her time to recover first. He needed to do this right.

Instead, he reached over and cupped her cheek with his hand. "Anytime. But now it's time for you to rest so you can get your strength back." He rose and laid a gentle kiss in her hair, drawing in the sweet scent of honeysuckle he'd learned to associate with her. "Sweet dreams." He turned to pick-up the tray and strode out of the room, an unfamiliar knot tightening in his stomach.

When Anna next awoke, sunlight poured through her windows. Abigail lay curled on the floor and thumped her tail when Anna's eyes opened.

"Hey, girl," Anna said, holding out a hand to the puppy. The dog came forward, tail fanning like a flag in a lazy breeze. As Anna scratched the silky hair between her ears, Abigail sat and gazed at her with a look of complete adoration. Something in the chair caught Anna's eye, and she sat up to get a better look, wincing at the pain. There lay a sprig of yellow honeysuckle and a slip of paper. She carefully picked them up and read the note. *Proverbs 31:10.*

Curious, Anna reached for her Bible on the bedside table and flipped to the verse. *Who can find a virtuous woman, for her worth is far above rubies.* Her mouth pulled into a smile and she fingered the flower, inhaling the sweet scent she had always loved. The note was written in Jacob's even hand. Did he think she was worth far more than rubies? She glanced down at the blanket covering her injury. She wasn't worth much of anything lying in bed. If only she could be up and moving again, working in the kitchen...*helping*. She wanted to be a helpmate to Jacob, just like the virtuous woman described in Proverbs thirty-one.

CHAPTER 28

Over the next few days, Anna strengthened and the pain in her leg lessened. She hated staying in bed all the time, but Jacob always brought her breakfast in the morning and read a couple of chapters from the Bible while she ate. He stopped in to visit throughout each afternoon when she wasn't sleeping, and at least once a day she would awaken to find a flower and a note on the seat of the chair. Aunt Lola was also a frequent visitor, and both Edward and Mr. O'Brien came by a couple of times each day to offer a cheery word. For the first few days, she slept much of the time, but as she was able to wean herself from the laudanum, she was awake more and more.

Jacob wasn't going out to work with the cattle. When he wasn't with her, he tinkered in the barn or did odd jobs around the house. It was strange. Nothing had kept him from the livestock before. Was he hanging around because of *her*? A warmth flooded her chest, but a seed of concern planted itself in her mind. She didn't like the idea of being so much trouble that Jacob couldn't even do the work he loved. She would just have to speak with him about it that morning. It was almost breakfast time, and Jacob would likely be coming up with her tray any minute.

As if he'd read her mind, boot thuds echoed up the stairway and down the hall, stopping outside Anna's room. She reached up to tuck a few wayward strands of hair behind her ears. It was bad enough she had to lay here in her dressing gown, but the least she could do was keep her hair styled. As soon as the pain had subsided enough for her to realize her state of disarray, Anna had engaged Aunt Lola's assistance in braiding her long hair so it didn't flow loose around her shoulders. Things may be a bit wilder and more practical in Texas, but she would make sure her sense of decency held strong.

The light knock on the door brought a smile to her face. "Come on in."

The door opened and Jacob peered around the edge. "You hungry?"

"Starved." Her stomach flip-flopped like that of a giddy school girl as Jacob approached. His strong jaw was freshly shaven and his short brown hair still slicked back since he hadn't yet donned his cowboy hat for the day. The royal blue shirt he wore didn't disguise the breadth of his shoulders and the muscles that played across his chest and arms with each of his movements.

As always, he wore the blue bandanna Anna had given him for Christmas, and she was struck again by how closely it matched his eyes. She studied it intently. The fabric was worn around the edges. She'd need to buy more fabric as soon as she could get to town. Too bad she didn't have the material now, for she certainly had time on her hands.

Jacob placed the tray on the side of the bed and folded his tall frame into the cushioned chair. "How're ya feeling today?"

"Much better. The pain's not as bad, and I haven't had to take the laudanum this morning." She bowed her head slightly and chanced a look at him. "Hopefully, I can stop sleeping so much, like I've done for the last few days."

"Sleep is what you've needed, I guess." He nodded toward the tray that she hadn't yet touched. "And food is what you need now. Eat up so you don't hurt Aunt Lola's feelings again by not finishing her food."

Anna's heart sank. "Oh, I'm so sorry. The food has been wonderful. I just haven't quite had my normal appetite."

A mischievous twinkle flashed in Jacob's eyes. "Don't worry yourself overmuch. I've been finishing off what you couldn't eat. Just didn't want to make the cook feel bad." He leaned back a bit and rubbed a hand over his flat stomach.

It took her a moment to absorb his words, then a giggle snuck out before she could catch it. "Well in that case, you might as well help me eat now instead of making me dine by myself." She pushed the plate with biscuits and strips of bacon in Jacob's direction. "I'll be doing good to finish the hotcakes with everything she's piled here. You eat these."

Jacob eyed the food for a second as if debating the sincerity of her words. He finally looked at Anna with a raised eyebrow then gave a slight shrug and leaned forward to pick up a piece of bacon. "I wouldn't want to make you eat by yourself." He popped it in his mouth.

Anna nibbled the hotcake, watching Jacob out of the corner of her eye. There was something intimate and comfortable about eating from the same tray. But why was she shy in his presence? She had to say something to break through her awkwardness. "Jacob."

"Yep." Elbows resting on his long legs, he raised his eyes to meet her gaze and the familiar tightening squeezed her chest at their blue intensity.

"You, um, haven't gone out with the cattle in a few days. Is there something wrong?"

Jacob studied her for a few moments, all traces of laughter

gone from his face, then looked down at the biscuit in his hands. "I thought I'd stay close for a few days...until things get back to normal."

Anna leaned forward and laid a hand on his arm. "I hope you're not staying here because of me. I love having you around, but I don't want to be any trouble for you."

Jacob stared at her hand on his arm as if deep in thought then lifted his gaze to look at Anna's face. A sheen of moisture covered the usually clear blue of his eyes. His voice was low and intense. "I… *We* almost lost you. When you were unconscious and I was racing to get you to the house so you could be doctored, I prayed God would keep you alive. I promised I would never let anything like that happen to you again. I'm just trying to keep my promise."

Anna's heart tightened at the pain in his eyes. "Jacob, God doesn't expect you to sit here and watch over me. That's *His* job."

He nodded, dropping his gaze back down to Anna's hand that still rested on his arm. "I know."

He sat staring at her hand for a long moment, then his Adam's apple bobbed and he seemed to recover himself. He leaned back in the chair and let Anna's hand slide down his arm and into the palm of his large, work-roughened hand. Anna relished the warmth of his skin.

"You finish eating now while I go talk to Pa for a few minutes before he heads to town. Anything you want him to bring back for you?"

Anna's eyes trailed to the bandanna around Jacob's neck. "There is something. If you'll get me a piece of paper, I'll write down a list for my aunt to gather for me at the store."

Jacob nodded and kissed her palm, sending a shiver up Anna's arms. Rising, he smiled with both brows raised. Something about the quirk of his mouth spoke a promise Anna couldn't quite discern. "I'll be right back."

The week had seemed like at least a month, but Anna was finally up and moving on the crutches the doctor brought her. She was determined to make it downstairs, but still didn't have the strength or stamina to sit upright in a chair for very long. So she settled for arranging herself on the sofa in the den in time for the family to gather after dinner and listen to Mr. O'Brien read from the Bible.

It was wonderful to be sitting, in a dress, not a dressing gown, with her adopted family all around. Mr. O'Brien, nestled in his overstuffed chair, read from the book of First Samuel while Aunt Lola rocked and crocheted next to him. The steady rhythm soothed the tension in her nerves and reminded Anna of early memories of her own Mama. Jacob inhabited his usual chair between the sofa and the fireplace and wiped down several bridles as he listened to the reading. He was always so industrious. Since Anna sat on the sofa with her leg propped across the extra seat. Edward had brought in a chair from the dining room and sat stroking Abigail's head. She gazed at him with her devoted-dog eyes.

Each person in this menagerie was so near and dear to her heart. Anna's eyes stung at the love that threatened to overwhelm her chest. At a gentle touch on her shoulder, she glanced at Jacob.

His brows pinched, shadowing his blue gaze. "Does your leg hurt?" He mouthed the words so he didn't interrupt the story of Samuel inspecting Jesse's sons to find the future king.

Anna flashed him what she hoped was a convincing smile and shook her head slightly. The truth was, the pain in her leg was getting worse the longer she sat there. She'd probably overdone it a bit for today.

Once again, Jacob seemed to read her mind. As soon as there was a break in the story, he stretched and yawned dramatically.

"I reckon I'm a bit tired tonight. Do you mind if we stop there so I can check the animals before turning in early?"

Aunt Lola 'harrumphed.' "Don't know how you could be tired from hangin' around the house all day. But Anna, on the other hand, has been up more than she ought. Reckon it's time for her to be turnin' in." Setting her needlework back in the basket beside the rocking chair, Aunt Lola pushed to her feet. "Come on, lassie. Let's be gettin' ya upstairs."

Two weeks later, Anna sat across from Jacob in the kitchen, her hands busy peeling potatoes for breakfast. She'd made Aunt Lola promise to sleep in this morning and allow Anna to resume cooking duties on her own.

As her knife flew around the potato almost of its own accord, Anna eyed Jacob. He'd been awfully quiet this morning...almost moody. Right now, he held a coffee cup in hand and stared out the kitchen window to some far distant place. He was going stir crazy missing the cattle and the cowboys, the life he loved. He hadn't said a word about it, though, so Anna wasn't altogether sure if *he* knew what was making him so gloomy. Of course, maybe he didn't mention it because he didn't want Anna to feel bad. If that was the case, then she needed to say something *now*. Anna took a deep breath. "I think they miss you as much as you miss them."

Jacob turned to look at her as if he'd just realized she was in the room. "What?"

"The cattle and the men. They miss you as much as you miss them."

He shook his head but didn't say anything.

"Why don't you head out with the boys today? I'm back on my feet now, so we'll be fine here."

Jacob's back stiffened. "You tryin' to run me off?" His words held a hint of defiance and Anna needed to tread carefully.

"No. I love having you here." She hurried to smooth his ruffled feathers. "I know you love working outside, and you've been cooped up here for three weeks. I could certainly understand if you were eager to get back in the saddle." The words spewed out one on top of the other, until she had to stop and catch her breath.

Jacob's back remained stiff for another moment, then he finally sighed and allowed his shoulders to slump. "I reckon you're right."

Anna released a breath. "I know you'll feel better when you're back on a horse."

Jacob sipped his coffee then placed the cup on the table and faced her. One look at the earnest expression in his eyes stilled her knife, poised over the potato while she waited for him to speak.

"If I go today, you have to promise me you'll stay *in the house.* Keep a rifle with you at all times. At the first sign of trouble, fire two shots and we'll be here in minutes. Do you promise?" His voice rose a bit with the final words, and Anna would have giggled at his overzealous worry if it weren't for the deep concern in his blue gaze.

Keeping her face relaxed but sincere, Anna set the knife on the table and placed her hand on top of Jacob's. "I promise."

CHAPTER 29

Anna hummed the tune, "Joyful, Joyful, We Adore Thee" as she pulled a loaf of apple cinnamon bread from the oven. The house filled with the aroma of apples and cinnamon baking, a scent that always put her in good spirits. She couldn't put her finger on the reason, but her skin tingled this morning like it usually did when something special was about to happen. To match her lively mood, she'd even dressed in the sunshine-yellow gown she tended to save for special occasions.

The back door banged shut and Jacob strode in carrying his usual bucket of milk and basket of eggs. "There are two hens setting now. We should have some little biddies soon." He set his load on the work counter with a thump and hung his hat on the peg by the door, running a hand through his short brown hair. Anna poured a cup of coffee from the pot that had finished brewing and turned to greet him with a warm smile. He offered a grin of his own when she handed over the steaming mug.

"I tell ya, a man could get use to this. Comin' in to a kitchen smellin' like the Garden of Eden, and a hot cup of coffee made by the prettiest gal in Texas."

Heat crept into Anna's cheeks, but before she could turn

away, Jacob set the cup on the counter and hooked an arm around her waist. With a teasing grin he pulled her to his chest and tapped a finger under her chin. "Yep, a man would sure like to get used to this."

Anna's breath caught and her heart fluttered like the wings of a hummingbird. His pulse beat strong under her palm on his chest. Every nerve in her body was aware of the strength in his arms as they wrapped around her. She braved a glance at his face and was suspended in the crystal blue of his eyes. She needed to say something, and she finally stammered out the first thought that made itself from her mind to her mouth. "Are you hungry?"

Jacob's eyes roamed down to her lips. "Very."

A tingle ran through her body as his blue gaze darkened and his mouth came down to hers. The touch of his lips was warm and strong, and their intensity flooded her even as her own body responded. Anna's hands crept up to his neck, through his thick locks, and down his strong jaw. Jacob's arms wrapped tighter around her body, pulling her against him. His hands slipped upward and kneaded her upper back. A little moan escaped from the back of Anna's throat as every part of her came alive. The sound seemed to quiet something within Jacob, and he pulled back slightly, resting his forehead on hers, faces inches apart. His ragged breathing mingled with hers and Anna's chest pumped as she struggled to catch her breath.

"Anna." Her name on his lips was spoken like a prayer.

"Hmmm..." She ran her hands back around his neck and gently fingered the short hair at his nape.

"Go riding with me today."

She drew back a few inches to scan his eyes. "Go riding?" She was sure the question played on her face. Today was Wednesday, a workday. Didn't he have work to do out with the cattle?

He rubbed his hands over her back again and pulled her to

him so her head rested against his chest. His strong heartbeat hammered next to her cheek. "Just for a few hours. I'll come back to get you around ten o'clock, and we'll ride down to the river before it gets too hot. Please?"

Anna remained quiet for a few moments, relishing the warm protection of being wrapped in Jacob's arms. At last, she stepped back and gave him a contented smile. "Okay. Now, you'd better get out of here so I can finish breakfast."

Jacob left with the men after breakfast, but true to his word, he marched in the front door promptly at ten. Anna was in her room upstairs, putting the finishing touches on her hair, when Abigail's soft whine and tail thumping on the floor boards signaled his return even before the front door closed. She'd tried a new hairstyle today, something other than the simple braid wrapped in a knot on her head that was her typical look. Today, a few curls framed her face while the rest of her mane was pulled into two braids that met in a low twist, offset on her neck.

Satisfied her hair was as good as it was going to get, she took one last speculative gaze in the mirror, eyes running over her yellow gown. She pulled the delicate gold cross and chain from under her neckline and straightened it, then headed downstairs.

Jacob was waiting at the bottom for her and Anna's heart skipped a beat at the sight of him. He was so tall, and his forest green shirt stretched across broad, muscled shoulders that contoured into a trim waist. His blue eyes held a twinkle as they followed her down the stairs. When she was almost at the bottom, he reached for her hand, halting her progress. His lips were warm as they placed a gentle kiss on her fingers, but his eyes never wavered from her own. A shiver ran through her body at the contact, but she kept a smile planted on her face.

Jacob guided her down the remaining stairs then tucked her hand under his arm. "M' Lady, your steed awaits," he said, with a flourish of his free hand.

Anna turned on her best Southern Belle drawl and gave him a coy smile, batting her eyelids. "Why, thank you, kind sir."

He chuckled and released her hand as she reached for her bonnet on the peg by the door.

"Let me just tell Aunt Lola you're stealing me away."

As they rode away from the house, a gentle breeze flapped the edge of her bonnet. Lifting her face to the sunshine, she released a contented sigh and stroked Bandita's neck. The mare bobbed her head, pulling at the bit in frustration at their slow pace. Anna shook her head at the mare's antics and gave her a final pat. "You ready to move out, girl?" She looked to Jacob and their gazes met. He had the beginnings of a grin on his face. "You mind if we jog for a ways?"

He nodded. "Fine with me, but just for a bit. You need to take it easy with your leg."

She arched an eyebrow at him. "I'll be fine."

As she squeezed her legs to push the mare into a jog, however, the familiar burning sensation pierced the outside of her thigh. But the pain didn't stop her enjoyment as Bandita's stride evened out into a ground-covering gait. It seemed like they had just begun when Jacob called them back to a walk. As they rode on, Jacob pointed out the changes to the landscape over the past few months and added in a story about the herd of deer the men had surprised one day last week.

"There were five or six does, each with a fawn, and the buck had a pretty good sized rack on him. They must have smelled us coming because they were running when we first found them. They sure were a sight to behold." His tone held reverence.

The familiar gushing of the river water sounded even before they emerged from the wide trail through the woods. As soon as she reached the river's bank, she slid off her horse, careful not to land on her bad leg, and stepped to the edge of the water. The breeze was stronger here, so she loosened her bonnet strings, allowing it to fall down her back so the wind could tickle her face and hair. The grass on either side of the water was always green no matter how hot the sun, and a few birds twittered to each other in the trees across the water.

Jacob stepped up beside Anna as she stood on the edge of the river bank. "It feels like heaven, doesn't it?" He spoke softly, not wanting to interrupt the spell of the beauty around them.

She turned to look at him and her hazel eyes glimmered more than usual. "I've missed this place."

His body moved of its own accord, taking a step toward her and reaching out a hand to stroke her cheek. The time had come, but how could he put into words what he wanted to tell her? He was a simple cowboy, definitely not an eloquent suitor. He took a deep breath. *God, help me to find the right words.* An image of his father popped into Jacob's mind, speaking a phrase he'd heard many times. *Son, just say what you mean.*

"Anna."

"Yes, Jacob." The sound of his name on her lips warmed his insides.

He placed a hand on each of her arms. "I want this to be your place, our place…always." She stared at him with a question in her eyes and he tried again. "I've always loved the ranch, from the beginning it's been a part of me. I never thought I'd find a woman who felt the same way." He brushed a wayward curl out of her eyes. "I didn't realize there was someone as special as you out there. And frankly, it took me a while to accept just how perfect you are." The corners of her mouth turned up, but her amber eyes remained locked on his. "And it took me a while to realize how much I love you. But I know it now, so I just have one question for you. Miss Anna Stewart, will you do me the honor of becoming my wife?"

Anna's eyes softened and her voice was low and sweet as she spoke. "I'd love to."

Jacob let out the breath he'd been holding and allowed a grin to spread across his face. His eyes drifted down to her lips. He could taste their sweetness already. He gave her a teasing grin and murmured, "Now that's settled." He lowered his mouth for a taste.

By jingo, she was sweeter than he remembered. Her arms around his neck spread a wave of desire through him and he pulled her closer. After just a few moments, he forced himself to break their seal, resting his forehead on hers. This woman was too irresistible to trust himself for long, but soon she would be *his*.

"So what do you think, should we go see the preacher this afternoon?" he said in a low, teasing voice.

Anna leaned back, her eyes forming wide circles. "Today?" she squeaked.

Jacob chuckled and pulled her back into his arms, tucking her head under his chin. She fit so perfectly there. "Right this minute, if you'll say yes." He stroked her back, enjoying her softness under his hand. "But if not today, you just tell me when."

CHAPTER 30

The next few days kept Anna busy, with the garden in full production and so much work to do, canning and preserving food for the winter months. Everything was different now. It would be her own family she prepared for. She was a little like the woman in Proverbs chapter thirty-one who *riseth also while it is yet night, and giveth meat to her household.*

"I don't know what kind of day you have planned, Anna." Mr. O'Brien's voice broke through her thoughts as they all sat at the breakfast table one morning. "But Aunt Lola and I are heading over to the Wallace Farm this afternoon and wondered if you'd like to come along? I need to take them a load of beef in trade for grain for the horses."

A bubble of excitement built inside Anna. She longed to see Ginny again and tell her about the wedding. It didn't take long for the bubble to burst, though. So much work waited for her, both in the kitchen and the garden outside. She only had a week and a half before the wedding and needed to get things done.

She gave him a gracious smile. "I'd love to, but I have so much to do here. I need to get started on things. Please give

Virginia my apologies for not attending with you. I'll send a basket with you, though."

"Oh, come now," he said with a wave of his hand. "What do you have that can't wait until tomorrow? And we'll be back in plenty of time to start supper."

Anna wavered in indecision for a moment, but another voice broke into the conversation.

"She'd love to go with you." Anna's head whipped around to the source of the voice, and Jacob eyed her with a stubborn set to his jaw.

"Wonderful." Mr. O'Brien beamed. "It's all settled then. We'll leave right after lunch."

Anna hustled through as many chores as she could during the morning hours, and by the time she settled into the wagon seat after lunch, she was exhausted.

When they arrived in the Wallace farmyard, Mr. O'Brien pulled the wagon to a halt beside a small building not much bigger than a large outhouse. Anna and Aunt Lola strolled toward the cabin in search of Ginny, while the men unloaded the brown paper-wrapped packages of salted beef from the wagon and stored them in the building. When the wagon was empty, they would load sacks of grain back into it from the Wallaces' barn.

Anna's knock on the door was answered by a pint-sized version of Ginny, complete with the head full of blonde curls, heart shaped face, and laughing eyes. The little girl's porcelain skin had a few extra decorations, though, by way of red smears around her mouth and cheeks. Probably strawberry preserves, judging by the shade of crimson.

"Hi, Katie. Is your mama inside with Lilly?" Anna bent down to be at eye level with the four-year-old.

Katie's thumb slipped into her mouth and she nodded.

"Can we come in and visit for a while? I'd love to see how good a big sister you are."

The little girl's eyes lit, and her head bobbed again. Anna chuckled, rose to her feet, and followed the child through the doorway, Aunt Lola on her heels.

"Ginny?" Anna called through the house as they trailed Katie toward the direction of the bedrooms.

"Anna? Is that you?" Ginny appeared through one of the doorways carrying a chubby baby on her hip. "And Aunt Lola. I'm *so* glad you've both come. Please come into the parlor and have a seat. Just give me a second to get cleaned up. Seems like I'm always changing diapers these days." She gave them both a wry grin, but her enthusiasm bubbled too close to the surface to be overshadowed. "Can I get you both a glass of lemonade? It's so hot for tea, but I can heat a kettle if that's what you'd prefer."

"Lemonade sounds perfect." Anna reached for baby Lilly and giggled at the way the little one ogled her with big blue eyes. "I declare, Ginny. She's gained ten pounds since I saw her last month."

Ginny flashed a proud smile, as she poured the golden liquid into mugs. "That little one loves to eat, for sure."

They settled into an easy chatter as Aunt Lola asked about the baby's health. Anna listened as her mind spun. How could she bring up her own news? She shouldn't have worried.

Aunt Lola turned to Anna with a gentle nudge of her elbow. "Well, bonnie lass, are ya goin' ta tell her or am I gonna have to?"

Ginny gasped. "Anna Stewart, are you holding out on me?" She leaned forward to perch on the edge of her chair.

Heat crept all the way up to her ears and her gaze dropped to the liquid swirling in her cup.

"Out with it." Ginny was never one for patience.

"Well." Anna stirred her lemonade. "It seems Jacob has asked me to marry him."

Ginny erupted in a squeal and leaped from her chair to hug Anna. "Oh, my friend. I am so happy for you!"

Anna giggled as she squeezed Ginny back. For some reason, she was self-conscious with Aunt Lola looking on.

The older woman's eyes held their usual twinkle, though, and her mouth broke into a toothy grin. "It's about time that boy got around to doin' somethin' good for him. I was beginnin' to think he was going to let this little lady slip away."

Anna's face heated from the teasing, but if she were honest with herself, she couldn't deny a little bit of pleasure from the attention. After a moment, she was able to turn the conversation toward the new things Ginny's little ones were into. The young mother's face lit up even more, if that were possible, as she went into detail about how Lilly was developing and what a great big sister Katie was. Ginny's bubbly personality had a way of brightening their home in a way that was infectious, and her two little girls were delightful. Anna spent much of the time playing with baby Lilly, and she couldn't help but yearn for her own little bundle of joy to love.

By the time Mr. O'Brien drove the wagon out of the yard with both Aunt Lola and Anna on the seat beside him, Anna's spirits were so high she couldn't keep from humming a tune under her breath.

"From the sound of things, you ladies must have enjoyed yourselves." Mr. O'Brien chuckled.

Anna's cheeks warmed, but Aunt Lola spoke up in her thick Irish brogue. "That Ginny is such a sweet, happy thing. You can just see the love of God bubbling out of her. And those young'uns are precious."

"They are that." Mr. O'Brien glanced at Anna, his cheeks twitching. "It'll be nice to have our own little ones running around the house soon."

Anna wanted to melt into the wooden seat.

"Oh hush, Marty. You're embarrassing the girl." Aunt Lola patted Anna's knee.

But Mr. O'Brien didn't appear to pay attention. He reined in the horses and pointed to a brown spec in the distance. A cow? No, it seemed to be too short and stocky to be one of the longhorns. A buffalo? They didn't usually wander this far east.

"What is it?"

Silence answered her for a long moment as they all stared at the creature clomping toward them. The horses fidgeted. Aunt Lola gasped, and Mr. O'Brien reached under the seat and pulled out a long rifle. What in the world? She turned back toward the animal in the distance. And then her blood ran cold. A large brown bear lumbered toward them, and it had picked up speed, now in a full-out, ground-covering run.

The horses were more than fidgety by this point, but Mr. O'Brien thrust the reins into Anna's hands. "Hold these," he barked. One of the horses surged into its harness, but Anna kept a steady tension on the heavy leather straps.

"Easy there, boys. Easy now," she crooned, despite the knot that churned in her gut. Anna's head swiveled between the bear, the horses, and Mr. O'Brien as he cocked the rifle and took aim. She tensed, preparing for the loud boom and the reaction of the horses. Horses that were used to pulling the wagon probably weren't accustomed to gunfire over their heads.

After what seemed like a very long time, the deafening retort of the Sharps carbine rang out. The horses danced in their harness, jerking at the reins. She continued crooning to the animals, focusing all her attention on keeping them from bolting. Runaway horses could be just as deadly as a grizzly bear.

For a split second, Anna looked up to make sure the bear lay dead in the distance. Her heart jumped into her throat. The bear was not lying dead or even injured. It still charged straight toward the wagon. Without slowing or missing a stride, it let out a tremendous roar that sent chills all the way down to Anna's toes. One of the horses released a frantic whinny, and she fought to keep them still.

A clicking sound beside her signaled Mr. O'Brien reloading

his rifle. He again took aim, and Anna's attention was drawn back to the bear. It was only fifty feet or so away from them now and moving faster. The thunderous crack of the rifle boomed again, and the huge body of the brown bear dropped in mid-stride. One moment it was charging, massive paws in the air, and the next it was lying on the ground in a great brown heap.

Anna sucked in a deep breath and let it out. Only then did her heart beat again, picking up speed until it thumped like a stampede in her chest.

"Thanks be to God." The quiet brogue whispered beside her. The older woman's wrinkled hand moved in the shape of a cross over her chest.

The horses were still now, though whether they were just being obedient or if they could sense the danger was over, Anna wasn't sure.

Mr. O'Brien reloaded his rifle more slowly this time, but his hands shook a little. "You did good with the horses, Anna."

She nodded her thanks then turned back to the brown lump in the field not twenty-five feet away from them.

Mr. O'Brien climbed down from the wagon and crept toward the form on the ground, the butt of his rifle tucked into his shoulder in case he should need to aim quickly. After an inspection of the body, he turned back toward the wagon. "He's a big one. Gonna take a couple of men to get him loaded. I'll come back out here with some of the cow hands to bring him in. It'll be nice to have a bear hide to keep warm this winter."

Anna shivered despite the hot Texas sun.

CHAPTER 31

Very little was said during the rest of the ride home. When they arrived, Anna headed straight for the kitchen and began preparing supper. It would have been easiest to make some kind of stew for tonight, especially since she'd been gone all afternoon. But Aunt Lola's specialty was stew, and she imagined the boys would have their fill of it while Anna and Jacob were gone on their wedding trip. A tickle of nervous excitement skittered down her spine.

Tonight's fare would be beef burritos, using meat from the steer they'd butchered this week. Spicy cornbread would be the side and peach pies for dessert. She'd made the pies that morning, so all she needed to do now was mix the cornbread batter, brown the meat with seasonings, mash and re-fry the beans, and melt cheese to pour on top of the wraps. That was a special trick Juan had taught her, and it added the perfect creamy flavor to soften the spices inside.

Anna folded the flour tortillas around the stuffing when a pair of large hands gripped her waist. She squealed and spun around to find Jacob with a wide grin across his face. His blue eyes danced as she let out a breath, one hand on her chest to contain her racing heart.

"Jacob O'Brien, you almost scared me to death." Her tone was scolding, but she couldn't hold back the smile that begged to join his.

"The smells coming from in here were too good to resist. I had to stop in and get a taste before dinner." His eyes drifted down to her lips and he pulled her close to his body. "Just couldn't wait to see you." As his lips found hers, Anna was again lost in the wonder of this man. He would soon be her husband. His kiss was sweet and gentle, yet full of longing. "I missed you today." His husky voice and warm breath in her ear sent a shiver all the way to the core of her being.

"Oh, Jacob." It was all she could manage. His lips reclaimed hers with an intensity that matched the fire burning inside her. But after a few more moments, he slowed, ending with a final caress of his lips. As he rested his forehead on hers, they both struggled to rein in their breathing and the emotions coursing through them. Anna ran her fingers over his strong jaw and whispered. "You have no idea how much I love you." Jacob pulled her tight against his chest, arms gripping her as if he would never let go. Anna breathed deeply of his scent, a mixture of man and nature and that something indefinable.

Too soon, his grip loosened and he ran his hands down the length of her arms, catching her hands in his. "I'd better let you finish supper or the boys'll be upset. Just about all they could talk about today was what you were going to cook tonight."

With a gasp, Anna spun around and flew into motion. "Oh, my goodness, I have to get dinner on the table."

Jacob stepped back to clear the way for her sudden flurry of activity. "Anything I can do to help?"

She kept her hands busy wrapping tortillas but glanced over at the stove. "Could you check the oven to see if the cornbread's ready? Use a towel so you don't burn yourself."

He picked up the rag from the worktable and opened the oven door. "How do you know if it's ready?"

Anna smiled at the picture Jacob made, his tall frame bent over to peer into the oven, a puzzled expression on his face. She leaned over for a quick glance inside. "It should be golden on top. Looks like it's just about right. Would you mind taking both pans into the dining room? Just make sure you set them on the leather pads so the heat doesn't burn the wood."

"You were attacked by a what?" Anna cringed as Jacob spat the words from his chair at the end of the long table in the dining hall. His eyes shot flaming arrows at her. Was she the cause of his ire? Good thing his father had control of this conversation. At the moment.

"Don't get your dander up." Mr. O'Brien drawled as if he were calming a spooked horse. "I shot him before he reached us and not one of us has a scratch. No one 'cept the bear, that is."

"How close did he get?" Jacob's voice was terse.

"He was about seventy feet away when I got off the first shot."

"You didn't answer my question."

Mr. O'Brien released a sigh. "Never got closer than twenty-five feet."

Jacob sucked in his breath. "What kind?"

"Brown bear. And like I said before, we're all fine." He turned toward the foreman. "Monty, do you think you could spare three or four men to go with me to fetch him tonight?"

From the finality in his voice and the change of topic, Mr. O'Brien was finished with his son's question-answer session. But Jacob continued to stew over his peach pie. His blue eyes were glaring a hole in his plate, but his mind appeared to be far away.

The men finished dessert and made plans for the hauling, skinning, and curing of the bear, then all rose and headed out to put the plan into action. Jacob rose, too, but remained standing behind his chair. He ran a hand through his thick hair and let out a sigh.

Anna gathered dirty dishes to take into the kitchen. She wasn't sure what to say. Wasn't exactly sure what was wrong, but it had something to do with them being in danger. Although, what could they have done differently to keep them from the peril? They hadn't *planned* to run into a bear. And each of them had reacted just as quickly and correctly as they should have. Like Mr. O'Brien had said, the end result was they were all *fine*. Except the bear.

She let the dishes slip into the clean water in the kitchen with a gentle *thunk* and headed back into the dining hall for another load. She froze in the doorway. Jacob was still rooted in the same spot, his hands on the back of his chair. He was just standing there, staring. His face held such an odd expression, she couldn't make it out. It wasn't anger anymore. Sadness maybe, or fear?

Anna's heart went out to him and she stepped in his direction. Ducking under his arm, she slipped herself between each stiff elbow and wrapped her own arms around his middle in a tight hug. He allowed his hands to rest on her shoulders at first, a bit stiffer than she was used to. Then they eased down her back and rubbed circles around her shoulder blades. She stayed in that spot, arms around his body, until his heartbeat reached a steady rhythm under her cheek and his shoulders relaxed.

At last, Anna loosened her grip and leaned back to study Jacob's face. His sky-blue eyes were clouded by a sheen of moisture, and he kept them focused on a point above her head. His jaw worked once, twice. She kept her gaze on his face and he finally lowered his eyes to meet hers.

"Doggone it, Anna. I don't know what I'd do if I lost you."

She stroked his jaw. "It's okay, Jacob. I'm safe. We're all safe." She snuggled back into his chest. "It used to kill me for Edward to do anything dangerous. After Mama and Papa died. Then we lost everything in the fire. It scared me silly to think I might lose him. It wasn't until those cattle thieves tied me to the tree that I realized I truly have no control. Not an ounce of it. God expects us to make good decisions, but then it's all up to Him. And He's got a pretty good plan when you look at the big picture. After all, if our house hadn't burned down in Columbia, we never would have moved to Seguin." She leaned back and offered a sweet smile. "And if we hadn't had so much trouble with the Union soldiers, I never would have agreed for us to hire on to your father's ranch."

"What trouble with the soldiers?" Jacob's brow creased as his eyes studied her face.

Oops. She wasn't sure she'd ever told him about that little bit of difficulty. "A few of the soldiers in town roughed up Edward, but I went to talk to their commanding officer and he put a stop to it."

His body tensed again. "*You* went to the Army camp? With your uncle?"

Anna shook her head, not looking him in the eye. "I went by myself, but the Major was nice enough. I can't say the same for some of his soldiers, but the officers seemed to be decent men."

"What do you mean you can't say the same for the soldiers? Did one of them touch you?" Jacob's gaze pierced as he ground out the last words.

"Just one." Anna scrambled to find a way out of this conversation. She hadn't planned to upset him again. "But the other soldiers came when I screamed and stopped him. He was punished then shipped off to another battalion in Virginia. Nothing to worry about now."

She kept talking to change the subject. "I remember the first time I saw this ranch. It's hard to believe it was less than a year ago. I was fiery mad about Monty hiring my brother and came riding all the way out here to tell your father what was what. Before I could talk him into firing Edward on the spot, though, he offered me a job." She smiled at the memory. "I decided it was the only choice we had at the time. Isn't it funny how something can look so bad when it's happening, but when we look back, it's apparent how God's hand was at work?"

Jacob shook his head then rubbed circles in her back again. "My Anna. Something tells me I'm going to have my hands full keeping up with you."

She flashed him a bright smile and snuggled back against his chest. "Don't you worry, Mr. O'Brien. I'll do my best to behave."

CHAPTER 32

The O'Brien men had been gone for two days. As Anna washed breakfast dishes the second morning, she forced herself to go through the motions. Jacob and his pa had gone to San Antonio to take care of ranch business, taking the wagon to bring back a load of wood from the sawmill and a few other things they needed for the barn. It was business, and Jacob wouldn't have gone unless he needed to, but the selfish part of her hated that he was away just one week before their wedding. Didn't he have things to do here? Maybe he didn't want the wedding to happen yet.

She was being ridiculous. This had to be pre-wedding jitters getting the best of her. What she needed was something special to do. Over the past two days she'd given the house a thorough cleaning and scrubbed all the laundry. The garden was picked and everything that needed canning had been prepared, pickled, and sealed in glass jars. She'd planned to wear her yellow gown for the wedding, so there wasn't a dress to make. She couldn't do any of the wedding baking yet, as it was still seven days until the ceremony. She could take Bandita for a ride to the river but really didn't have any desire to be alone with her thoughts right now. They might eat her alive. Maybe she should find Aunt Lola and ask if there was anything with which the older woman needed help.

Anna peeked into the front parlor. Aunt Lola nestled in the petite chair that fit the small Irish woman like it had been built around her. Aunt Lola was reading her Bible, but looked up with a pleased smile when Anna entered the room.

"And what might ye be up to this fine mornin', Anna dear?" She studied Anna and the wrinkles above her eyes scrunched together in concern. "Ye look like yer mind's about to torture yer poor heart." She patted the sofa next to her chair. "Come sit down and tell me what's botherin' ya."

Anna sank onto the couch and released a sigh. "I guess I'm not sure what to do with myself. I was hoping I could help you with something."

Aunt Lola chuckled. "I'd be more than happy to let ya read to me from the Good Book and save my poor eyes, but I think what ya need is to move around a bit. Why don't ya head into town? I have a letter to mail and you could visit with your aunt and uncle a bit."

That appealed to Anna more than anything else she'd come up with. Maybe she could pick up lace to add to her gown while she was there. It'd be nice to have a little something special for her special day.

"I suppose that might be a good idea. Is there anything I can pick up for you in town? I can borrow a wagon from the livery and get supplies while I'm there."

"Nay, I sent my list with Marty and Jacob. They'll be bringin' everything I need. You take that mare you like to ride so much and make a day of it. I'll cook supper for the boys tonight, so you don't need to be back until dark time. And I promise I won't make stew…this time." The twinkle reappeared in the older woman's eyes and the skin above her cheeks bunched into the usual smile lines.

Anna couldn't stop the impulse to hug the sweet lady and plant a kiss on her cheek.

Aunt Lola only laughed and returned the embrace then made a shooing motion. "Off with ye then."

"You're not going to make a wedding dress?" Aunt Laura's gaping mouth and raised eyebrows evidenced her shock. She looked almost as appalled as if Anna had said she was going to dance down Live Oak street in nothing but a corset and petticoat. Now *that* would be true cause for the expression Aunt Laura was now aiming in her direction.

"But there's no time," Anna defended. "And I don't want to delay the ceremony. And my yellow gown is lovely. I thought I could add lace to the white ribbon on the edges and it will look brand new." She gave her aunt a cheery smile, but it ricocheted off the woman like a pebble off a coat of armor.

"My dear, no Stewart woman has ever been married without a wedding gown as far back as I can remember. Not one who was born a Stewart. And not one who married a Stewart. Your mother would turn over in her grave if she knew you were considering such a thing." Aunt Laura shivered.

Anna forced her face not to reveal her amusement at Aunt Laura's ranting. It didn't seem the situation required such dramatics. Maybe in the 'old days' women always wore a bridal gown for a church wedding, but much had changed with the war. Many brides didn't have money for a new dress, especially one that couldn't be worn many times after the wedding.

Aunt Laura stood in her kitchen, frowning, hands on her hips. Her toe tapped the floor and the lines on her forehead were scrunched into deep grooves, evidence of her mind working. "I suppose if we start right now, we could most likely have it ready before the wedding. I could work on the top half and you could take the...Wait!" Her face lit and she spun around, striding down the hall toward the bedrooms. On a mission.

Anna wasn't sure whether she should follow or stay but sat quietly in her ladder-back chair at the kitchen table. The whole episode was a little funny, but maybe she should put more effort toward decorum. It honestly hadn't seemed like a bad idea to wear the yellow gown. She wanted to focus more on making sure *she* was ready for the marriage than spending unnecessary time preparing her wardrobe for the ceremony.

Within two minutes, Aunt Laura strode back into the room, carrying a large fluff of white material. "I think I have the perfect thing." Her eyes shone as she gently laid her load on the table.

Anna's jaw dropped. Her gaze roved the yards of material then trailed back up to her aunt's face. "Your wedding dress?" Anna's voice squeaked.

Aunt Laura nodded, a smile budding on her face. "We'll need to add a flounce at the bottom to reach over your crinoline, and maybe tweak a couple of seams, but I think it will be perfect."

Anna rode home later that afternoon with a full heart and a spring in her step. Aunt Laura had been just the right medicine to settle her jitters and help Anna focus on what needed to be done before Saturday. Now it was time to get down to the doing.

As she made her way down the long lane leading from the main road to the ranch, a brown object stopped in front of the barn. A wagon? Her heartbeat picked up its pace. She hadn't expected Jacob and Mr. O'Brien back until tomorrow or possibly Monday. Since it was a day's ride each direction to San Antonio that would have left only one day to take care of all their business and pick up supplies. Still, it did look like their wagon.

She pushed Bandita into a jog. They were too close to home to canter, since the mare wouldn't have time to cool down afterward, but a jog wouldn't hurt anything. As she neared the yard, half a dozen of their cowpunchers unloaded long, mill-cut boards from the wagon and carried them into the barn. She scanned the faces for Jacob's. Edward. Bo. Donato. Miguel. No Jacob in sight.

She sat back in the saddle, easing Bandita to a stop in front of the wagon, then slipped off the mare.

Edward stepped forward to take her reins. "Jacob's inside, sis. I'll take care of this girl if you wanna go on in."

Anna's pulse leaped but she glanced at Edward's face. "Are you sure?"

"Yep." He gave her an impish grin but didn't say anything more.

She almost kissed his cheek but stopped herself in time and settled for a hand on his arm. He might be her little brother, but he was doing his best to grow into a man and didn't need a mother hen to coddle him just now. "You're the best."

She scurried toward the house as quickly as she could while trying to appear somewhat ladylike. As she climbed the steps, the front door opened and Mr. O'Brien stepped out, settling a wide-brimmed hat on his head.

"Mr. O'Brien." She offered him a wide smile. "Welcome home."

"Why, thank you, Anna. It's awfully good to be back."

"We didn't expect you both back for a couple of days yet."

He chuckled softly. "I've never seen Jacob get so much done in twenty-four hours. I think even if we hadn't taken care of all our business, he still would have left out of San Antonio this mornin'." He patted Anna's shoulder. "You're good for him, my dear. Now get on in there. Unless I miss my guess, he's hangin' around the kitchen somewhere."

Anna's cheeks flamed, but she forced a mumbled, "Thank you, sir," as she made her way past him.

As Anna's eyes adjusted to the dimmer light in the house, she met Aunt Lola at the base of the stairs. The older woman carried a small parcel wrapped in brown paper. The older woman's shoulders seemed even more hunched these days than when Anna had first met her.

"Can I help you carry that upstairs?"

"Nay, lassie. It's just a couple o' books the boys brought back for me. These ol' bones need a little work ever now and then to keep 'em strong. I think you might be needed elsewhere, though. Why don't ya head on in to tha kitchen an' see." Her blue eyes twinkled.

Anna shrugged and shook her head as she headed down the hall. Everyone seemed eager to send her to the kitchen this afternoon. Stepping into the room that was her special domain, she stopped short at the sight of Jacob seated at the table in his usual chair, coffee in hand. Jacob rose when he saw her. A squeal escaped as she catapulted into his arms.

"There she is." He chuckled, wrapping her tight in his long, muscular arms. "I figured if I waited here long enough, you'd show up."

After a few short moments, he gently disentangled himself and held Anna at arm's length. "What do you say we head outside for a bit? Maybe you can help me find a place for the rest of the things we brought back."

"Sure." Hesitation echoed in her own voice, but it was odd for him to ask her to help with the unloading. Maybe there were supplies for the kitchen? Aunt Lola had promised to take care of the evening meal and the aromas wafting from the cookstove smelled like she had things well under control.

Jacob hooked Anna's hand in his and led her to the back door. At the top step, she froze.

Her head swiveled from one side of the stairs to the other as she took in the four sprawling green plants. "What are these?" she breathed. Each bush sat in its own sand-colored earthen pot. Golden blossoms dotted the plants like little suns emitting bright rays of life to everything around.

"Yellow roses." Anna answered her own question, her eyes coming up to search Jacob's face. "You brought us roses?"

"I brought *you* roses," he corrected. "And they were harder to come by than ice in the desert."

Anna skipped down the last two stairs and stooped to caress one of the delicate blooms, inhaling its light aroma. "They're amazing." She infused her tone with the reverence due the gesture and stood to bestow a smile on her future husband. How much trouble had he gone through to get four perfectly-formed yellow rose bushes?

His hands slipped into his trouser pockets and he ambled down the steps to join her. "The storekeeper I ordered them from said they're considered the flower of friendship and joy. I figured that was pretty appropriate for a wedding gift, since I'll be marryin' my best friend." His words warmed Anna's chest like nothing else he could have said. She planted a kiss on Jacob's cheek. A princess rewarding her knight in shining armor.

CHAPTER 33

Anna stared at her reflection in the mirror of Aunt Laura's little apartment above the mercantile.

"You're the most beautiful bride I've ever seen." Aunt Laura fastened the last two buttons on Anna's stunning white gown.

"Oh, Aunt Laura, it's the dress that's so beautiful. Thank you so much for letting me wear it."

"Darlin', I'm not just letting you wear it. It's yours to keep and pass down to your own daughter. I'm sure not planning to use it again." She chuckled.

The gown was made of light muslin with a close-fitting bodice and a full skirt, layered with three lace-trimmed flounces. Aunt Laura had expertly added the bottom layer for Anna, to accommodate the extra fullness of the current crinoline styles. The entire gown was covered with a sheer ecru organdy jacket with a lace ruffle around its edging. The effect was stunning, and the wreath of daisies crowning the veil in her hair created the perfect finishing touch.

Examining herself in the mirror, a little shiver ran down her arms. It had only been two weeks since the special ride to the river, but it seemed like a lifetime had passed. Today was the day she would become Mrs. Jacob O'Brien. Today she would marry the most wonderful man she'd ever met, her best friend.

A knock sounded on the bedroom door, and Aunt Laura opened it. Edward poked his head inside. "How's it comin', sis?"

"Good, I'm almost ready." She grabbed Edward's arm and pulled him into the room.

"Wow, you look beautiful." His voice held a mixture of surprise and awe.

Anna giggled. "You don't have to sound so shocked."

He pulled a hand from behind his back and pushed a bouquet of yellow roses toward Anna. "These are from Jacob."

Anna held them to her nose, inhaling deeply. Tears pricked her eyes at the beauty of the simple gesture, and she remembered the sweet words Jacob had said when he gave her the rose bushes. *I'll be marrying my best friend.*

She blinked to clear her eyes and turned back to her brother. He stood with his hands in his pockets, looking down at his boots as they scuffed the floor. He looked awfully handsome in his borrowed white cotton shirt with high neckline, vest and matching trousers, and long black cutaway coat. His cowboy boots, cleaned and polished, peeked out from underneath the pants.

"I think Jacob's gettin' nervous, so you'd better hurry. Either that or he's just plain hot. I know I sure am." Edward tugged at his collar for effect.

Anna spun back to the mirror to make sure everything was in place and straightened the gold cross around her neck. Finally satisfied, she faced her aunt and brother. Letting out a deep breath, she allowed a smile to spread across her face. "I'm ready."

~

Jacob stood in the front of the church between Reverend Walker and Pa. He was trying his best to remain calm and collected on the outside, but the longer Anna took, the tighter his stomach coiled. What was it exactly that had him so tied up in knots? It didn't matter, really, he was just ready for this shindig to be over.

At last, a hushed commotion near the back of the church caught his attention, and Anna appeared on the arm of her brother. The sight of her uncoiled his stomach and everyone else faded into the distance. She was the prettiest image he'd ever seen, carrying the bouquet of yellow roses.

Her eyes stayed fixed on him as she strolled toward the front of the church. His chest constricted as the reality of the situation settled over him. This woman was about to become his wife. This beautiful, amazing woman would be bone of his bone, flesh of his flesh. As Edward placed Anna's hand into Jacob's, she flashed him a brilliant smile, soothing the last of his nerves. With Anna by his side, things would be just fine.

~

The women of Seguin had prepared a feast for supper on the church lawn that rivaled that of the Independence Day celebration. It looked like the entire town had turned out for the event, and even the mixture of blue Yankee uniforms in the crowd didn't squelch the festive atmosphere.

Anna stayed by Jacob's side throughout the meal, and even afterward when the editor of one of the local papers pulled out a fiddle and the dancing commenced. Of course, many of the boys approached to request a dance with Anna, but Jacob would have none of it. Not even Monty was allowed the honor.

They sat enjoying the revelry before them, until the fiddler began to play "The Yellow Rose of Texas." Jacob stood and held out a hand to Anna. "Mrs. O'Brien, would you give me the honor of a dance?"

The name sounded almost foreign to Anna, and she replayed it silently on her own tongue as Jacob led her onto the dance floor. He swept her into a lively waltz while the music played their own special song. Jacob piloted their progress around the dance floor, maneuvering expertly around the other couples.

Anna took the opportunity to feast her eyes on Jacob's face. His strong chin and ruddy features were set in perfect proportions, creating a flawless background for his amazing blue eyes. She certainly hoped their sons would look just like him. Anna's mind wandered to the making of those sons, and her heart flip-flopped at the same time her mouth went dry. Jacob chose that exact moment to look down at her. As though he could read her thoughts, his eyes darkened a bit.

With a smile touching his lips, Jacob leaned down to whisper in her ear. "As much as I love dancing with you, this party's getting a bit old. Think we could sneak away?"

Anna gave him a coy smile. "Sir, I am at your disposal." That seemed to be all the encouragement he needed, for Jacob swept her to the edge of the dance floor and escorted her straight toward the buggy waiting by the hitching rail. Anna stopped, forcing him to pull up. "Wait. We need to say goodbye to everyone first."

A hint of frustration touched his face. "Darlin', you can have the rest of your life to say goodbye or hello or whatever you want to them all. But if we stop to speak to our family and friends now, they'll keep us here all night." He dropped his voice to a low tenor and stroked a finger across Anna's cheek. "And *that* would be a tragedy."

Anna swatted his finger playfully. "You're just impatient."

"Why, yes, ma'am," Jacob said, his face an image of mock seriousness. He reached for both of Anna's hands and raised them to his lips. "But, I've never been able to say no to you, and

I'm afraid I can't start now." He gave a martyr's sigh. "Let's go say goodbye to them all."

Anna stared into his blue gaze in indecision. She supposed people would understand if they slipped out. She allowed a grin to slip out. "I guess they won't miss us."

After spending their wedding night in Seguin's grand Magnolia Hotel, they drove the thirty miles to San Antonio in a rented buggy. It was so much better than the bumpy, crowded stage.

They finally rolled into San Antonio on Sunday evening, and Jacob reined the buggy to a stop in front of an impressive two-story building. Its beige exterior appeared to be made of the same limecrete material of which most of the buildings in Seguin were constructed. Windows spanning the front on both floors were taller than Jacob. The three center windows on the second floor were topped by rounded arches reminiscent of Grecian architecture. Above the arched windows were the words 'Menger Hotel' in large block letters, topped by a triangular arch rising above the limecrete wall. A balcony spanning the second floor across the front was bordered by an ornate black metal railing.

Anna couldn't help but stare in awe at the elaborate exterior. She hadn't seen anything this impressive since leaving Columbia.

"Would you rather sit here all night or should we go in?"

Anna blinked, pulling herself from her reverie. Jacob had already disembarked and waited patiently next to the buggy. His eyes held their familiar teasing twinkle.

"I suppose we might as well see the inside, too," she bantered, allowing him to lift her to the ground. His strong hands could almost span her waist, fingers touching on either side.

The interior was a hundred times more grandiose than the outside. The center of the lobby was a huge open space that rose all the way to the dome above the second floor. Massive round pillars supported the vaulted ceiling, with marble bases that were taller than any of the men in the room. Elaborate metal railing ran around the interior balcony on the second floor. White porcelain tile with a black fleur-de-lis design gleamed from the floor, with an ornate oriental rug spanning the center of the room.

Where should her eyes feast first? She was barely conscious of Jacob's hand on the small of her back, nudging her toward the long gleaming desk that seemed lost in one end of the massive room. The murmur of male voices droned in the background, as Anna took in the rich royal blue of the velvet curtains and the large artwork adorning several walls.

Upon hearing "Mrs. O'Brien," she forced her attention back to the gentleman behind the desk. He motioned them toward a young man dressed in a smart uniform. The lad's black coat was buttoned to the neck with a double row of polished silver buttons. Black pants met with black shoes, and the entire display was topped with a smart black cap. The young man would have appeared rather somber if not for his shock of sunshine yellow hair and a white, toothy grin.

He gave a sharp salute and, with a spin of his shiny black shoes, led the way to the grand staircase that wrapped the west wall. She might have been the Duchess of Wales ascending the palace stairs as they made their way to the second floor and down a long, opulent hallway. The attendant marched to the end of the corridor, jangled the keys that hung at his waist until he found the right one, and swung open the large mahogany door with a flourish.

"Here you are, Mr. and Mrs. O'Brien. The bridal suite. Our finest room in the hotel." His chest puffed at his words and his grin flashed as if he'd personally built the room.

Anna had prepared herself for a well-appointed room but nothing so extravagant as this lavish sleeping chamber. The oversized canopy bed was centered on the east wall, with a dressing table and a large picture window taking up much of the north wall. Its burgundy damask curtains blended nicely with the burgundy and gold spread covering the bed.

Anna's eye was drawn to two doors on the west wall of the room. Was this room connected to a sitting room or another bedroom?

She strode to the doors and cautiously turned the handle of the first. It opened to reveal a small closet with rods stretching from one end to the other, hangers dangling loosely in preparation for garments.

"Look, Jacob. A closet!" She couldn't help the excitement in her voice. She'd known a girl who spent her summers in a plantation home with closets for hanging clothes built into the bedrooms. It had always seemed like a lavish waste of space, although practical if one was wealthy enough to have too many gowns for a wardrobe cabinet.

Anna eyed the other door with curiosity. She turned to glance at Jacob where he leaned against the wall watching her. His legs and arms were crossed casually and he had a devilish twinkle in his eye. He raised an eyebrow at her expression. "Why don't you open it and see?"

Anna spun back to the door and twisted the handle. When she pulled the door open, a curious sight stood before her. It was a small room with washbasin and pitcher on a stand. To the left of the basin was a low, round seat with a cone-shaped base.

Anna looked back at Jacob. "What is it?"

He grinned and pushed away from the wall then stepped behind Anna. His arms wrapped around her waist, chin resting on the top of her head. "It's an indoor outhouse with plumbing. Just like the fancy hotels in Boston and New York."

Anna whirled to face him, loosening his grip in the process.

"I've heard about those. I had no idea they were here in Texas, though."

Jacob's arms tightened around her waist again, and Anna rested her hands on his chest. She raised her gaze to meet his. "Jacob, this whole place is amazing. I never expected anything so lavish. I would have been perfectly happy in a little boarding house."

He slid his hands up and down her sides and one corner of his mouth quirked. "Only the best for my gal."

CHAPTER 34

Anna's eyes opened in the dim pre-dawn light as she tried to place the strange surroundings. A warm, contentment settled over her like a blanket as the details of the hotel room became clear. Their wedding trip. She snuggled deeper into the warmth of Jacob's body. He mumbled something incoherent and Anna placed a soft kiss on the tender part of his forearm.

"G'mornin'." Jacob's voice was thick and husky from sleep as he nibbled the ticklish part of her neck. His warm breath and prickly whiskers brought goose bumps to tingle her skin.

Anna giggled and turned over to face him. "Good mornin'." She rubbed a hand over the stubble on his jaw and looked up to heat darkening the blue in his eyes. Jacob leaned forward and planted a quick but less-than-chaste kiss on her mouth. When their lips separated, Anna lay back against his arm with a contented sigh and traced his jaw with her finger. Jacob's stomach grumbled to voice its complaint about the lack of food at such a late hour. Anna couldn't help but grin. "I think we'd better feed you."

"Mmm... Come to think of it, I guess I am a bit hungry." He

grinned, mischief sparkling in his eyes. "The food here is good but not as tasty as what I'm used to. You know, that is why I married you. Couldn't let your food get away from us." She threw a pillow at him, but he winked and slid out of the bed.

Less than an hour later, Anna sat across from Jacob at a little round table in the hotel's dining room. As the waitress poured coffee for them both, Anna used the opportunity to scan their surroundings. The room was full of genteel people, mostly dressed in suits and elegant day gowns. The quiet conversation murmured over the soft clink of fork against dish.

She turned back to Jacob. His rugged good looks helped him fit into any setting, but his blue long-sleeved shirt that brought out the color of his eyes clearly identified him as a cowboy. Warmth flooded Anna's chest. *Her cowboy.*

A familiar scene flitted through her mind of the group around the large dining table at the Double Rocking B. Such a comfortable picture it made. The haphazard group of cowboys had become her extended family. And she was one of the women of the house now. She really belonged there and had a gold band on her finger and a marriage license to prove it.

Jacob reached forward to lay a hand on top of Anna's. "Everything okay?"

She brought herself back to the present and smiled. "I was counting my blessings."

"Would one of those blessings be the breakfast I smell cooking?"

She raised an eyebrow. "Maybe."

When it arrived, the food did look awfully good. Crispy bacon, buttered toast, warm eggs, sausage and grits. Jacob had ordered an extra plate of hotcakes, just to make sure he had enough to hold him over until lunch.

As they bowed to ask God's blessing on the food, Anna's eyes drifted open to stare at the shiny ring on her left hand. A warmth spread through her. This was the ring Jacob's father had given to his mother as they began their beautiful and lasting marriage. And now, Jacob had given this same ring to her as a symbol of all their own marriage would hold.

She sneaked a peek at Jacob and drank in his perfectly-formed features. His rich voice and the adorable pucker between his dark brows revealed his concentration on the prayer. Anna's conscience pricked. She quickly bowed her head and raised her own heartfelt thanks to the Father.

"So what would you like to see tomorrow?"

Anna strolled on Jacob's arm along the river walk next to the San Antonio River where it ran through the center of town. The sky held the dusky aura that comes just before a magnificent sunset.

"Well," he contemplated as they ambled along, "the San Fernando Cathedral we saw today was somethin' else, but I think my favorite is still the Alamo we toured on the first day. You could just about hear the bullets still ricochetin' off the walls in there."

Anna chuckled. "A real piece of history for sure."

Jacob paused his strolling to turn and face the water, hands deep in the pockets of his trousers. The river was wide in this spot and flowed slowly. Not as much like the Guadalupe that bordered their ranch. No birds sang in the trees here, or rabbits bounding into the underbrush. Actually, no underbrush at all. Still, there was the earthy smell of the water and the gentle murmur it spoke.

"The clerk at the hotel told me the San Antonio springs are only four miles north of here. He said there's one spring in particular, the Blue Hole, that's a pretty sight and would be worth the drive. Whatd'ya think?"

Anna allowed her smile to blossom. "It sounds perfect for our last day."

Jacob glanced over to gauge her expression. "Are you sad we'll be leavin'?"

Anna turned to face the river, the breeze ruffling her hair. "In some ways, yes. It's been a little bit like heaven to have you all to myself." She cast a sideways glance at him then focused on the flowing water again. "I miss home, though. And Aunt Lola, and the boys, and my kitchen. And our own river."

"Mmmhm."

They stood there for a long time. Like trees on the river's edge. The breeze caressing, the water flowing. No words needed. Just silent companionship.

~

The weather couldn't have been more perfect, sunny but with a little bit of breeze that tasted almost like fall was in the air. The hired gelding kept up a steady jog until Jacob reined him back to a walk when they reached a sign that read *The Blue Hole Spring ahead*. An arrow pointed to the left toward a wide trail that led from the main road.

When the spring came into sight, Anna gasped at the vision that lay before them. Water shot several feet into the air, spraying over thick green foliage and moss-covered rocks. The play of light through the clear water created a rainbow of colors, and the effect of it all was stunning.

"It's amazing," she breathed.

Jacob set the brake on the buggy and leaned back in the seat, propping a boot on the buckboard and an arm on the seat back behind Anna.

"It is that," he agreed in a low, reverent tone.

Anna nestled into Jacob's arm and the two sat for a while admiring the natural beauty God had created in this place.

Anna was the first to speak. "I wonder if there's a spring like this at the head of the Guadalupe?"

"I heard an old rancher one time say it starts up in the Texas hill country and comes from two river forks that join together near Kerrville. Maybe we could take a trip up there to check it out one day."

She gave him a hopeful grin. "I'd love that." After a few more peaceful minutes, Anna gave voice to her thoughts. "As pretty as this is, I miss our own river. It feels like I've lived a lifetime there on the banks of the Guadalupe."

Jacob chuckled, "Me, too, Darlin'. Me, too."

Thursday dawned overcast, but as long as the rain held off, Jacob figured that would probably be the best weather to travel in. Not as hot if the sun wasn't beating down.

He sat in their hotel room in one of the overstuffed chairs by the fireplace, working the buttons on his shirtsleeves into place. Anna stepped from the washroom and brushed her long wavy brown hair in front of the full length mirror. His fingers itched to touch it again. There sure was something special about his woman's hair.

Anna's eyes caught his in the mirror and she flashed a shy smile. "What is it?"

"Oh, I'm just sittin' here thinkin' how lucky I was to get the prettiest gal in the state of Texas."

A mischievous light twinkled in her eyes. "Lucky, huh? Seems to me luck didn't have much to do with it."

Jacob nodded and rose to his feet, grabbing his hat from the table. "Reckon' I know better than to argue with a lady." He strode forward, laid his hands on Anna's shoulders, and nuzzled a kiss on the side of her neck, breathing in the honeysuckle scent that always clung to her. "I'm gonna head downstairs and send for the buggy. I'll be up to get you shortly."

Anna leaned back against him, and he was tempted to forget all about the buggy for a while.

"I'll have things ready when you get back." Her words helped him refocus on his mission and he pulled himself away.

Before long, they were on their way, headed back toward Seguin. The trip was a long one, almost thirty miles. He usually dreaded it, especially in a buggy or wagon instead of on horseback. It seemed to pass more quickly this time, though. It surely helped to have Anna snuggled in next to him. How was he ever really happy before her?

They made it to Seguin by suppertime and stopped at the café inside the Magnolia Hotel. They were almost home.

It seemed like everyone in the restaurant stopped to congratulate them on the marriage. By the time the fifth person had approached their table, Anna stopped turning pink from all the unexpected attention. Most of the people knew them both from church, but Jacob spied a plump, matronly woman moving toward them whom he doubted Anna had ever met.

"Here comes Mrs. Catherine LeGette," Jacob whispered, preparing his wife for the approaching guest. "She lives in the big Sebastopol house over on Zorn Street. The one that looks like a Grecian temple."

Anna's eyes widened as she pressed the cloth napkin to her mouth.

Her response was cut short by the delighted pitch of the lady's shrill voice. "Oh, if it isn't the newlyweds." Mrs. LeGette stopped in front of their table, panting a bit as if striding across the café had winded her.

Jacob stood politely. "Mrs. LeGette. Always a pleasure, ma'am."

She waved him down. "Sit, sit. I thought that was an O'Brien man when I saw you from the door." She turned to Anna.

"These O'Brien's, you can spot 'em in a New York crowd. Broad shoulders, tall, and the prettiest blue eyes you ever did see. And wearin' cowboy boots like they was the latest in Paris fashion. Mmmm..." She looked like she might eat him up right then and there. Jacob caught himself edging backward.

Anna's soft chuckle soothed his nerves. "It's a pleasure to meet you, Mrs. LeGette. I'm Anna O'Brien. And how do you know my husband's family?"

She raised a single eyebrow, a half-tilt to her mouth. "Oh, every single gal in Guadalupe County knows about the O'Brien men. The two most eligible bachelors around." She spun back to Jacob. "And now you've gone and broken the heart of every maiden under the age of thirty-five. Tsk, tsk." She released a dramatic sigh and Jacob wanted to sink right down under his chair. She was drawing the attention of people at nearby tables, too.

Before either one of them had a chance to respond, Mrs. LeGette turned back to Anna. "But I hear he's made an excellent choice, my dear. I couldn't be happier for you both. And I insist you come and visit me the next time you're in town. No advance notice needed, just stop by my home. It's the one with columns along the front over on Zorn Street."

Anna's eyes lit. "That's so thoughtful. I'd love to. I've seen your home from the street and it's beautiful. The architecture reminds me of something from Ancient Greece or Rome."

The matronly woman puffed a bit at the praise. "They call it Greek Revival style, and my brother Joshua built it for me about ten years ago. We always dreamed of traveling to exotic lands when we were little, and I guess we never got it out of our systems." She almost giggled.

Anna rested a soft hand on Mrs. LeGette's arm. "Well, I hope you'll give me a tour when I visit."

The older woman bloomed like a rosebud after a rain shower. It was amazing the effect his genteel wife had on people. "I'll be counting on it. Now I'll leave you two lovebirds alone to enjoy your supper." Sending a final pert look in Jacob's direction, she said, "You take care of this gal, Jacob O'Brien. You hear?"

"Yes, ma'am."

The food at the café was decent, but these bland hotel meals were losing their luster. They didn't hold a candle to the food that came out of Anna's kitchen. After the bill was paid and Anna rose to her feet, Jacob stood and stretched his long arms, feeling a bit crowded in the little tea room where they stood.

"Well, would you like to stay in town tonight or head on out to the ranch? We have another hour of daylight left before the sun'll start to set, so I'm fine either way."

Anna chewed her bottom lip and peered up at him through her long lashes. "If you're not too tired, I'd love to go home. It feels like we've been gone for ages." And then her eyes went wide and her cheeks pinked. "I mean…it was a wonderful trip, though. I enjoyed every minute of it."

He couldn't quite hold in a grin. He reached for Anna's elbow and guided her toward the front door. "I know it, darlin'. I'm a bit homesick, too."

~

Jacob kept the bay gelding in a steady jog for much of the road to the ranch. As the familiar live oak tree came into view that marked the corner of the O'Brien land, he reined the horse back to a walk. As much as he was looking forward to seeing the family again, it was like a little slice of heaven having Anna to himself. He hated to break the spell just yet. An idea began to form in Jacob's mind. He turned the horse and buggy off the road and into the meadow, heading toward a familiar line of trees in the distance.

Anna sat up beside him, her hand touching his forearm. "What are we doing? Is everything okay?"

He tried to keep his face as stoic as possible, but this was going to be fun keeping her guessing. "Everything's fine. We're just taking a little detour."

Anna didn't say anything else, but her fingers twisted the blue muslin of her skirt. It was eating her alive, not knowing where they were headed. Well, hopefully the outcome would be worth the suspense.

When the buggy rolled onto the road through the woods that led toward the Guadalupe River, Anna's shoulders relaxed and she leaned back into his side. He avoided looking at her until the river was before them and he'd reined the horse to a stop.

He finally dared a glance and was caught up in the delight that had spread across her face. "Do you wanna get down or enjoy it from here?" He spoke softly so he didn't break the magic of the place.

Without answering, Anna lowered herself from the wagon and stepped forward to the edge of the water. He strolled up beside her, and Anna reached for his hand without moving her gaze from the flowing river, entwining their fingers together.

For a while they stood like that, listening to the gentle murmur of the water and the twitter of birds in the nearby trees. The sun was making its progress toward the western horizon and flashed brilliant oranges, pinks, and purples across everything in its path. The way the colors illuminated Anna's face only served to enhance the pure pleasure there. She looked like an angel.

"Jacob." She still hadn't looked at him, and for a moment he wasn't sure if she'd actually spoken.

"Yes."

She finally turned to face him, love shining in her gaze. "Welcome home."

Did you enjoy Jacob and Anna's story? I hope so!
Would you take a quick minute to leave a review?
It doesn't have to be long. Just a sentence or two telling what you liked about the story!

To receive a FREE short story and get updates when new Misty M. Beller books release, click here: mistymbeller.com/freebook

And here's a peek at the next book in the series, *The Ranger Takes a Bride* (Edward's story!):

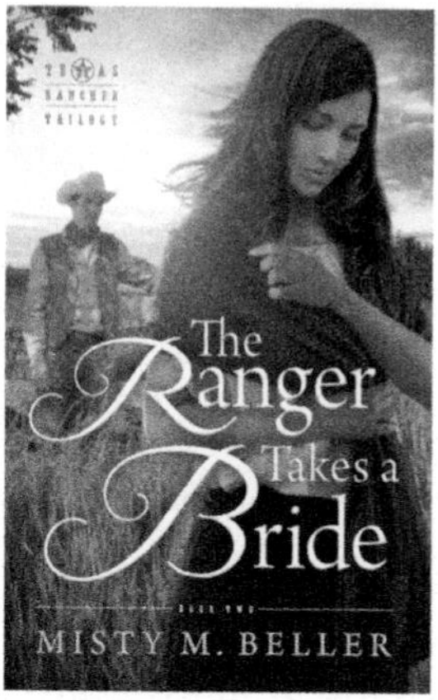

Chapter One

NOVEMBER 20, 1875
RANCHO LAS CUEVAS, TAMAULIPAS, MEXICO

Alejandra Diaz picked her way across the rocky ground, a band of dread tightening her chest. This was not a message she wanted to give, but desperation compelled her.

Reaching the rough wooden door of the adobe hut, she rapped lightly with one hand and pushed it ajar with her other. "Mama Sarita?"

"Sí, mija."

As Alejandra's eyes adjusted to the dim light of the room, she focused on the slender figure standing by the work table. Mama Sarita held knife in hand, poised over something on the counter. Red peppers most likely, judging by the sweet aroma lacing the air. But the woman's eyes focused on Alejandra, and the love that usually shone there mixed with wariness and fear.

Forcing her feet to carry her forward, Alejandra blinked back tears as she stood in front of the woman who had become as dear to her as her own sweet mama had been. But Mama Sarita wasn't her mother. She was Luis' mama. The *madre* of her *prometido*—promised one. And now he was gone, and it was up to Alejandra to break the news.

"Mama Sarita." Alejandra stopped to force moisture into her parched throat.

"What is it, child?" Mama Sarita raised a hand to cup Alejandra's cheek. The calluses on the woman's work-roughened fingers were the touch of love.

Alejandra's eyes and throat burned with the sting of tears. "Mama. The news is bad, *es terrible*."

Mama Sarita's palm dropped from Alejandra's cheek to clutch her hand. "My Luis? And Ricardo?" Her grip tightened on Alejandra's palm, but it was a welcome pain.

"I'm so sorry, Mama." Alejandra couldn't hold back the tears anymore, as they streamed down her face. "The soldiers killed them both. And my papa, too. Señor Salinas and eighty men. All gone at the hands of the...American Rangers." Alejandra spat out the last words, almost choking on them.

Mama Sarita pulled her into a tight embrace. The feel of this madre's arms was more than Alejandra could resist, and she allowed the sobs to overcome her body. First her own mother had been murdered at the hands of French soldiers all those years ago. Now Papa. And Luis, her promised one and best hope for a suitable husband. And Papa Ricardo, Luis' padre.

A wave of realization washed over Alejandra. Now she and Mama Sarita had only each other. In one fell swoop, the soldiers had left them both alone and abandoned.

Alejandra clutched the woman's swaying body tighter. As long as there was breath in her body, Mama Sarita would never be alone.

Alejandra ladled the atole into a bowl, then settled a spoon into the thick, grainy liquid. Mama Sarita liked atole with plenty of ground corn so it was more like a porridge than a drink, so that's exactly how Alejandra made it. Mama Sarita said it kept her menfolk full longer, so they could work harder. She always patted Papa Ricardo's muscular shoulder when she said the words. The love between them always lit the small adobe dwelling. Pain seared Alejandra's heart at the memory—partly because she mourned the loss of the three men who had meant the most to her, and partly because of the agony Mama Sarita must be experiencing. Papa Ricardo and Luis had been her world.

Swallowing back fresh tears, she carried the bowl to the front doorway and sat next to the hunched figure seated on the stoop. "I brought your breakfast. Thick, warm atole."

Mama Sarita accepted the bowl Alejandra placed in her hands, but her eyes stared out across the narrow dusty road that ran in front of the hut. The trail passed by each of the ranch worker huts nestled in openings in the trees, and eventually ended at the Rincon de Cucharras outpost of the vast Rancho Las Cuevas.

Rancho Las Cuevas had been her and Papa's home for these six years, but much longer for Mama Sarita. How long had Luis said? They'd come here when he was but a child of five. And now, he would have celebrated his veinte años in less than a week. Twenty years. Except the American soldiers killed him. Alejandra fought the urge to hit something. But instead, she raised her hand to finger the scar that marred her right cheek, extending from her cheekbone to the base of her ear. Yes, soldiers brought nothing but pain and heartache.

"What was the fighting about, mija?" Mama Sarita's voice drifted through the tirade in Alejandra's mind.

She turned to look at the older woman. But Mama Sarita still stared into the distance, over the road and into the woods beyond.

Alejandra swallowed. "I'm not sure exactly. There was trouble with some cattle. I think our *vaqueros* brought the animals across the Rio Bravo, and the *soldados Americano* wanted to take them back. They killed Señor Salinas and eighty of our vaqueros."

"So the cattle belonged to the Americanos?"

Alejandra jerked her attention to Mama Sarita's face. The leathery skin between her brows pinched, as if she were trying to decipher a mystery.

"Sí, mama."

"And they took the animals back across the river?"

"Sí." What was Mama Sarita trying to determine? If the Americanos were in the right? Of course not. They were soldiers, invading a land that wasn't their own and murdering innocent people. Murdering Papa.

The thrumming of hoof beats in the distance finally brought Mama Sarita's head around. Through the trees, a rider became visible. A man wearing the wide-brimmed hat of a vaquero. As he reined his bay to a stop in front of them, a cloud of dust rose into the dry air. He removed his hat to swipe the dust away, exposing unruly black hair and thick brows, a perfect match to his long mustache.

Alejandra rose to her feet in deference to Señor Vegas, one of the foremen at the outpost. Mama Sarita didn't leave her perch on the step.

"Buenos dias, Señora Garza. Señorita Diaz. I'm glad to find you together." He nodded to them both, his mustache curving down as his mouth pinched.

"Señor Vegas." Mama Sarita's greeting held a quiet authority.

"My news is not good. You know of the fighting with the Texas Rangers, si?"

Alejandra nodded.

"Many vaqueros were lost. Your men among them." He paused and eyed them both, as if assessing whether they'd heard the news already.

The now-familiar burn pricked Alejandra's throat and stung her eyes. But through her blurry vision, she glimpsed a nod from Mama Sarita. Did the older woman not have any tears left? Or was she still in shock, not fully understanding what had happened?

The man continued. "As you know, the houses you both live in are ranch property. For the vaqueros and their families." His fingers squeezed the round crown of his hat, crunching it like soft cotton. "Since you don't have men to work on the ranch…." he stopped to clear his throat, "you must plan to leave."

He looked down, apparently lacking courage to meet their expressions. And that may have been a wise choice, but Alejandra still did her best to burn a hole through him with her gaze. How dare this man throw them out of their homes?

A motion in the corner of Alejandra's gaze caught her attention, and she turned to watch Mama Sarita slowly unfold herself from the stoop and rise. An Aztecan queen never moved with such regal bearing, such quiet nobility. She stepped forward, stopping a length away from Señor Vegas.

"Señor." Mama Sarita's voice was strong. "I would like to inquire after work—at the main house or one of the outposts. I am willing to clean or cook for the Don and Doña. Alejandra would make an excellent nurse for the wee babe."

The man shook his head before she was half through with her request. He held up a hand to silence any further words. "Señora. So many vaqueros have left wives. There is not work enough in all Tamaulipas for them to be cooks and housekeepers. You must go."

With those final words, he jerked the horse's reins to spin the animal around. The unsuspecting gelding threw up its nose, eyes wide, before it acceded to the pull and spun toward the road.

Señor Vegas reined in the animal after only a few strides, then turned in the saddle to look back at them. "Señora, it will be a few days before the new vaqueros arrive. You may have until Saturday to move your belongings."

Three days. They had three days to close out the remnants of life as they knew it and create a new purpose.

As the anger that had coursed through Alejandra's veins dissipated, despair filled its place, pushing down on her shoulders like layers of thick woolen ponchos.

Mama Sarita turned, still standing near the road where she'd spoken to the foreman. Her face mirrored the same weariness that pressed down on Alejandra's spirit. Mama Sarita wasn't an old woman—barely past child-bearing years. But the deep lines that formed around her mouth, eyes, and forehead gave the appearance she had lived more than one lifetime.

And maybe she had. After all, hadn't she grown up in *América*? Living in another world, until Papa Ricardo won her heart and brought her to live in Mexico. *Como México no hay dos,* Papa Ricardo always said. Mexico is second to none. After living so many years in this land, Mama Sarita almost looked like a native now, despite her dark brown hair and rich cocoa eyes. Her skin had leathered under the Southern sun, and she spoke the language like any countryman. Yes, Mama Sarita belonged here.

A surge of love welled in Alejandra's chest, and she stepped forward to take Mama Sarita's arm. "Come, Mama. Eat, and then we will make plans."

~

NOVEMBER 21, 1875
SAN ANTONIO, TEXAS

Edward Stewart gave the outlaw a shove as the man shuffled into the small jail cell. Neither of them spoke while he swung the metal door shut and turned the key. A click radiated through the small room, and he gave the door a sound shake to make sure it was secure. The man inside grunted as he plopped into an old spindle-back chair, then folded his greasy head into his hands.

Edward spun on his heel and strode out of the jail area, into the front office. They'd been traveling most of the day without stopping for food or drink, so the prisoner would need rations. He couldn't bring himself to hurry, though. It was hard to pity a man who would steal from innocent women and children.

As he tossed the jail key on the deputy's desk, a rush of adrenaline blasted through him. Another assignment complete. Another scoundrel behind bars. The Texas Rangers were victorious again.

He met the deputy's gaze with a nod. "He's locked up and still cuffed. Might get a bit hungry soon, but I'm not worried about 'im."

The deputy stroked his mustache. "We'll keep him secure 'til the judge comes around. Just leave yer report."

Edward turned, lifted his hat, and scraped a hand through his hair. "I'm a bit short on grub. I'll write out the details while I eat a bite at the Riverwalk."

He strode out the front door and through the gate that surrounded the jail and courthouse, then fell into stride on the road with the other passersby and wagons. A sea of people going every direction. And where was he headed? Where did this vacant spot in his chest tell him to go?

For two years now, he'd been a Texas Ranger. Part of the family of men who'd built a reputation as tough lawmen, the bravest in any territory. And among the Rangers, he worked hard to be one of the best. A far cry from "Little Brother," as the cowpunchers called him when he'd worked on his sister's ranch back home. So why wasn't it enough?

Edward stepped up on the boardwalk, then veered around a well-dressed couple strolling down the center of the wood plank walkway. The woman wore gobs of lace and finery, and her laughter tinkled like a bell on the breeze.

Maybe he needed a woman. A pretty little flower to walk on his arm and laugh at his jokes. But when exactly would he have time to escort a wife around town? Ranger assignments kept him traveling for days at a time, with a short night or two at home before he climbed back in the saddle for the next job. Nope. There was good reason why most Rangers remained unmarried.

So what is it, Lord? What am I missing?

The question reverberated in Edward's chest as he pushed through the swinging doors of the Riverwalk Café. There'd be time to dwell on that empty feeling later. Now was his chance for a decent meal, before he had to saddle his horse and track down another desperado.

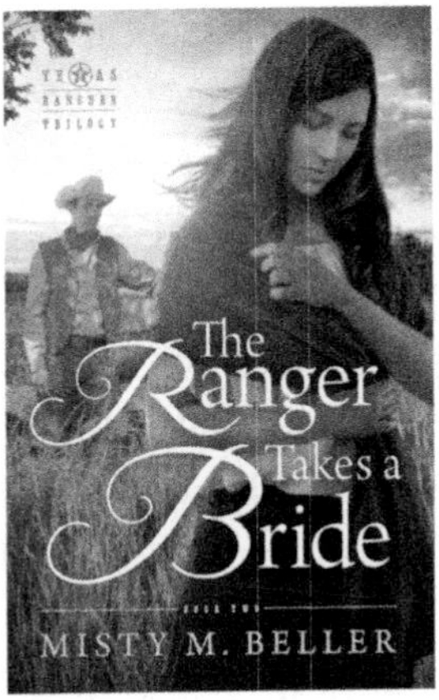

Get THE RANGER TAKES A BRIDE at your favorite retailer.

ABOUT THE AUTHOR

Misty M. Beller is a *USA Today* bestselling author of romantic mountain stories, set on the 1800s frontier and woven with the truth of God's love.

She was raised on a farm in South Carolina, so her Southern roots run deep. Growing up, her family was close, and they continue to keep that priority today. Her husband and children now add another dimension to her life, keeping her both grounded and crazy.

God has placed a desire in Misty's heart to combine her love for Christian fiction and the simpler ranch life, writing historical novels that display God's abundant love through the twists and turns in the lives of her characters.

Connect with Misty at www.MistyMBeller.com

ALSO BY MISTY M. BELLER

Call of the Rockies

Freedom in the Mountain Wind

Hope in the Mountain River

Light in the Mountain Sky

Courage in the Mountain Wilderness

Faith in the Mountain Valley

Honor in the Mountain Refuge

Brides of Laurent

A Warrior's Heart

Hearts of Montana

Hope's Highest Mountain

Love's Mountain Quest

Faith's Mountain Home

Texas Rancher Trilogy

The Rancher Takes a Cook

The Ranger Takes a Bride

The Rancher Takes a Cowgirl

Wyoming Mountain Tales

A Pony Express Romance

A Rocky Mountain Romance

A Sweetwater River Romance

A Mountain Christmas Romance

The Mountain Series

The Lady and the Mountain Man

The Lady and the Mountain Doctor

The Lady and the Mountain Fire

The Lady and the Mountain Promise

The Lady and the Mountain Call

This Treacherous Journey

This Wilderness Journey

This Freedom Journey (novella)

This Courageous Journey

This Homeward Journey

This Daring Journey

This Healing Journey

Printed in Great Britain
by Amazon

38908119R00148